Bring the Rain

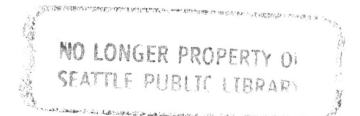

Bring the Rain

a novel

JoAnn Franklin

SHE WRITES PRESS

Published 2019
Printed in the United States of America
ISBN: 978-1-63152-507-0
ISBN: 978-1-63152-508-7
Library of Congress Control Number: 2018953150

For information, address:
She Writes Press
1569 Solano Ave #546
Berkeley, CA 94707

She Writes Press is a division of SparkPoint Studio, LLC.

Dedicated to Richard

ONE

Painting the outside trim of my house in Southport, North Carolina, was boring and monotonous, which is why I was daydreaming, while standing on a ladder, about an historic, beautiful palace in Salzburg, Austria. The ballroom's ceiling and columns gleamed with gold leaf, creating a place of light and beauty. Hundreds of scholars and leaders, all experts on poverty, stood before me in that cavernous room. They smiled as I took the podium. Their applause caused my ears to ring.

We had a week together at the prestigious Salzburg Global Seminar. A week to brainstorm how we could erase poverty and ease humanity's suffering. Not enough time, but the work would start . . . and caught up in my exuberant fantasy, I must have ignored that the ladder wobbled when I stretched to reach the last bit of trim. I did feel my body lean into nothing and remembered thinking, *How odd. No one is smiling anymore.*

My unconscious mind, the Sentinel, reacted before I could consciously take action. With speed and exquisite care, the Sentinel centered my weight. By the time I realized I was in danger, he had me upright again, my body plastered against the ladder, pinning it into place.

I had almost fallen. I looked a long way down, shuddered, and

1

looked up. Overhead, the sun shone in a cloudless sky, and I felt its heat on my face. I heard the ocean waves and, when a gust swept the paint fumes away, I could smell the salt air, for the Atlantic Ocean was my front yard.

Several deep breaths later, I realized what had happened. I hadn't been paying attention. *No more daydreaming*, I told myself, and eased my grip on the ladder, to look up and away from the ladder, to finish the job, this time without the daydream. That's when I saw what I didn't want to admit. I'd missed a spot.

I couldn't believe it. The ladder wasn't steady. Every muscle ached because I'd been up and down all morning painting this stupid trim plus standing on my tiptoes to reach impossible places, like the spot I'd missed that I didn't know how I'd missed— although now that I knew the dinginess was there, that was all I could see. I was afraid of heights but living in a two-story house that is over a hundred years old in a climate of salt and humidity makes upkeep a constant chore. No matter how many times I told myself to let it go, that no one could see the dinginess from the ground looking up, the rationalization didn't matter. I knew that I'd missed a spot, and that wouldn't do.

I would have to move the ladder again. Ten, twelve, what looked to be hundreds of feet below me, a gigantic beautyberry bush loaded with purple berries blocked the way. Couldn't move the ladder over. I looked up. Climbing higher on the ladder, to that last rung, made sense, except my mind kept shouting, *You're going to fall. Don't move.*

Academics spend their lives immersed in the nuances of specifics. My research focus is decision-making, which is why my unobtrusive Sentinel hadn't fooled me. As a scholar of the mind, specifically the conscious (what scientists call System 2) and the unconscious (what scientists call System 1), I know the Sentinel likes his own way. But I'd always believed that I, not the Sentinel, was the one in control.

Yet I hadn't saved myself from falling. The Sentinel had hijacked my body to yank me back from space. It happens to everyone, but I study this stuff. I'm aware that I'm not in control, but I can never bring myself to believe it. Which is why I'm so shocked that I can't, no matter how hard I try, bring myself to step up on that last rung and finish the job.

Should have hired this job out, I told myself for the fifteenth time.

But that didn't matter either. I'd started the work. I'd finish it. If I couldn't go up or down, I'd have to go over, without moving the ladder. That meant leaning out over nothing. Something I didn't want to do.

I dipped the brush into the bucket of white satin trim paint that hung on my ladder and reached out, then hesitated. Reconsidering, I dipped the brush again into the paint because I didn't have the nerve to lean out over nothing twice to reach what I'd missed.

The paint-loaded brush touched the trim.

Just a few brush strokes. That's all that needed done. Then I could quit for the day.

My arm trembled. My elbow ached, so did my wrist. The brush weighed a hundred pounds. I could do this, and I leaned farther out. My back spasmed.

The paintbrush dropped from my hand.

I grabbed air.

After that, I don't remember much. Except I thought falling might hurt worse than it did.

That's when I realized I was still upright, trembling enough to make the ladder shake. The Sentinel had made numerous calculations in nanoseconds, then moved my feet and hands, and twisted my torso in space to center my body weight against the ladder. This time he'd moved me two rungs down from where I'd stood. Normal behavior for the Sentinel because that decision, the calculations, the hijacking, all movement made without my conscious participation, had saved my life.

The unconscious never sleeps, they say. *Thank God.* I hugged the ladder like my nephew used to hug his old brown teddy bear.

Through the rungs, below me, I saw the brush on the brown mulch, its white-coated bristles splotched with fine particles of hardwood. That could have been me, lying there, spattered with wood chips, startled blue eyes wide open, staring up at the sky. I shivered and closed my eyes.

Then I looked down again because I'd seen something else below me. Patterns, compelling patterns grabbed my attention. Splattered white dots on ripe purple berries and shiny green leaves. Intriguing patterns. I started to connect the dots of white, purple, and green.

I don't know how long I stood there tracing, retracing, connecting the multiple patterns that linked purple to green to white, green to purple to white, purplewhitegreen.

I do know the pain in my feet brought me back to reality. Released from whatever had kept me focused on that pattern of dots below, I closed my eyes and laid my cheek against the warm ladder. My head felt hot from the sun overhead.

What had happened to me? I'd been standing, staring at those dots for a long time. Maybe for half an hour or more.

I flexed my toes. Opened and closed one hand, then the other, all the while searching for what really happened because this dissociation from reality didn't make sense. Not for me. I had a reputation for hard work, common sense, insight, and intellect.

The first incident, the Sentinel hijacking my body on the ladder, I could understand. My unconscious did that all the time with a seamlessness I never noticed. Tracing phantom patterns on a bruised beautyberry bush though, that meant something else had hijacked my mind, something that wasn't normal behavior, not for me or for the Sentinel.

I'd never before found dots of paint compelling. In fact, I hated painting the trim, the walls, the floor—anything that involved a brush and paint. I started to tremble from the implications of what I couldn't accept. That I'm a psychology professor who studies decision making didn't make one bit of difference to how I felt because, although the Sentinal held me safe from that first skirmish for control, the fury I didn't know was within my mind wouldn't give me a second chance. How could my mind be a place of fury, and I hadn't noticed? Yet I had no reason to doubt the passage of time, the ache in my feet, the hot burn on my scalp, all the evidence that said I'd been standing staring at paint patterns on a bush for way too long. The facts blazed with truth. The Sentinel, an entity more intimate to me than my body, an entity I relied on every second of every day, had stuttered. And that glimpse into my own mind terrified me.

Lost in a mental confusion that wouldn't let go, I looked up at the sky. The sun blazed hotter. I looked down at the ground. The paintbrush hadn't moved.

I gripped both sides of the ladder and slid my fingers down the rail as I moved one foot off the rung to the one below. What happened to me today while painting the trim could have happened to anybody. Rationalization wasn't a wise choice, but those psychological miscues the Sentinel put up had cascaded into denial. Closing my eyes against all external stimuli, I told myself that I had good reason to reject the metaphor of my mind as a battlefield. I moved my other foot to join the first one. Then I stepped down to the next rung. Within the total hours of the day, this was a small blip that would be forgotten once I climbed down off this ladder, got a cool drink, and relaxed for a bit.

~

Susan heard me come inside. "Done with the trim?" she asked as, without looking up, she laid down her Mahjong tile on the dining room table and said, "One bam."

"You missed lunch," Mary Beth said, choosing a tile from the Mahjong wall. "We left you a sandwich in the refrigerator."

The four women who had rented rooms from me for almost a decade—Classy, Susan, Lynn, and Mary Beth—were playing Mahjong as if nothing had happened. Sunlight filtered through the lace curtains at the large windows. The beams highlighted the lighter accents of lilac and pink in the soft gray floral rug my mother had put under the large dining room table more than fifty years ago.

They played the game every weekend that found all of them home. Each of them rented a bedroom from me, and my home had become theirs, a place of refuge and sanctuary. And by making them founding members of The Raindrop Institute, a think tank I'd started five years ago, they had another purpose for living, although sometimes I felt they preferred to play Mahjong than to untangle complex messy problems.

"I almost fell off the ladder."

"You didn't," Lynn said, looking up at me, refusing to believe that what I'd done had been that dangerous. "You were only up one story."

"I hate ladders. I'm hiring someone to paint the rest of the trim."

"We told you, but would you listen?" Classy shook her head and turned away to draw a Mahjong tile. "Oh no. You had to do it yourself."

That stung. I'd almost died out there. "Don't know how I'm going to pay for it. Guess I could always raise the rent."

"Good luck with that." Susan turned back to the game, but Lynn and Mary Beth didn't.

"You okay?" Mary Beth asked.

No. But I couldn't tell her I'd been staring at dots for half the morning.

Nothing to worry about, I told myself for the ten-thousandth time since I'd climbed off the ladder and picked up the paintbrush. People my age had brain farts all the time. I'd have that sandwich Mary Beth mentioned, a drink of water, and relax for a bit. Everything would be fine if I didn't get back up on that ladder.

"Your letter came, Dart." Lynn inclined her head toward the single chair at the farther end of the table and the pile of correspondence.

I stiffened as once again space opened beneath me. Patterns, but this time coming to an end.

Atop the pile of business correspondence for our weekly meeting of The Raindrop Institute, which I would convene this afternoon, sat a legal-sized envelope. I made myself walk over, pick it up, and examine the address. As Lynn had indicated, my name was there in old-fashioned cursive writing. Once I saw the return address that was embossed on the envelope, I knew I was about to learn whether I'd finish the trim or pack my suitcases.

My throat dried up. My vocal cords couldn't work. I felt all the aches and pains in my body and, again, I was falling into that yawning space that wanted me.

"Open the letter, Dart," Classy said.

"Don't you think I might deserve a bit of privacy?" I said, clearing my throat.

"Our fate as well," Susan said. She discarded a four bam.

"Don't you dare take that into the living room or up to your bedroom," Classy said. She picked up Susan's discarded four bam, laid the tile face up on her tray, added two more four bams, and discarded a three dot.

"If you don't inherit, we all have to go," Mary Beth said.

The others nodded. This insubordination is what comes of inviting people to share your home. They'd morphed from tenants into friends and then crossed over the line to become family.

They weren't playing Mahjong any more. They were watching me, but I didn't like their scrutinizing. None of their blood, sweat, or tears had revitalized this house. This morning, they hadn't been high above the ground on a ladder painting the trim. No, they'd been inside the house, playing Mahjong while I worked in the hot sun.

Small favors.

Had they been watching, they would have carted me off to the hospital.

"If your father's fancy-pants lawyer sold this house out from underneath us"—Classy's voice yanked me from my thoughts—"I'm going to dig up your dad and hurt him." Classy's eyes flashed determination. Anger heightened her color, snapped her blond hair out of place because, as usual, she'd raked the curls back from her forehead when she became impatient.

My father and I had found one another five years ago in those long days after his accident, and before he died, I'd learned that he trusted *me*—not my brother David, not my cousin, not my sister-in-law, but me. Then I opened his will and found I would pay penance for five years—not my brother, nor my cousin, but me.

I remembered the words as if I'd read them yesterday. "I want you to put that fancy schooling of yours to use, Dart," he'd written in his will. "Do something about civilization collapse. And while you're at it, solve poverty. Martha would like that. If you don't succeed in five years, your land and the Southport home will be sold and the proceeds given to your favorite charity. Don't let your mom and me down. Love, Dad."

I liked to think he'd been sorry for that moment of frustration and fear when he'd changed his will to spite his own flesh and blood, but I knew my dad. He'd had no regrets.

My mother's home place. I looked around at the dining room, the living room, the hallway to the back bedroom, the stairs up to the second floor where my tenants slept. Mom had grown up here and then brought my brother and me for summer vacations on the ocean. That had been magical for me.

What I'd done to keep the place was launch The Raindrop Institute, what we called TRI, a think tank whose ambitious goal was to prevent civilization collapse, which has happened several times in human history, and to think differently about poverty. But although we'd been successful, we hadn't eradicated poverty or pushed back civilization collapse. That's why all of this could be gone—because The Raindrop Institute had tried to do too much and failed. TRI should have focused on unraveling one of those problems, not both, although to be fair, that also was unrealistic. Complex messy problems had been around for a long time. They provided job security for researchers like me.

The letter would tell me the lawyer had sold this house with the lace curtains at the dining room windows, the rug, the old table, and the china hutch with my mother's best dishes and glassware inside. The walls glowed a soft pink rose, accented with the tiny rosebud border of wallpaper against the high nine-foot ceiling. I'd worked myself silly to bring this house into shape. I'd painted, patched, refinished, and the house still demanded more money, time, and effort—and it might not be mine.

"You fulfilled your obligations, Dart," Susan said. Her long gray dreadlocks swung about her face as she leaned across the dining room table to persuade me that I'd done everything I could, but I knew I hadn't, I knew I could have done more.

"Your father wanted a good faith effort, and he gave you five years to get that done," Mary Beth said.

"You sent the lawyer all the press releases, the good deeds, the evidence that we have made a difference, all the proof your father demanded in his will, copies of letters people have sent, and thank you letters when our suggestions worked." Lynn gestured to the portfolio under the letter. "TRI has been successful. You've got nothing to worry about."

Maybe they were right. If what we'd accomplished in the past five years wasn't enough to make this house mine, I'd start over somewhere else.

As if that would be easy at sixty-three.

Enough.

I sat down at the end of the table, picked up the envelope, and ripped it open. Action at last, Classy's features said. Satisfaction beamed from Susan's smile. I felt none of those emotions.

They knew the verdict before I comprehended what I'd read. Classy threw her folder into the air, and pages fluttered everywhere, a swirl of jubilation that matched the spontaneous laughter around her. "What did he say?" Didn't matter who asked, all of them wanted to know.

I read the brief lines aloud.

"That's it? After all we've accomplished, that's it? Congratulations . . . exclamation point . . . The house and the farm are yours . . . period." Classy stood in protest, and papers swirled from her lap onto the gray rug, like swamp magnolia tree blossoms spiraling down onto pine straw, where they made beautiful abstract art on the forest floor. "I can't believe the brevity."

My eyes followed the drifting papers. The sun high in the sky. Dots of white connecting patterns of purple and green.

No. Focus.

The Sentinel couldn't get caught up in that undercurrent again. I forced myself to pay attention to what was around me, who was around me, not the shapes, the undulations that swirled in enticement, so intriguing I could watch them forever.

Meet their eyes. Tell them you don't deserve this. No matter what the letter said, what we'd been doing these past five years wasn't effective. Never mind that the pile of business correspondence under the letter, a haphazard stack of brown, cream, and white, said otherwise. The Raindrop Institute may not have eradicated poverty or stopped collapse, as Dad had wanted, but those pleas awaiting our attention . . . they were evidence of our success.

But I couldn't ignore what I knew. He'd expected more from me, and I'd let him down and I'd let myself down. And, now that

the house was mine, I couldn't ignore the guilt and disappointment that TRI hadn't done more.

I had the social clout, and I had the content knowledge to make
The Raindrop Institute stand out in the noise of our culture. What
I didn't have was the right vehicle to transport those ideas. Which
is why I hadn't wanted to open the letter, why I didn't want them
to watch me. No matter what the letter said, I didn't deserve my
inheritance.

I also knew I wouldn't have the courage to reject his gift.

Failure, that feeling I couldn't put into words, made me tremble for the third time that morning and tears start to my eyes. I
put the letter down and rushed from the room.

"Aren't we going to celebrate?" asked Lynn. "This is great news."

Mary Beth called after me. "The house is yours. The farm is
yours. You're set for life."

No, I wasn't. The keys to the Volvo were at the front door. I
grabbed them and opened the front door. I kept moving through
the open doorway. They wouldn't understand.

I'm not sure I did.

"We're not going to move out, Dart, so Ash can move in," Classy
yelled after me from the open doorway. "You can't kick us out."

"And we're not giving up TRI," Susan hollered from behind her.
"That's what you want, isn't it? But we're not giving up, Dart, and
you can't make us."

I left them standing in the doorway of the home I'd just inherited and drove away, toward Wilmington and Ash, the man who
might explain all of this to me. Maybe Ash would understand the
only alternative I had, the one thing I didn't know how to do, but
that my father's letter had forced me to face.

TWO

ACROSS THE COFFEE TABLE, Ash arched an eyebrow. That gesture translated to an unsaid comment. *You messed up.*

"My father would have said I hadn't done enough," I said.

"Dart, your father's dead. He's been dead for five years."

"I know." But I didn't really. I found it easier to look at the beauty of Ash's landscaped yard, and his neighbor's impressive landscaped yard and more impressive house—anything to evade the mental image of my father lying in a hospital bed struggling to breathe.

I thought Ash would understand. He wanted me to move in with him, here in Wilmington, where life was civilized with the theater, arts, historic homes . . . and cutting-edge medical services. Spring Haven, one of Wilmington's more prestigious suburbs, had beautiful homes, I'd give him that, but his view didn't compare with the one I had at home. The Atlantic stretched beyond my lawn in Southport, and my thoughts could travel everywhere. Here, my ideas flew into trees, tile, brick, and snagged themselves on shingles.

"I haven't accepted that he's gone." I brought my gaze back to Ash. "I know he died five years ago, but I still had to meet his expectations, and that kept him close, all the time, in my mind, my heart. I read that letter and the last link with him vanished. That's why I ran from the house tonight." I rubbed my eyes so he wouldn't see the tears. "My tenants must think I'm crazy, rushing out of the house like that."

"Not the Raindrops," Ash said. "What are you going to do now?"

"Grieve, cry, although I did all of that five years ago," or so I'd thought. "Classy and Susan think I'm an heiress."

"You are an heiress."

I shook my head, no. That word didn't describe me.

My mom's home place where I lived now gobbled more money than I'd ever have. The Illinois farm ground and the barns, sheds, and fences needed improvements, and the one way I could realize any cash was to sell my portion of the farm, and I couldn't do that. That farmland didn't belong to me, even if my name was on the deed. Nor could my brother, who owned the other half of the farm but not the Southport house, afford to buy me out.

I took a sip of the tea Ash thought might calm my nerves. The warm drink, a blend of sencha and matcha, tasted good. "I never thought of kicking the Raindrops out of my house. I owe them everything. How could they believe that I'd leave them without a home?"

And that was the problem. I was going to leave them behind when I revamped TRI, and they wouldn't be happy. They liked the story they'd crafted of themselves as super heroes fighting against civilization collapse's impending disaster. Dismantling poverty wasn't nearly as headline grabbing.

"Dart. . . ." Ash looked exasperated but not angry. "You, not your tenants, gave The Raindrop Institute a national reputation. Now you have the financial means to do anything." He threw his arms wide. "Anything you want. You don't need their rent money."

"I never let them stay for the rent money." I tossed a pillow on the couch into the opposite arm rest. "They had no other place to go. Every one of them was down on her luck when I took her in. That's why I let them stay."

"From their perspective, you needed the money once, now you don't. You've shared that TRI isn't working. If you don't need their money and if they aren't Raindrops, why do you need them?"

His level gaze nailed my indignation down, and I saw over that emotion to the vast horizon of possibilities my father's bequest had opened for me, and why the Raindrops were afraid. Ash saw freedom. I felt a heavy weight of responsibility.

"Nothing has changed."

"You're spending more time with me, and now that you're an heiress, I'll never let you go."

Surely, he was kidding. Wasn't he?

"We'll spend more time together, travel to exotic places on Daddy's cash. I'll buy you a fur, and you'll buy me a castle in the Alps because I've always wanted one of those."

"Ash, don't be dense," I said.

Then I understood. My eyes must have widened, or maybe my mouth dropped open in the O of surprise people make when they discover the hidden pattern, for he nodded. "They think you're moving in, or that I'll move in with you."

That's what Classy had shouted at me as I left the house.

Ash grinned. He patted my hand, his fingers warm against my skin. "I'd hoped you would."

What? Wait.

Ash and I hadn't been intimate. We were just good friends. I didn't understand move in with me, but he hadn't said that, he'd said he hoped I would move in with him. In dismay, I shifted my gaze from Asher's handsome face to the window, seeking the vast expanse of sky, buying time to think. I pulled my hand from under his.

"That can't happen."

His smile disappeared, and he leaned back away from me. "Only because you, Dart, have the belief in your head that I'm still in love with my dead wife."

"That's because you are, Asher."

Jennifer, his wife, had been gone two years now, but she'd been ill for a long time. He was in denial about Jennifer as I had been in denial about my dad. And when he woke up to reality, his pain would be agonizing.

This time I sought the intelligence behind those blue eyes, not the view in the distance. If Jarvis Asher Wright, dean of Stratton College at North Carolina University Wilmington and my boss, didn't get confirmation I'd heard him, he'd keep repositioning the idea in our point-counterpoint relationship. We'd discussed this, more than once, including how our path together had come to be. If the faculty hadn't ganged up on me and appointed me as spokesperson to tell Dean Wright to shape up after his wife died, I wouldn't be sitting in his house.

We'd had a stormy history. Once upon a time, five short years and eleven months ago, he'd threatened to deny me tenure and promotion. I'd defied him and gone on to achieve both as an associate professor of psychology. Then, he'd done the impossible and supported my promotion to a full professor the following year.

I like to think it was because he knew my worth. More likely, with his wife in the last stages of frontotemporal dementia, he'd caved to the demands of the provost and president, both of whom wanted The Raindrop Institute, which had achieved moderate success by then and showed promise of greatness, to stay at the university.

"You were a mess, my friend."

"I didn't like that the faculty thought I needed a sabbatical. I took it out on you."

"I know." I sipped more of my now tepid tea just to take a break from the intensity and to consider the opportunity. Ash didn't talk about that time, those months after Jennifer died when he came to work unshaven, without showering, and stayed later and later until the weekend the janitor caught him sleeping on the office couch at three a.m. and called me.

That he was open to discussing our relationship and that dark time allowed my own frontotemporal lobes to ignite with hope. I juggled data for a living, which was an occupational hazard when I transferred that skill to finding patterns in my personal relationships.

I sighed. What I hadn't foreseen was that I'd fall in love with my boss. I'd always hoped that love would come my way, despite my wrinkles. I knew the reality because that had a pattern as well. Men saw women like me—older, gray hair among the black waves, wrinkles, an extra pound or twenty, plus an inheritance and a good-paying job—as a purse and a nurse, and if that made me cynical, so be it.

"Have you told your renters about the episodes?"

Episodes, that's what he called my brain's sputtering, *episodes,* and I resented the plural. I'd had two, and that wasn't twenty or two hundred. Two, just two, in the space of twelve months, and I'd been able to stop the third today when the papers swirled from Classy's lap. I still saw the abstract art pattern on the floor, and even now my mind found the shifting patterns fascinating, but

I'd stopped myself from connecting the dots. I wouldn't let my brain go there.

That ability, being able to stop the episodes, I reasoned, could make my brain spasms anything, anything at all, like a deficiency in vitamins, minerals—not enough spinach, or broccoli, or turnips. I never have mastered how to eat properly. Even when I was married to Emory and was responsible for all the cooking, we ate out more than we ate in.

Living with the Raindrops wasn't much better. We'd had hot dogs and chips last night because Classy, who had fixed dinner, knew less about nutrition than I did. Tomorrow night would be better. Mary Beth always prepared a balanced meal. I'd eat double my portion of vegetables.

As for exercise, my fingers got plenty on the keyboard and so did my brain, but not the rest of me. Lately, walking up flights of stairs at work left me winded. That's why I'd vowed for the rest of this year, I would walk up and down three flights at work at least three times every day.

"There's nothing wrong with me, Ash." I wasn't going to tell him what had happened to me on the ladder this morning. I didn't want him to fall back into a pattern of caring for someone because that's what he knew, what made him feel useful and wanted.

"You're traveling too much, Dart."

He might have had a point there. I'd presented at two conferences this month, one in San Francisco and the other in Germany. I'd stumbled off a plane yesterday morning. I hadn't been in any shape to paint the trim. Lack of sleep and jet lag had bungled that opportunity, I could see that now. And in between that trip and the one before, two weeks ago, I'd prepared for my online class; edited my fifth book, which the publishers said would be a best seller; and completed another paper on conscientiousness and how cultivating that personality trait could impact poverty.

I could feel the latent power within that idea. Intriguing. Americans didn't value conscientiousness. The trait had been lost in get-rich-quick schemes, and the me/my movement. If The Raindrop Institute became the vehicle I knew it could be, if I had the support of the Raindrops, then maybe this odd idea about how to eradicate poverty by changing the culture and making conscientiousness a super meme might have merit. All I had to do was convince my tenants I wasn't dismissing their contribution to TRI.

I would address their concerns, and we could put all this doubt behind us. Really, I thought they knew me better than to think I'd desert. . . .

"Dart?"

Ash brought my thoughts back to him with another touch to my hand. Touch was the emotional connection that kept me in this relationship. Thankfully, Ash needed touch as much or more than I did.

Funny how all humans craved that sensation, and we were so conscientious about it, hugging others when they needed consoling, or when we wanted to share joy, or when we were overcome with happiness. Touch kept us connected, in tune, aware of ourselves and one another, but that wasn't the whole truth because touch said you are not alone. Robbie, my nephew, was the only person I knew who didn't yearn to be touched.

Ash looked at me with concern. "You okay?" he asked, and I filed my observations about Robbie and conscientiousness back into my mental to-do folder. I'd call my nephew and my brother this week to see if they had inherited their portion of the farm, although I couldn't see why they wouldn't, and I'd do some more research on how conscientiousness impacted the emotional attributes of poverty, maybe this afternoon while Ash watched football.

"I'm fine, Ash. I shouldn't have tried to paint the outside trim on the house this weekend. I'm not as young as I used to be. Plus, I'm worried about Ellen." The cousin I loved like a sister. "She texted me while I was in Germany." Again, I looked out the window seeking the gray-blue Atlantic that wasn't there. I couldn't move here, no matter how many times he asked me. Southport's ocean view allowed me to breathe and think and create.

"What about your cousin, Ellen?"

"She thinks the cancer has come back. Says Bill will leave her if it has."

"I didn't leave Jennifer when she was diagnosed with FTD."

Now I'd offended him.

Frontotemporal dementia. He never said the name, just the initials, as if that hard, abrupt thunderbolt of consonants explained how the diagnosis had wrecked his life and Jennifer's. I reached across to hold his hand. "You didn't nurse Jennifer through twenty years of cancer either. Bill's out of patience. If this test comes back positive, he'll call it quits. Ellen says he's tired of taking care of her."

Ash started to protest.

I leaned toward him, stopping his words. "Not you. No reflection on you. No one could have cared for Jennifer as well as you did. But Bill's different. He's watched Ellen struggle, and he can't watch her go through this anymore. He's done."

"Ellen's not done." Ash got up with an abruptness that told me how agitated he had become. "He can't be done. She needs him. She's beaten this twice before; she'll do it again. He'll regret that decision—if she's right and that's what he does. But I don't think

Bill will leave. And if he does, he'll find himself reminded every day of his life with her. Those memories won't go away."

Ash lowered himself back into the chair. "So many little things lie in wait for me. Two years now, that's how long she's been gone, and I still come out of the shower expecting to see my suit, shirt, and tie laid out on the bed for me. I didn't care what I wore, but Jennifer was convinced that if I didn't look good, the day wouldn't go well."

Moments like these broke my heart. He kept showing me how much he missed his wife.

"Today's Saturday, and you don't need to wear a suit to walk the beach."

He grinned that Asher grin I loved, the one that said he saw me and not Jennifer. "Is that what you have planned for today?"

"I thought we might fit it in around that football game you want to watch."

"And what are you going to do while I watch football?"

"I'm going to construct a strategy that will convince my Raindrops that they won't be forgotten when The Raindrop Institute recruits more women."

"More women? You didn't tell me about this."

The man was gone, and my boss had returned.

"I approved the link to TRI's website on the college's web page, Dart. You said nothing about changing the structure of The Raindrop Institute when you asked to build TRI's online presence."

But I knew how to deal with the boss as well as the man.

"I spent five years driving the wrong distribution vehicle because my father and you pushed me into that decision." At his wry grimace, I added, "Despite my social credentials and the Raindrops' content clout, the think tank hasn't done what I conceptualized it to do. That has to change, or the day will come when I won't be able to step foot in my own house because of the guilt."

Dad had left me his achievements, the farm and the house, with one intention, to help me realize my dream, building my think tank to a place of prominence in thought leadership, a touchstone for complex, messy problems. Now, he'd left me without excuses for my failures and a compulsion to make an odd idea reality.

Who tied conscientiousness to the eradication of poverty? No one except for that crazy woman at Stratton College who ran The Raindrop Institute, they'd say, and they would mean me.

But the idea made sense. I'd created the think tank to help women, and a few intrepid men, think past symptoms to the problems underneath. The problem was the idea I had for TRI's metamorphosis was too difficult, too odd, too big for me to contemplate, or at least it had been before I'd had this conversation with Ash.

And I was scared to death of the thing because, despite my best intentions to shoo it away, like I'd done as a child with the chickens in my father's barnyard, the idea that TRI had to be more wouldn't leave me alone. Which is probably what my father had planned from the very beginning, because if anyone knew how to play me, my father did.

He'd left me that farm and the house, not because I deserved either one, but to spur me on to greater accomplishments through TRI. I would see this idea through plus find a way to make TRI more accessible to a larger community.

As I drove home from Ash's house, I started laughing as I drove by the grocery store, because an old commercial started playing in my head. The Sentinel had a sense of humor, but I was going to need more than a bowl of Wheaties to make this transformation happen.

~

When I got home later that evening, none of my tenants looked up from their Mahjong game. I pulled out a chair at the dining room table, sat down, and decided how to begin.

"Sorry, I ran out on you—"

Classy frowned and held up a warning finger. She laid down a tile and said, "One dot."

Fine. If that's how they were going to play it, I would ignore their request as well. "You see, as long as I could fulfill the requirements of the will, I never had to say goodbye to my dad because we were always connected, because I still felt as if I were working with him, for him. Then the letter came, and. . . ."

Susan looked up from the game. "Five years go by and you didn't know your dad was dead?"

"Of course, I knew he died." They knew as well as Ash did, but how to explain? "I hadn't accepted that he was dead."

No one said anything.

"I'm sorry I ran out on the celebration."

They turned back to their game. They were still mad.

"Ash is not moving in." Maybe that reassurance would get me back into their good graces.

"Sssshhhh." Classy held up her hand as if to stop me talking and picked up a tile, considered, then racked it again.

"And I'm not moving out," I added.

No one looked up. I wasn't deterred.

"I should have shared my doubts with you from the moment I started thinking about changing TRI."

"Now she tells us," Classy murmured as she rearranged her tiles on the rack.

"You're not kicking us out?" Mary Beth asked.

"Of course not. We've got a Raindrop Institute to run and a meeting to convene. Lynn, would you please get the folders?" Then I held my breath, hoping she would comply.

She did. I breathed out. Maybe this would be okay now. At least they were listening to me.

"Ash won't be happy living with a bunch of old women." Classy pushed away her rack with a sigh, as did the others, and tiles clacked, clattered, and clicked against each other as they filled the trays with tiles from the table. Susan put the game away. Lynn brought the folders to the table and distributed them.

"Didn't you hear me, Classy? He's not coming to Southport."

Classy got up and brought back a bottle of wine that she put on the table. Susan picked up the wine and filled the glasses.

"To Dart," Classy said as she raised her wine glass. The crystal gleamed in the ambient light of the overhead chandelier.

"And to her father, Will Sommers," Lynn said.

"May her house always be ours," Susan said.

Reluctant crusaders. That's what they were. What I was. In the dear faces around the table tonight, I saw what I had known but refused to admit for some time. They hadn't realized that TRI had been drowning. We had gathered around this scarred, worn dining room table once a month for the past four years to discuss pleas for help, but no matter what we did, the pile of letters kept growing every month.

When I mentioned that, Mary Beth put down her wine and said, "Why do we have to do more? Why can't we have one evening where we feel good about what we've accomplished?"

Classy was trying to organize the unwieldy pile in her folder because when she'd dropped it earlier that day, she had stuffed every piece of paper every which way. "You've got the house now." Classy adjusted a few more letters before sighing in defeat. "Mary Beth's right, we can sit back, relax, and take our time."

No, we can't, because humanity is a hot mess that is getting hotter, and catastrophe will be here soon, maybe in as little as fifteen years. Scientists are already saying we're in a sixth mass extinction, and humans are to blame. I reined in the thoughts and arguments I'd constructed around civilization collapse and instead said, "I thought TRI was my best effort, but then I realized it wasn't. I can't accept what I haven't earned."

"You're being ridiculous," Classy said as she turned on me. "The farm and this house are yours. You're the one who made the requirement more than that, Dart."

"I'm not going to give it up."

"Praise be," Classy said, and the others echoed her comment.

Smart aleck.

"I'm not an idiot, but I am going to change how The Raindrop Institute works." Once I figured out how to make that odd idea happen.

"I've always thought civilization collapse and poverty were too big for us," Lynn said, "and that we should focus on one or the other."

Both problems needed solving. They weren't going to go away, but Lynn had seen what my father's death made me realize. "I agree. TRI's efforts are too fragmented." My dad had wanted me to eradicate poverty. If I could focus the Institute on poverty instead of splitting our energies between both initiatives and any-thing else we thought we might impact, the Institute could start to make some real progress.

"We need an intellect as big as the ocean to deal with the

heartbreak out there," Susan said as she considered the logic I'd presented. "This was fun, Dart, when we first started." She flipped through the papers, her dreadlocks swaying, the tips of them just brushing her shoulders. "I suppose the faces weren't real then."

In other words, Susan understood, but she didn't want things to change. I knew that feeling.

"Here's a letter from a mayor in Arkansas," Lynn said. "He wants to rename his town Daylily because the economy blooms for one day when folks cash their monthly relief checks."

Mary Beth picked up a letter. "Here's one from a citizen in Oklahoma. She's concerned about the farmers who are losing generational farms because of low grain prices."

"Some of these pleas for help are dated from several months back." Susan looked across the table at me. "Why haven't you shared them with us?"

Her edgy tone made me wonder. Had she heard the rumors about the bad blood between me and Kathleen Hendrix? Kathleen was her friend. They had lunch quite often. Is that why she seemed so antagonistic tonight? Stratton College, where the three of us worked, was in a small town, and gossip spread like the flu. Susan worked as a research associate in North Carolina University's provost's office. Cushy job for someone with a brain like hers that liked numbers, facts, and stats, and the provost's office heard all the gossip.

"We don't have the funds or the manpower to go that far from home," I said.

"Then why aren't we dreaming up solutions to that little problem?" she asked.

"I can always use more money," Classy added.

"Money isn't the problem."

Classy indicated the inheritance letter that was still on top of my folder. "Not if you have farm income and a house on the Atlantic Ocean worth a cool million."

She'd never understand that I felt like the caretaker of these properties, not the owner, even though my name was now on the deeds.

"This model isn't scalable. Five women sitting around a dining room table discussing and solving one problem a month won't stop anything. At best, for every beached plea we've thrown back into the sea, we've left thousands that contribute to the growing unrest. We need more minds at work on the problems that face humanity. We've had some great successes, local and statewide. And gratitude for our efforts has made us a name in North Carolina. When we got the Oprah interview. . . ."

"We didn't get that interview," Classy said. "You did. Your research. Your books. Your ideas. We just helped."

"You did more than help. You launched TRI." I took a sip of wine, caught my courage, and dared to verbalize the idea that refused to leave. "Why don't we find a way to train more women not local women, but the ones who are living in these cities and towns and dealing with poverty every day?"

"How would we do that?" Susan asked.

"You mean create more Raindrops? Everywhere?" asked Lynn.

Mary Beth looked dazed with the possibility.

"We're the Raindrops." Susan rejected the idea out of hand and started leafing through the papers, searching for information she already knew. "We should charge for our services."

"They don't have the money to pay our travel," I said, "which means they don't have the money to pay us. We can't travel that much because we're gainfully employed. Perhaps we could train older women in those towns to think outside the memes without putting our own jobs in jeopardy or our bank accounts."

"I don't have a bank account," Classy said, twirling a curl with her index finger, "and I don't know what you mean when you say *memes*."

If I tried to curl the waves in my salt-and-pepper hair, my friends would say, stop embarrassing us. With Classy, we all watched those blond curls twist up and bounce free. I envied Classy those curls.

"Memes are infectious ideas that spread from person to person within a culture," I said as I leafed through the letters in my folder. "And the lack of a bank account is a problem a lot of these folks have as well," I said, indicating the letters I had been leafing through. "You are not alone."

"We took two years to get up to speed, Dart," Susan said as Classy frowned.

"Memes are like the flu?" She cocked her head to one side considering that.

"Kinda," I said, "but it's a cultural phenomenon, not a bacterial one."

"Can we please get back to the subject," said Susan. Classy looked miffed, and I almost smiled. "How would we train women we don't know, can't see, and can't talk to about a problem that has plagued humanity forever?"

"Books, websites, blogs, videos."

The Raindrops weren't enthused about the idea. They wouldn't meet my eyes. That frustrated me. I knew firsthand that technology held the answer to creating communities that made a difference because this semester I was scheduled to repeat a massive open online course, a MOOC, that I had taught for the first time the previous semester.

Lynn stated, "All these backwater towns have in common is poverty."

"Don't call them that." I'd grown up in a town like these, and so had Lynn. I didn't understand her remark unless she was putting the town down to validate her reason for leaving. "People live in these towns, like I did in Hawthorne, like you did in your hometown, Lynn." She had the grace to look ashamed. "Like we live in Southport," I said. Their glances suggested I'd gone crazy.

"This is a small town when the tourists are gone."

They relaxed once again. "Okay." Lynn said. "The question remains, how can we help these people?"

"They have to help themselves," Classy said.

"Most of them have no desire to improve their lot in life," Susan said.

"That's not true." I gestured to the fat folders in front of us. "That's evidence to the contrary, but you're rejecting these letters because the evidence doesn't confirm your bias."

"People aren't motivated to get out of poverty. Everyone knows how well they live," Classy said.

Like Classy, I used to believe the same stereotype, but no more, not after the last five years. "They know that their lifestyle isn't optimal, but finding the money, the energy to get out is difficult."

"You can't believe that," Classy said.

"One woman worked two jobs until one night she parked her truck in a no parking zone because she was late to work. The truck was impounded. She didn't have the cash to pay the fees, couldn't borrow the money, didn't have bus fare, and as a result, lost both jobs because she no longer had transportation."

"That old rock keeps rockin' back in every time you think you're out from under," Lynn said. She had lived at the edge of poverty for most of her adult life. She knew better than anyone at the table how banal poverty could be.

"Has to be intelligence then," Mary Beth said, "that differentiates the superrich."

"Intelligence isn't a determining factor," Susan argued. "Read Diamond's *Guns, Germs, and Steel*. He makes a pretty good case for opportunity or lack of it as the culprit."

"Dart and Susan have those fancy degrees that open doors for them," Classy said. "That's why. . . ."

"Men do the same thing," Mary Beth said. "They open doors for their wives—"

"—until the bastard doesn't." Susan's face twisted. She'd had a tough marriage and a tougher divorce. Most days she wasn't bitter, but tonight the pain was real again.

"I think we should take from the rich and give to the poor," Classy said. At the collective groans, she pointed to the stack of emails I'd printed. "A lot of them agree."

"You're thinking about this wrong," I said.

"No, I'm not," Classy said. "If everyone had money, poverty wouldn't exist."

Classy's heuristic wouldn't go away unless I could erase that shortcut thinking. "Wealth is a sexy word, but producing objects of value isn't sexy. But that's why people are wealthy. They produce items that others are willing to pay for. You can give the poor all your money and the next day the imbalance will be back because the wealthy, not the impoverished, produce things of value."

"If the poor had money, they could create items of use." Classy wasn't going to give up.

"Money is a technology," I said. "A vehicle we use to buy things of value. If you want to solve poverty, we have to focus on giving those who are impoverished opportunity to create things of worth. That's different from giving them money."

"Lots of beliefs standing in the way of that one, Dart," said Susan.

"You're saying poverty isn't a result of unequal distribution of money, but rather a symptom of the underlying problem?" Mary Beth's fingers tapped the table as she considered what that meant.

"Eradicating symptoms does nothing to solve the problem." I was getting tired of repeating myself, but unless I kept putting the data points up for consideration that I wanted them to incorporate into their decision-making about the poor, they would ignore everything I said. "And the problem has many, many parts. Only one of which is the unequal distribution of the capability to produce things of value."

"We have to bring the rain then," Mary Beth said.

My dad always liked rain, but that's not what Mary Beth meant. "That's right, we have to approach the problem from every angle we can and patch all the holes in the roof, not just the one, like wealth distribution."

"That's because you earn money." Classy twirled her blond curl. "Thinking differently about nothing still leaves you with nothing."

The unconscious at work again. With that heuristic, that simple little go-to formula that solved, although it didn't, a complex mess, Classy could ignore the problem. She'd shrugged her shoulders and decided there was nothing she could do. Problem solved. We might as well sacrifice a virgin or two as the Mayans had, and hope that sacrifice would work if we were going to ignore hundreds of thousands of conflicting data points as irrelevant.

"Not for the first time, we've spun ourselves in a circle," I said.

Susan grinned.

"We're ignoring what Dart has been trying to get us to do." Something in Mary Beth's voice caused Classy to stop twirling her hair.

"For a psychology professor, she's clueless."

Classy's indignant words stung.

"She's dating the dean. She's got money and a roof over her head." Classy ticked the points off on her fingertips. "She doesn't need us anymore, and she sure doesn't need to solve problems like poverty because that doesn't affect her, not anymore."

Funny, if I were rich, I'd hire someone to paint the trim. But I wasn't, and that meant I'd be back up on that ladder tomorrow. However, I did have the resources to buy a long extension handle for the brush that would reach the spot I'd missed without my getting back on the ladder.

"We've been successful," Susan said. "We could charge for our suggestions, and I think with our track record people would pay our way."

Translation: nothing I'd said had assured them.

But I had made a decision. Like my paintbrush, TRI needed a longer reach. I'd hoped that all these years of working together would smother their fears and their persistent unconscious voices, but I would have to go on without them. The data were too strong to ignore. I might not have the evidence to back up my odd idea that conscientiousness could combat poverty, but I knew in my soul that conscientiousness was key.

THREE

"**D**R. SOMMERS."

Lea Wilson, the postdoc whom I'd hired to run the MOOC, the university's only and ongoing collaboration with Stanford, came up behind me on the east wing stairs at Stratton College. Her timing couldn't have been worse. I was out of breath and wondering why I'd thought climbing the stairs instead of taking the elevator was a wise decision. The most I could manage was to return her smile and wish I were anyplace else while taking deep breaths that didn't begin to ease my need.

Tall, five ten at least, with the mixed features of an Irish, Polish, German, and African-American heritage, Lea prided herself on not belonging to one race but held allegiance to her individuality and intelligence. Her grandparents had survived the Dust Bowl, and maybe those genetics had allowed Lea to escape from Cabrini–Green, a public housing project near downtown Chicago known for murder, drugs, gangs, and misery.

Her research interests in risk taking and decision-making matched my own. We'd been working together for a year to expand the research I used for the MOOC and also for TRI. She had both energy and ambition, and she had published over ten journal articles—a phenomenal number for someone who'd finished her PhD a year ago. She'd been considered for the Early Impact Award from the Federation of Associations in Behavioral & Brain Science (FABBS) and this year had won the Hillel Einhorn New Investigator Award from The Society for Judgment and Decision-Making.

Plus, she'd experienced and survived an impoverished childhood. That experience growing up in Cabrini–Green, and not the awards, is what got Lea the job with North Carolina University at Wilmington. Childhood experiences like hers didn't normally transition to an academic setting. If individuals like Lea could succeed, logic highlighted that poverty could become obsolete. Now I was eager for a longer discussion around my idea of conscientiousness as the meme that could serve the poor, if I could catch my breath to speak.

Lea's quick grin of welcome that made her friendliness contagious faltered.

"So," I said, stalling for time to gather oxygen and my thoughts from petty squabbles, "how long have I been standing here staring at you?"

"Just a few seconds, Dr. Sommers."

She smiled as if that were the most natural thing, even though we both knew it wasn't. In academe, we're all independent of one another, but try to reach above your means and the rest will reach up to pull you back down. Add the few professors who forget to take their meds, and no wonder things become unstable. Much is tolerated under the glamour of supposed brilliance in this environment.

Probably several minutes then. Now I was positive she'd want to run TRI's online presence and work with me if I could convince the Raindrops to take TRI online. No one else would have confidence in an absent-minded, elderly, out-of-shape professor.

"Dr. Eggers told me he parked his car at the library yesterday and locked it. When he came out two hours later, the car was still running," she said.

How sweet to try and put a positive spin on my forgetfulness.

"Someday," I said, "we'll go over to the math building and watch the professors think about where they parked their cars that morning." I didn't add that sometimes the same thing happened to me, because she seemed pleased to anticipate that joint excursion.

"What can I do for you, Lea?"

That light of pleasure on her face evaporated. I'd come across as abrupt when all I wanted was not to waste her time or my own. People thought me emotionally remote. That wasn't true, although I did have a hard time expressing my feelings.

My father hadn't liked jubilant behavior or expressions. He tended to make fun of them, so I had repressed much of my natural exuberance. In the five years since his death, I'd regressed a bit, but much of the repression was now ingrained. Who I could have been was not what I had become.

"If you tell me how I can help you, Lea, I can answer, then go to my office and hyperventilate in private." I expelled what little air I had, to take more in and give my oxygen-deficient lungs some relief.

She laughed and the awkwardness eased between us.

"My paper was accepted," she said. "The one that posits good decision-making doesn't rely on high levels of fluid intelligence or abstract reasoning."

I frowned. "I'm not sure I understand."

"This outdated thinking, that people of high intellect are best at decision-making, has constrained human potential and influenced our policies, government, welfare practices—everything in our society." She threw her hands wide to illustrate everything. "We're wrong to think that way. As long as a person understands risks, that individual can make informed decisions. That data has tons of implications for poverty, for The Raindrop Institute, for the MOOC."

I frowned because tossing aside accepted memes like high intelligence equals good decisions wouldn't be easy.

"People who make bad decisions don't understand the risks involved. If we improve risk literacy and couple that with adaptive technology like computerized tutors, decision-making improves, regardless of intellect."

I thought of an Illinois neighbor who sold his farm for four hundred thousand dollars and lost all that money in eight minutes of gambling when he went on vacation to Las Vegas. A lifetime of work and heritage wiped out because he hadn't fully understood the risks in his decision to gamble. Once again, I found breathing difficult as I lost myself in the enormity of change the concept presented. We'd put the U.S. economy at risk with its lottery, sports gambling, and casinos if we overturned that meme.

Lea nodded and smiled. "Intellect has always been tied to better decision-making, and we've been wrong. This study said intellect didn't matter."

Our whole society, how we provide aid to people in this country and overseas, all of it is based on an acceptance that high intellect is needed. If Lea was right, what made a difference was understanding risks and considering risks involved in making decisions, and anyone, high intellect or average intellect, could be taught to do that.

If we could slow down the unconscious decision making, but I didn't pay that errant thought much attention.

Add conscientiousness to the mix, and TRI had another tool to use in the fight against poverty. I needed Lea to develop assessments that helped people evaluate and be aware of the risks involved in decisions about money.

"Lea," I reached for her hand with both of mine, "the dean has approved a link to TRI on the college website." We'd never had any social media presence before. "Can you build that website for us? I'd like to put your risk assessment quiz on the site, we can profile your research, and we can let our followers know that with training, visual aids, and diverse programs, people can climb out from under the consequences of bad decisions."

I told her about the charity that had gone into Africa filled with good intentions and how the charity urged the local inhabitants there to plant tomatoes on a verdant field by the river. The locals said it couldn't be done, but the charity didn't agree and soon the tomato plants they planted were red with fruit. They were feeling quite good about the crop when the hippos came up from the nearby river and trampled everything into a pulpy mess.

"The lesson learned was to listen to the people they are helping. That's what they're doing with further efforts to improve lives in that area."

"We should do that with the poor in this country," Lea said. "They have ideas as to how to improve their lives and charities— volunteers and government officials should listen to them, not preach to them."

"Could we incorporate The Doomsday Clock into that risk assessment?"

"Inciting dread doesn't lead people to action." Lea frowned at me as if she thought I should know that. "Comprehending the risks involved in decisions leads to positive action."

She had a point. "We have one resource to tap, and it's not our emotions," I said.

"The brain," Lea said, the amusement bubbling through her thoughts, "the same resource that's conceptualized the Doomsday Clock."

"Ironic, isn't it?"

She laughed.

"Did you know that for the first time in a century, over half of the population lives in cities. That's going to put enormous strain on infrastructure and resources in those urban areas."

"Speaking of disaster," Lea said, "that's why I caught up with you. Dr. Hendrix . . . .."

Uh oh. Hendrix had never been a fan of mine because my imagined slights against her had grown fossilized over time. I don't think she ever forgave me for having the temerity to disagree with her decision and that of Catherine Alvarez, who had left the university after she served as the chair of the promotion and tenure committee, to not grant me promotion to associate professor or tenure. That had been five years ago, and my ideas and the recognition they received, plus the credit that got me a full professorship the following year after I went up for associate, hadn't helped quell her dislike. If anything, that promotion had intensified her aversion.

"What about Hendrix?" I wasn't smiling when I said those words.

Lea looked a bit frightened, but she managed to say, "She asked me to write a chapter with her for that new book from Harvard on brain theory, but I'd rather write with you, Dr. Sommers. What we've been discussing interests me."

"Dr. Hendrix won't be happy if you write with me."

"You hired me, but I'm not hers, or yours, or anyone's—whatever it is you all think I am."

I'd felt that way once in my long career. At a conference in Salzburg, Austria. Class, race, religion, good looks, money, my father's disappointments, his expectations, and all the other data measurements I used to evaluate myself faded to nothing while I was there.

Maybe that was why I wanted to go back. I'd grown so much during that week, stretched my thinking, that I came back to NCUW a different person, at least intellectually. Although I don't know for sure, I'm certain that The Raindrop Institute had its beginnings in that overseas adventure. I'd been forced to focus on decision-making and, oh, how I wanted to go back someday, to share who I'd become, where my research had brought me, my successes. And I'd take Lea with me, if they accepted my intention to host a symposium on world poverty and conscientiousness, what I'd been daydreaming about when the Sentinel saved me from falling off the ladder.

But that was in the future, and Lea had a problem in the now. "Hendrix will vote on your tenure and promotion bid, if you are selected for the assistant professor position we have available. Did you submit your vita for the position?"

"I did, but if I have to align myself with someone, I'm on your side, not hers. I want to collaborate with you."

"Then tell Hendrix that you've already agreed to work with me on a chapter and that we are exploring the theory that the brain's role is to coordinate body movement."

Lea's beautiful sea-green eyes narrowed as her pupils widened. "That's very controversial."

Increased pupil size indicated engagement. Good, I had her attention.

"Keep in mind, that's not Hendrix's area of research. She can't piggyback on our efforts if we write about this theory. Conducting research on how the brain coordinates or doesn't coordinate movement might be of interest to a lot of people. Remember? I sat next to you at the last faculty meeting when you shared your sister's experience lifting the car off her puppy."

I didn't tell her the other reason I was interested. The research might explain why I'd stood so long gazing at a pattern of white, purple, and green dots. Or why the patterns of light and dark highlighting Lea's hair at this moment challenged my own sense of rightness. I clenched my fist to stop the urge to touch her hair. That didn't lessen the compulsion to follow those shades of light into dark and dark into light.

"My sister shouldn't have been able to lift that car, but Sadie did. I still don't know how she managed to save her puppy." Lea ran her hands through her tousled chestnut and blond hair, evidence of the genetic war inside her pitting Irish curls against African texture. She wore it loose today, a change from her preferred braids.

The gesture rippled the patterns of light and dark, and my compulsion to capture the light grew stronger. When my hand involuntarily lifted, I clenched my fist tighter and brought the involuntary movement under control. It wasn't easy.

I knew better than to touch a student. I never did except for a hug at graduation, which was fine in that time and place. Nor did hair fascinate me, although I have to admit, hair fascinates a lot of the students at this university. They spend excessive amounts of time and money on hair products and tools.

The pattern of light and dark that played about in Lea's hair drew me just as the pattern of dots had kept me standing, staring down at purple, white, and green. She shifted to stand in the shadows, and the patterns vanished. My entrancement disappeared, the compulsion eased, and my fist unclenched.

Bewilderment was on her face. I noticed because I could think again. What had we been talking about? Had she noticed my restraint? My half-lifted hand?

I remembered. We'd been talking about her sister. "Was she hurt?"

"A jammed finger," Lea said.

"I'm going to use that for next week's lecture in the MOOC."

Because I too had had a similar experience of the Sentinel chemically hijacking my body. I'd been standing at the foot of the stairs watching my nephew Robbie come down the stairs with his father when he twisted out of David's grasp, tucked, and started to roll. Before he'd tumbled down four steps, I'd thrown myself up the flight of stairs to pin his fifteen-month-old body against the wall. He'd been laughing when my shoulder slammed into his stomach. The wonder of that? He was okay, and I had a jammed finger to show for my rescue act. None of what I had done was a conscious decision.

"The brain hijacks the body," she said.

"The unconscious, actually," I said.

"And you find yourself doing something without any conscious effort to take that action."

"Thinking is not the brain's primary function. Survival is." And unlike movement theory, there was plenty of research to back up that claim.

"But that doesn't explain why Sadie risked her life or injury to save Nico." At my smile, she stopped trying to explain what

I couldn't say. "So that's what I tell Dr. Hendrix, that we're interested in a theory of motion as the primary function of the brain."

"That's what you tell her." Relief that Lea understood eased into a smile. "She'll dump you as fast as I was breathing earlier. Kathleen's take on neuroscience research is that the brain is all about thought, not action. That bias of hers won't tolerate any deviation."

"Will this hurt me when it comes time for promotion and tenure—if I get the job, that is?"

"Not if your annual reviews are good for every year you are here. She can say anything about you that she wants, but those annual reviews, those are the documents that matter."

"Then I would be honored to write that chapter with you, Dr. Sommers, on the brain and movement, with a concentration on how the unconscious can hijack the body"—and I thought, *and the mind*—"and I'll collaborate with you to build the online presence of The Raindrop Institute."

Lea held out her hand, and I shook it, the bargain sealed.

"If we are going to collaborate with one another, call me Dart. Our deadline is just a short month from now for that chapter. There's a wonderful TED talk about our topic. View it, take some notes, and we'll start fleshing out the pros and cons tomorrow. Does that work for you?"

Lea hurried away to get started on the research we needed.

That's when I saw that, two doors down the hallway, Hendrix's door stood half open, and I'd bet a thousand hours of library research she was inside listening, her mouth tight with displeasure. Lea had gone the opposite direction, back to her office. That was good, but I had better confront the fire ant in her office before she spread stinging rumors neither Lea nor I needed.

~

Before I could argue with myself as to other options, I rapped my knuckles on the half-open door, then pushed open the door and leaned against the door jamb, trying to convey the impression that this was a friendly visit. I should have known better.

Scribbling words on the margin of a student's paper with enough emphasis to make my jaw hurt, the woman who lived to make my professional life miserable looked up at me, but only after she'd finished her comments. That poor student. He or she wouldn't get any pleasure out of those red marks.

"Stay away from her, Dart." Hendrix put the pen down with precise movements. Despite her bulk she moved with grace. That straight, short gray hair framed a wide face with small brown eyes made smaller by drooping eyelids. The sun hadn't been kind to her.

"Stay away?" I asked. What did that mean? To be prudent, I remained standing just inside the doorway.

"You don't remember?" Scorn coated every consonant and vowel as she looked up at me without a smile of welcome on her face.

I didn't remember.

She grew impatient with my ignorance. "Rosa."

Rosa. Why Rosa?

The only Rosa I knew was Rosa Gonzales, who had come to work in Stratton College for one semester three years ago and then had jumped to Harvard when they offered her a job the following semester.

"You drove her away."

"Lea's still here."

"Rosa." Her jaw clenched so tight she couldn't get the words out. "Rosa Gonzales."

I stopped leaning on the door jamb. If Kathleen decided to attack me, I had to get out of her way before she got around the desk because if she reached me, she'd take me to the ground as she weighed twice what I did.

"You drove Rosa away."

"Ah, you were the one. . . ." The clicks fell into place. I knew now what had never made sense before. I'd been hurt that a colleague I'd made every effort to be friendly toward had lied about me, but Rosa hadn't done the lying. Hendrix's lie was what Ash had believed when he'd called me into his office, the dean's office, three years ago and chewed on me for unbecoming conduct toward a colleague.

Nor had he apologized when I showed him my calendar for the semester Rosa had been with us. I hadn't been in the office that much because I'd been on sabbatical and traveling for interviews and meeting with business leaders and K–12 educators about The Raindrop Institute. My jaunts had paid off, but I'd always felt a bit guilty that I hadn't interacted with my new colleague, although we'd become friendlier after she left.

"You made life hell for her."

"You're the one who told the dean I drove her away."

"Well, it doesn't matter, I suppose, who said what."

The heck it didn't.

"The result was we lost a great researcher because of you." Hendrix shifted in her chair and aligned the red pen precisely along the edge of the dissertation she'd been reading. Or at least I thought the pile of papers thick enough to be a dissertation.

"Your behavior and that of Professors Mendoza and Wilson, that's what made Rosa leave," I said.

"Lea has a chance at a good career here if you leave her alone." She glared at me, eyes narrowed with intent. "I'll stop you from harming this one."

Old resentment flared. "When Rosa had her exit interview with the dean, she didn't mention my name."

"Of course, she didn't. She's too professional to sling mud, but we all know what you're like."

She hadn't gotten over those three graduate students who had deserted her and asked me to chair their dissertations. Via the grapevine, I'd heard that Hendrix considered their decisions my betrayal. Emotion again. People think emotionally, and they don't see facts. If she made herself more approachable to the students, maybe smiled at them once in a while, they would respond in a positive manner and not desert her; but no, Hendrix preferred cold disdain as inspiration.

And, to be frank, in the past that demeanor had worked to her advantage. But times had changed because she and others like her had been so successful in fighting to bring professors and students of color to this university. White males had once dominated Stratton College, but no longer. We had more women than men now and more women and graduate students of color than Caucasians. And younger professors of color like Lea wanted to work here because we valued their capabilities and ideas.

All of that happened because of social justice efforts from warriors like Hendrix. Yet the fight had left her wounded. Slinging slights, insults, and hatred—the very missiles that had once been directed her way—she refused to see that her glamour of faded splendors obscured reality. She'd spent forty years fighting dis-crimination, and the warrior hung onto past glories and insults.

I should have understood what I now observed, for I studied this stuff, the flawed decision-making dependent on heuristics and biases that no longer worked in a changing environment, but I didn't. "I made a mistake when I left Rosa Gonzales to your care," I said.

My regret left me feeling disappointed in myself.

Hendrix thought I had admitted wrongdoing. I could see it in her smile, and I knew she'd be at Ash's desk within the hour, shar-ing that confession. So be it. I could handle Ash, but I wouldn't let her hurt Lea. Women like Lea were the future of this college, of this university. I stepped closer to the desk, stopping when my thighs touched its edge. She settled deeper into her chair, her brown eyes wide because she had to tilt her head back to stare up at me looming over her desk. Her jowls fell back from the clean line of her jaw.

"Lea will be working with me on that chapter for Professor English's seminal book on neuroscience."

"But I've invited her—"

"Yes, you have, and I hope you'll not withdraw that invitation. To do so would send the message that you were—how did you put it?—'making her life hell,' and I'm sure you don't want to do that. Book chapters don't count for much in this place. You made sure of that when you were on my tenure and promotion committee, but two book chapters in such a prestigious publication will. If we work together for Lea's benefit, she'll be more successful than we are."

"How dare you imply that Lea doesn't have my support?" She stood up. "I always support students of color. She has the talent and potential you never had. We should never have given you tenure. You're the one who is an affront to the institution, to this college. We have too many like you roaming these halls."

I had turned to go, but now reconsidered. "What do you mean *like me?*"

"Your research methods are shoddy, your experiments can't be replicated, and this department doesn't need more theory about civilization collapse. We're the laughingstock of academe because of you."

Because I didn't trust myself around her any longer, I turned away again. Five years ago, she and Alvarez would have won if Ash hadn't listened to the university lawyers and to reason and given me tenure. She'd made my life hell during that time for no other reason than she could. I'd once thought she and I could be friends because we had so much in common, both of us older white females who as young women had aspired to be more than what society at that time deemed appropriate. I'd been wrong.

She called out just as I was about to quit the room: "And leave that ratty ol' bear in your office next time you roam the halls. This isn't a confinement center for the mentally ill."

Anyone in the hall could have heard her, I realized as my firm steps faltered. Hobbled by a new and unsettling suspicion, I looked down. Brown Bear dangled by one paw from my clenched left hand.

∼

Closing the door of my office behind me, I leaned against it and considered Brown Bear. Then I hugged Robbie's old teddy bear close to my chest before I set him on the table and turned away, trying to forget I'd made a fool of myself holding a stuffed teddy bear while walking through the building. What had I been thinking? How many of my colleagues had seen my odd behavior? What must they be thinking?

I glanced at Brown Bear. He hadn't moved except to slump a bit. Poor thing. I reached out to stroke his fur, just the tip of one finger, but that was enough to soothe me again.

Think of something different.

Not Hendrix.

Sunlight. Sunlight was good.

Focus on how that splotch of light drapes itself across the high-backed ergonomic chair at the desk, as if the sunshine is prepared to take dictation. Your eighty-page vita resides somewhere inside that computer.

I came back to myself. I noticed the diplomas of the three degrees I held hung on the wall above the silent machine. The PhD certificate with my name on it hung above the work station. I had graduated from the University of Illinois, a prestigious school, with that final degree in psychology. Numerous awards sat on the deep window sill. More hung on the wall to the other side of the window. My eyes touched each award.

Data. Look at all the data that says she's the one who's crazy. Connect those dots, not her scorn. So what if I'd carried a teddy bear through the office? The cesspool of Hendrix's disdain faded as I took stock of who I'd become. I wasn't an affront to this college. On the contrary, my output surpassed Hendrix's, and she'd been here thirty years longer than my measly ten and a half years.

The library shelves. *Look there.* Along the wall. Opposite the computer. The floor-to-ceiling bookcases contained at least five books with my name etched on the spines. The last two had achieved best-seller status. None of the professors in my department, including Hendrix, could match my accomplishments. My books, articles, co-authored chapters—all evidence of something different from her perceptions.

I pulled out that ergonomic chair in front of the computer, set Brown Bear on the desktop, uh oh, I'd picked him up once again and carried him around with realizing what I was doing. My thoughts as confused and slow as my movements, I sat down, my eyes on the bear, fearing what I didn't want to admit.

I wished I'd never brought Brown Bear to North Carolina. I'd found him in my father's house the day I closed and locked the door on that life. I couldn't leave him because he didn't deserve to molder away in a cold, empty farmhouse that the mice invaded every fall. Robbie had loved Brown Bear, but then he'd given him up. Something had happened—what I didn't know, nor did I know why—but Robbie had given him up, and the bear had been forgotten until I found him that morning I'd left the farm.

I should have left him there. The chair back was warm from the sunlight. After a while, I spun it around so that I could look out the window and forget the confusion I felt, but the fear, the need to know why I was disintegrating, wouldn't leave me alone.

Two weeks ago, at the faculty meeting, the dean had declared that online learning was the new direction of the college, and he'd used my MOOC as an illustration of what the future held for us all. That praise hadn't endeared me to Hendrix. But he was right, the students liked online learning. They didn't need to drive to campus. They could work on lessons at home in their pajamas at three in the morning if they wished without anyone being the wiser.

The internet could serve more students than did limited

seating for two hundred in an auditorium, without the cost and upkeep of drafty old buildings that needed sustained expensive maintenance. The university liked limitless web enrollment which translated to more money in the university's coffers with minimal expenses.

The acquisition of money and protection of money drove universities, which meant more endowments, more grants, higher tuition and fees, hiring more and more adjuncts and professors of practice rather than tenure-track folks like myself. In other words, not letting associate professors except those who were stellar apply for full professorships kept costs down. What made the whole thing funnier than my father's suspenders was that professors supplied the energy that kept the lights on.

We hadn't done ourselves any favors. Our very ubiquity worked against us and, until the lights went off, we were our own worst enemies.

I was the future Hendrix dreaded. That's why she'd attacked me. Psychology had a term for this: transference. She would harm me so my notoriety couldn't illuminate her shortcomings.

I'd been indulging in transference myself. How had I'd gotten Brown Bear off that top shelf? More importantly, *why* had I carried him around?

What had I been doing before I went for that walk up and down the stairs where I met Lea?

The dissertation. I'd been reading a student's dissertation. I looked over the smooth expanse of my desk to the round table beyond. I'd left my chair pushed back away from the table. Instead of fretting about Hendrix and Brown Bear, I should finish editing that dissertation.

Remembering the texture of the silk against my bare feet

had me standing up again, going over to the table, slipping off my shoes and digging my toes into the plushness of the Persian carpet, with its threads of turquoise, aqua, and Santorini blue. They were soothing colors, and I'd spent hours tracing the pattern of those threads as I thought my way through complexity. I thought I'd picked up my red pen. But when I looked up from the rug, sunlight no longer doused the chair, and the red pen hadn't been moved.

Lost again.

The afternoon had waned, and I still sat at the table, my toes buried in the plushness of silk while my hands stroked Brown Bear. I hadn't picked up the pen. I hadn't marked a single sentence on the dissertation. I had brought Brown Bear with me to the table, and I'd been sitting there petting him for at least an hour. An hour doing nothing. An hour I couldn't remember.

I would put him down now.

I would.

Instead, I fussed with his ribbon, the smooth, scarlet ribbon with the frayed edges that felt like silk against my fingertips as I arranged those smooth bits of fray around his neck. Shaking again, for a different reason, I clasped my hands together to stop that reaction. And when my mouth wouldn't stop quivering, I pressed my fists against my lips to hold myself together.

Maybe Ash was right about how stressed I was. I could relax for a bit, take my time with reshaping TRI, go away for a while and veg. All these people pulling at me, that's what was wrong with me. If I could just go away and forget about all of them, forget that Ellen might be dying, forget that the Raindrops were mad, forget that Asher loved his dead wife more than me.

But I couldn't do that. My dad always said to face what I feared.

I put Brown Bear down and went to my desk. The afternoon sun may have gone, but the chair was still warm. I pulled a piece of paper toward me, picked up another red pen, and started writing down the odd things I'd been doing.

- *Body hijacking, noticeable only because I know I didn't consciously move myself on that ladder.*

- *Standing on the ladder, looking at dots of paint on the beautyberry bush. (Mind hijacked)*

- *Papers swirling like swamp magnolia flowers falling to pine straw.*

- *Stroking Brown Bear.*

- *Pattern fascination with Persian silk rug.*

Putting the pen down and studying the words, I realized I'd forgotten something.

- *Pattern fascination with lights and darks in Lea's hair.*

I read and reread what I'd written.

My conclusion?

The data are inconclusive.

Carrying a teddy bear? A little unusual for a woman in her sixties, but with all the pressures of work and Ellen's illness, plus the farm and the Raindrops, that too could be rationalized as normal, soothing, comforting behavior. And I hadn't seen patterns in the rug, I'd noted the colors. To test that assumption, I glanced over at the rug. Nothing unusual engaged my mind, not even the blue that reminded me of Santorini's caldera.

No pattern repeated into obsession.

I looked at the list, ignored the line that read pattern fascination with lights and darks in Lea's hair because I couldn't fathom why that had happened. We'd worked together for a year now, and I had never been interested in her hair. Still, wasn't that a pattern? Even now I wanted to trace it, find how it worked, how the light blended into the dark and then glinted again through that darkness.

Crumpling the paper up, I tossed the mess into the wastebasket. This had been a weird day, and I should go home and get a good night's rest. I gathered my things and walked away, then paused at the door, something nagging at my brain that said *you forgot me*, and with my hand on the doorknob, I turned around.

Brown Bear sat on my desk.

Leaving him sitting alone in the dark didn't seem like a kind thing to do. Maybe if I put him back on the top shelf where I'd found him earlier, that would be better. He'd be safe there.

That anxiety taken care of, I went home.

Around two that morning the sheets rustled as I stretched and came awake because my mind had another rationalization for me. I lay still in my bed because I knew if I moved, the thought would disintegrate.

Everyone experiences little slips—hesitations, forgetting words, forgetting keys—as they age. The episodes, as Ash called them, were nothing to worry about. Just overwork. Stress. I hadn't committed a crime, hadn't murdered anyone although Hendrix had made me feel as if I had. Things would be better tomorrow after I had a good night's sleep.

But what about that impulse to touch Lea's hair? That thought kept me up for a while until I snuggled Brown Bear close, turned on my side, and closed my eyes.

FOUR

SUNDAY EVENING FOUND ME lost in the minutiae of returning emails from colleagues and students in my doctoral classes. The rain had started an hour ago. When the plant beside my desk shivered, I convinced myself what I'd seen from the corner of my eye wasn't real. Then the plant shivered again. I touched the leaf. Wet. My eyes went to the ceiling. A droplet of water there . . . falling . . . and the leaf shivered again.

Classy opened the door into the living room just as the plant shivered yet again. From the street, a car engine revved and then faded as her boyfriend, Sandy, drove away.

"Hope you hire that handyman who did the repairs last month," she said, looking at the quivering plant. "He looked good in a tool belt."

"Nice night?"

"We met Bill and Ellen for drinks."

"What did you do?" I asked, my attention returning to the emails I was reading.

"Talked." She smiled, and in that moment, in that light, she looked young again, dressed in black tights and a shapeless turquoise top that slouched off one shoulder. Her bra strap was black lace. Sexy, even for Classy. "About your inheritance, what you

54

should do with the Raindrops, Ellen's cancer, and how grateful she is Bill and Sandy are friends."

"I don't believe the cancer is back. That would be too cruel," I said. "And TRI will survive, Classy. We'll just do things differently." I typed a response to one email. "In a way, our jobs will be easier."

She walked over and sat down in the easy chair next to my computer desk. "Then let me lighten your burden a little more."

"TRI is not a burden." Why did she have to make this difficult? "We're not making enough progress. The problems are bigger, people are still impoverished, and we're running out of time. If problems get too complex, they snowball and then everyone is crushed as they run to get out of the way."

"Dart, look." She held out her hand between me and the computer screen and wiggled the third finger of her left hand.

The diamond was small, but the facets twinkled in the dim living room lights. All my fears of marriage as a trap for women rose in resistance. "But you said. . . ."

"Doesn't matter what a woman says if the right man comes along, and Sandy is the right man for me."

"It's just so sudden."

She laughed. They'd been dating for six years.

"Be happy for me, Dart. Ellen and Bill are."

"Classy," I sighed and looked down at the keyboard. "You're compounding all your problems if you marry him."

"Don't ruin my evening. I've had such a good time."

She wasn't thinking this through. "Sandy's younger than you are, but his health is worse than yours. And yours is bad enough. You can't climb up on the bar at Zack's anymore." She'd done that more than once in the time I'd known her, climbed up on the bar and danced, all the men looking at her and she didn't care.

"With me cooking for him and taking long walks together, we'll get his health and my flexibility back."

"Might let him do the cooking, Classy. He'll live longer."

"Now you're being mean."

"Sandy wants what you want, someone to take care of him. And that's going to be your lot in life. Why don't you just let things be?"

"I could die before he does."

"But you won't. You'll end up taking care of him, changing his diaper, his bedclothes, pushing him around in a wheelchair, trying to make him laugh when he doesn't remember how. Why can't you enjoy him now without putting yourself in that trap? Marrying him will pull you under, Classy. It'll pull you under so far you'll never get back."

"You aren't willing to risk that for Ash, but you were willing to drop everything and take care of Emory."

"My ex-husband has nothing to do with this conversation. He was dying. I couldn't throw him out."

"Sandy loves me, Dart."

But I didn't hear her because I still felt a little bit of guilt about Emory. He'd spent a lot of time alone before he spent his last days with me. "You told me, all of you told me, I had a bigger obligation to humanity than caring for a man I'd divorced twenty years earlier."

"I'm not you, Dart, and Sandy's not Emory or Ash. He's not in love with his dead wife." She tugged her hand out of mine. "Or, for that matter, his ex-wives. I don't have a fancy job at a university or a title or a contribution to make to society. I work in a bar, and my back aches when I come home from the night shift. Sandy will be there to rub those aches out for as long as his hands work. He'll be there to bring me hot tea for as long as his legs work. And when his body quits, pray it won't be soon, then I'll be there to bring him tea and to massage his back. This is what I can do, Dart. That is my contribution, to love one old man and care for him."

"The reality won't be as romantic as the wedding."

"I know. I've been married before."

Like three times before.

"He'll take your money and property, and your assets will support his next wife in the style to which she is accustomed."

"Dart, honey, I don't have any assets other than my outgoing personality, wicked sense of humor, and a body that won't quit."

Remorse jumped up. Who was I to judge what she did? Classy and Sandy might have ten or twenty years ahead of them, and if she wanted to risk all for that time with him, then, as her friend, I should have been happy for her.

"We're not going to talk about sex again, are we?"

She knew with that wacky question I'd accepted her decision. "Not if you don't want to, but engaging in safe sex with Ash might help you relax a bit. If the dean won't oblige you, then find someone else. You're wound tighter than I've ever seen you."

"I think my brain is dying, Classy."

"That's good news."

Now who was daydreaming? I confide my deepest fear and she says that's good news. At my sharp glance, she gestured toward the screen and the email displayed there. She'd been reading my email and hadn't been listening. The relief of that was as quick as a news flash across my phone screen. I read what she'd seen.

"They want you."

The new email came from The Salzburg Global Seminar. I read the message again, so quickly the words blurred. "To host. Do you know what this means? I'm one of five finalists to host the

Salzburg Global Institute Summit on World Poverty next year. This is what we've dreamed of, Classy."

"Do they meet in that castle?" She pointed at the picture of the building made famous by the movie *The Sound of Music*.

"A restored Schloss." The same place I was daydreaming about when I almost fell off the ladder. "Beautiful place. Like a fairytale. You'll love it there. If I'm chosen, we're all going."

Her face lit up, which made her young again, then she shook her head. "Sandy won't want me that far away from him. Mary Beth never leaves the house. Susan has her job. Maybe Lynn can attend."

My gaze fell to the diamond on her hand because she was twisting it around and around; that tiny rock that meant Sandy had already taken her from me.

"You must go." Thought leaders from across the world would be there to share ideas and insights into the biggest problem that humanity faced. I couldn't do this without the Raindrops. "All of you have to attend."

"Sandy and I are getting married as soon as we can get a license."

"They let women wear wedding rings in Salzburg."

"I'll be moving out tomorrow." She must have seen pain or fear in my face, or felt the pounding of my heart. "Sandy's my life now, Dart. You're strong enough to take on the world, but I'm not. I just want my little corner of it to include Sandy."

She got up then, patted me on the shoulder, and said as she left me, "Let the Raindrops go, Dart."

The plant near the computer shivered, then shivered again. Water glistened on top of the dirt. Glancing at the ceiling, I held my tongue against the roof of my mouth. The pressure dissipated my panic as I counted the droplets of water that plopped onto the plant. The mental note to contact the roofers moved to the top of my to-do list. No wonder my mind sputtered every once in a while. No one could stay sane with my responsibilities. The constant drain on my finances and energy made me crazy. Although I didn't know what it was like to be hungry, I had something in common with those in poverty. There never seemed to be enough money to fix their problems either. Another plink, another quiver.

Maybe Classy was right, maybe I should sell this place and move in with Ash. I stood up and moved to the window. *Let us go, Dart.* The words wouldn't leave me alone.

Moonlight glistened on the ocean. More droplets fell. With a sigh, I got up from the computer and retrieved a bucket from the kitchen, set the puddled plant inside, and put both back under the roof leak. Then I sat back down behind the computer's bright promise and wondered what I was going to do. This was a chance of a lifetime, to host at Salzburg, but my think tank had disintegrated, and now Classy had left and my guess was that others wouldn't be far behind. Another drop of water, then yet another, pinged against the bottom of the tin pail. If this rain kept up, the plant would drown in the middle of my living room.

I turned back to the computer. I'd always wanted to go back. If they chose me, I'd find a way to drag everyone there, even if they didn't want to go.

~

I stood at the podium, ready to tape the first MOOC lecture for the fall semester. I'd postponed this taping several times. Lea hadn't been pleased, and if she hadn't done so already, she'd tell Ash and then he wouldn't be pleased. We had to get this done today.

Online teaching wasn't for me. I missed the rows of students sitting before me and the energy they generated that kept me invigorated. I missed their puzzled glances, cues that spurred me on, their small frowns that meant I should supply more data, and I appreciated their sighs of impatience when I dithered on about something they didn't think was important.

Alone with Lea, the camera, and the small desk inside a hot, cramped room that smelled stale, I started to sweat. I was the one person in the room capable of bringing life to the ideas, thoughts, and theory about issues that threatened human existence, which was the topic of this semester's class. I should have taken the time to relax, but I didn't.

That's why the text on my phone grabbed my attention. Ellen. She . . . and like that day on the ladder, the Sentinel yanked me away from the podium, the phone, until my shoulder blades hit the classroom's corner walls.

Drop the phone. I heard that inside my mind as if the Sentinel had shouted the words.

Emotional demands and fight or flight chemicals distorted reason, and I had to think. I had to. Another fragment of logic harnessed another emotion, and only then did I remember to breathe, deep gulps of air that calmed my response.

Lea grasped my elbow at that moment, when I was most sensitized to my mental confusion. Maybe that's why I jerked away from her, prepared to run again. Her shocked look—had I thought she was going to hit me?—stirred consternation and guilt.

"Ellen, the Sentinel," I said, trying to explain how my unconscious had hijacked my body, how I'd ended up hovering in a corner.

"What's wrong?"

"Pulled me away."

Go to her!

Again, I resisted the imperious demand, the compulsion to run, but it cost me.

"You were trembling when you backed away from the podium. Maybe you hit your head." Her hand went to my hair.

I shook off her concern. "Not my head. The Sentinel inside my head. Ellen."

"There's no one here but us, Dr. Sommers."

"He hijacked me." *Again.*

"Let me help you to a chair so you can sit down." She took the cell phone from my hands and brought me back to the podium.

"He hijacked me," I said again. "Now and this morning." I'd realized that I couldn't remember how I got to work this morning, and there were other incidents. My unconscious was out of control. *A text?* What was the danger in a text?

"Men try that with me all the time." Lea set the phone down, at the very edge of the desk, so I couldn't reach it.

"No. Me. Driving this morning."

"I lose track of time when I drive," she said and I knew she was humoring me. "But your Sentinel. Who is he?"

I leaned against the desk, my arms and legs quivering from the receding chemical push that had shoved me away.

Lea frowned. "Maybe I should call the campus police and have them send an ambulance."

The police couldn't help me. "I don't remember how I got to work this morning."

She reached for her phone. I made another effort to explain.

"The Sentinel moved my legs to brake, to accelerate, my hands to turn on the turn signal. I lost track of time."

"So, you don't know how you got to work this morning?"

"The Sentinel. Chemical hijacking. That's what happened to me just now and this morning."

But a few minutes ago, I hadn't been in danger. I kept coming up against that bit of data that didn't fit the pattern. The Sentinel had acted to keep me from harm. That was the evolutionary agreement for how he came to be. *But I hadn't been in danger.* Not from a text.

"I think you've had a stroke, Dr. Sommers. I'm going to call nine-one-one."

Ellen needs you.

This time I listened to that still voice. I straightened and tried to pull myself together. "I'm fine. Let me take a break." I drew a deep breath. "I'm fine. Ellen's cancer is back."

"Let me call nine-one-one."

"A little rest, I'll be fine." As soon as I talk to my cousin. "Let's reschedule."

"The dean won't approve."

"Ash will understand."

"You've already rescheduled twice. People are beginning to talk."

I'd been holding things up, stalling, even before Ellen's text had the Sentinel backpedaling my body away from what I didn't want to know. A colleague believes the neurons in our brains are feral, fighting among themselves in the struggle to stay alive. All that mental warfare, he says, makes us more creative, more intuitive, and more prone to mental illnesses, obsessions, and smaller tics. Lately, I'd been reading his research, trying to find answers to the vague feeling of not being well that troubled me, but I couldn't get my head around the complexity, or perhaps more accurately, the simplicity of his ideas.

I haven't considered my mind as a place of fury. But since that day on the ladder, I've wondered.

"If you insist, I'll stay, but I need to go to my cousin." I moved to the side, hoping Lea wouldn't notice that movement, and she didn't. She heard what I said, didn't see what I did, and bless her, she did as I wanted. Lea put my phone down on the desk and moved back behind the camera.

"Now," Lea was all brisk efficiency, "if you're sure you're okay?"

I nodded that I was. Lea smiled at me from behind the camera. Why small triumphs like posing as the professor seemed significant to someone of her intellect confused me. Then I remembered. Frustrations reduced perplexity to its least common denominator. And Lea was very frustrated with me. Unless I performed well, she would be out of a job. She reminded me of myself when I'd first started out in academe, uncertain of everything and everyone and vulnerable to any misbeliefs.

"Talk to the camera instead of your notes, so students feel as if you are speaking to each of them."

"That's not a logical expectation." Her glare indicated that telling her she wasn't logical might not have been the most tactful way of saying what she needed to hear. "We have almost thirty thousand students across the globe who have signed up for this class. The students know I'm not talking to them individually, but I will try if you think it will help." I dropped my gaze from hers, shuffled the papers I'd brought as props, and glanced at the clock. The hands hadn't moved.

"Stop doing that, Professor."

I inched my hand closer to my phone as I raised my eyebrows to question what it was I was doing that aggravated her.

"You're a clock watcher. This is the fifth time in the taping session you've done that. Pay attention to me, Dr. Sommers. Don't let your students down, not now."

Lea wheeled the camera closer to me, and I took that moment to palm the phone and put it in my pocket.

Straightening my jacket, squaring my shoulders, I looked into the lens. I kept smiling at the camera for the close-up she had framed. Then I noticed my frightened face on the TV monitor at the back of the room. Gruesome image. I didn't look at all professional and self-assured. Why had I thought I would with the emotional load I carried? My hair, more gray than black, needed combing, my lipstick was gone, and my blue eyes looked scared. Lea said this class had to be taped today because the MOOC's first lecture would go live next week. Eleven more lectures to do after this one.

The intensity of that odd feeling grew. And of course, the dean had shared what professional and personal consequences would be mine if this experiment failed. An unsettling emotion grew more intense. The camera loomed bigger, larger. I couldn't fathom why I'd wedged myself into the corner of the classroom, out of sight of the cameras that were trained on my every expression.

I had to talk to Ellen. *This made no sense. Why had I moved to protect myself when it was Ellen whose cancer was back?* Text messages weren't harmful, and the Sentinel knew that as well as I did.

Something is wrong.

Of all my cousins, I felt closest to Ellen. She understood who I could be when others never saw my potential. I felt as obligated to live up to her expectations as I had my father's. But I'd let a plant drown in my living room a week ago while I sat in dry comfort behind the computer. Logic supporting an irrational decision does not make that decision right.

And, this time, the Sentinel had nothing to do with my conscious decision.

"Professor Sommers?" Lea's anxious voice trailed after me as I quit the room before she could get out from behind the camera. I found myself in the hall glancing both ways, uncertain and unsure of myself. My hand curled around the phone, my determination sweeping everything aside. I'd make Ellen talk to me.

"I was pretty sure all those rumors I heard about you being crazy were false." I was halfway down the hall and moving fast, but that accusation made me stop and look back. Lea stood in the doorway, a tall Amazon with golden hair, green eyes, folded arms, and a resigned expression.

I wasn't crazy, although I did have to admit that not many professors carried a brown teddy bear around. But they didn't have the pressures I had.

"You're beginning to worry me."

I was beginning to worry myself. Too many people pulling at me. They all wanted something. But Ellen needed me now.

"I'll be back," I said, and I started for the stairs before Lea could hold me hostage to her demands.

∼

Unlocking my office door, I slipped inside and closed it with a snick of the lock. The quiet dampened my fears. The blue sky outside my window had a few clouds competing with the sunshine.

I pulled my phone out of my pocket, keyed up her text even as I pressed her contact button, went to the window to stare outside, and listened as the phone rang and rang.

Finally, I hung up and reread the text.

Lung cancer back. Have refused treatment. Don't call.

Forget that.

I dialed again. My call went to her voice mail.

She was there, with her phone in hand. I knew it. She always had her phone with her, a link to everyone important in her life. Just as I did.

Should I call Bill? No, I didn't want to talk to her husband. Ellen was who I wanted to talk to. So, what to do since she wouldn't answer the phone?

Going to her house wouldn't work. I could camp on her porch for months and she'd find a way to avoid going out the front door. Ellen was nothing if not resourceful. She could stop me from every action, I realized, but thinking . . . and texting.

How's Bill taking the news?

Nothing. More clouds now outside my office window and a few birds in the sky. Seagulls? Despite living on the coast, I didn't know the species of birds that well other than the usual suspects: seagulls, pelicans, and those little brown ones that pecked, darted, pecked. There was one on my beach that had lost a leg. The loss didn't hamper him any.

If he leaves you, don't let him take my mother's rocking chair that she gave to you.

The phone remained dark and silent. Beguilement wasn't working. I'd have to try harder to break her resolve. Clearly, she didn't care if Bill left or not, and that wasn't good, wasn't good at all.

She was doing her master's work on Nietzsche's beliefs, such as they were. I'd tried to tell her he was passé in light of the current brain research, but she'd argued with vigor that he wasn't, that his insights still had relevance.

Nietzsche misunderstood. God not dead.

That didn't work either.

Your family sucks eggs.

No response to that old farm insult from my past. As a middle-schooler in my hometown of Hawthorne, I always got angry when someone said that to me. Don't know why I thought a grown woman might respond to it.

Life is unfair. Get over it. Call me.

Nothing.

Someone knocks on the door of a home decorated for Christmas. The home owner opens the door, looks down, and says, why did u bring them? Because, said the Christmas tree bulb, when one of us goes out, we all go out.

Nothing . . . again

I'll buy you chocolate if you'll talk to me.

No response, then just as I was typing in the first letter of another inane thought, her reply lit up the phone.

That was a lousy joke.

Seasonally appropriate.

Christmas 3 months away.

Never too early for cheer.

I may not be here.

Good thing I told you the joke.

My church group said cancer back because I'm evil.

You need to change churches.

What if they're right? What if I am evil and that's why I have this again?

Fight.

What's the use?

I didn't like the defeatist tone. That was new for Ellen.

Cancer and I weren't acquainted, but I did know that

motivation to beat the disease back mattered. I could hope that she could rally. Cancer wasn't a death sentence these days, or at least it didn't always need to be.

Answer when I call.

No. Don't want to talk.

I'm not going away.

Tomorrow. Okay? Tomorrow.

I'll stop by.

Text only.

You can't hide.

Don't want to. Just need time.

Don't like.

Don't care.

How could she not care? I loved her like the sister I'd never had. Maybe over the weekend, I'd stop by.

The bird with one leg wasn't there when I looked out the window. No, wait, I was confused. The bird with one leg was on my beach at home, not outside this window. I glanced at my watch. Fifteen minutes had gone by, and Lea would be coming after me if I waited much longer.

Lea was sitting in a chair at the student tables in front of the podium when I walked back into the classroom. She put both hands palms down on the smooth Formica top as if bracing herself against me as I walked to stand opposite her.

"Your unwillingness to teach this joint collaborative class has caused a great deal of concern, Dr. Sommers," she said, looking up at me with a sad expression. "Dean Wright knows you haven't been cooperative. He told me that Stanford wants to substitute one of their professors in your place. People are talking. Last semester you enjoyed this class. You're the reason

Stanford is partnering with us again. I don't understand what happened."

She was right. Last spring semester and the semester before, I'd loved teaching this course. This semester I felt as if I'd been set up for failure from the beginning. Had this been a regular classroom, students would have sat with her behind those creamy white expanses of tables, their notebooks, laptops, phones scattered about. I missed that interaction with students. No, whatever this was was more than that. Conscientiousness kept me coming to work these last few weeks. The fact was that I'd lost interest in doing my job.

My eyes went once more to the phone Lea had put down when I came in. Had she called? I must have spoken the words aloud.

"No, I didn't call. You told me not to. This lab is booked all day for taping your class, and I want that to happen, more than anything. I believe you can put NCUW and Stratton College on the map with this class."

I handed her the stuffed toy. Lea looked confused but she took him out of my hands. "I call him Brown Bear."

"Of course you do."

"I don't have students here, Lea. I'm talking to an empty room."

She seemingly understood for she stood up and settled the small brown teddy bear on top of the camera. He looked quite silly there astride the blunt-nosed lens, his single adornment a ragged red satin ribbon.

"This will help, won't it? I should have realized." Lea slipped behind the camera and bent her head to look through the lens. Then she popped her head back up and gave me an okay sign.

I could do this. I went behind the podium, squared my shoulders, and straightened my dark blue suit coat once again. My keys were in my pocket, the phone was on my desk where I could see if Ellen might call. I was ready. Gathering my thoughts, I found the courage my father had struggled to strengthen.

"Welcome," I said, and stopped because I couldn't bear that camera lens looking at me. "Lea," I said, fighting the urge to run, and when she popped up from behind the camera, I breathed again. Brown Bear seemed to smile at me.

She saw immediately what I needed. "One minute." She ducked behind the camera, made some adjustments, and stood upright again. "Now, start again and look at me. I won't go anywhere but where you can see me."

Another deep breath. Again another try.

"I'm happy to be here with you"—I stared into Lea's eyes and imagined thousands of students out there listening to me—"for this continuing collaboration between North Carolina University at Wilmington and Stanford University. This class examines decision-making and the roles System 1 and System 2 play in decisions.

"For those of you who are rusty on the psychology, System 1 is our unconscious. Most of the time we're unaware of its presence, and the unconscious, what I call The Sentinel, likes it that way. System 2 is the logical, reasoning part of the brain. That's the part you will use or think you use for the class. But be aware, System 2 usually backs up the decisions that System 1 makes. Most of the time, all this works fine . . . except when it doesn't.

"We'll be framing that discussion within the context of poverty. Your final project for this class will be to identify and resolve a problem that contributes to poverty. And—underline this with a red pen—*symptoms* of poverty are not the underlying problem that creates poverty. Societal and individual problems lead to poverty. How can we eradicate those causes and, through that process, eradicate poverty?

"At this point, some of you may be planning to drop this course and find something else." I smiled to show them I understood how overwhelming this class could be. "Don't do that. You'll be working in teams via the internet, and this is your chance to use your brain, to examine stereotypes, political leanings—right, left, and centrist—and whatever else is standing in our way to make a difference."

By the time I'd brought my lead slide up on the screen, and the camera shifted to focus there, I was as relaxed as if I had been taping online lectures for decades in classes like this. Lea's reaction drew my attention away as I followed the cues in her green eyes and facial expressions, and I adjusted my voice, stance, and emphasis in response. That was better, much better, almost as good as having a roomful of students.

"This compilation of advances in brain research comes from an article in *Scientific American*," I said, indicating the slide out of habit rather than necessity as Lea had focused the camera already on that information. "'Ten Big Ideas in Ten Years of Brain Research,' by J. Calderone, does a good job mapping out the main advances in areas of neurogenetics, brain mapping, brain malleability, knowing our place"—noting Lea's frown at the terminology I explained the term, "grid cells" then continued with the list, "memory, therapy advances, optogenetics, glial cells, neural implants, and decision-making. I would add an eleventh area of research—insight—to Calderone's summary. In fact, I'd move it to the top of the list in importance."

I paused, as if there were students in the room, to let those online take in the impact of that statement. "All of this knowledge,"

I indicated the slide, "hasn't kept humans from stumbling into poverty. System 1, the Sentinel"—I knew that if I didn't make it personal, my students wouldn't understand the difference between the two systems—"will destroy us, not through intent, but because of good intentions. As one of my fellow scientists said, 'The brain uses heuristics that allowed humanity to survive saber-toothed tigers. Those heuristics don't translate to complex messy problems like poverty.' Most of the time, the Sentinel works just fine, but complex problems like poverty or civilization collapse don't fit how the brain likes to work."

Lea straightened from the camera. "That wasn't in the script the dean approved." She stopped filming. "Give the students more hope. The advances you mentioned can't go by the wayside . . . because you think intuition is the solution." At least she had cut the camera off before she interrupted. We wouldn't have to tape all that introduction over again. I doubted I could recapture those moments.

"Not intuition, Lea. Insight." I wasn't surprised at her intrusion or the dean's. "We're already deep within a cycle of mass extinction. The evidence is quite clear. That can't be denied."

"Just because we are, doesn't mean that we will continue to be," she said.

"I'm not alone in thinking civilization is precarious. Atomic scientists have moved the Doomsday Clock closer to midnight. Silicon Valley startup executives are having Lasik done, not for cosmetic reasons but because when collapse comes, and they are certain it will come, they don't want to be compromised physically. Glasses and contact lenses won't be available because manufacturing businesses will have shuttered their stores. Those executives are also buying motorcycles instead of Teslas and Mercedes to get them to their getaway properties in small towns across the West.

"Silicon Valley executives don't understand that the brain has a built-in negativity bias. It helped us survive back in the days of saber-toothed tigers, but it doesn't do so well with modern day problems. The brain is working through evolution—a slow process from a human standpoint—to develop more tools like insight, but our democracy is a wonderful, grand experiment that is starting to fail because our brains haven't caught up with the world's complexity. That's what I'm trying to explain." I glanced at the clock. Arguing with her wasted time.

"Let's finish this," I said.

At her nod, indicating she was ready, I told the students about how the Sentinel held us to beliefs and not facts. Then I explored insight and poverty, and outlined the course's intent. "For the rest of this semester, we'll examine research on what keeps people impoverished—religion is one culprit but not for the reason you think. Food is another. Some of those discussions might make you angry. I ask one thing only, that you understand the purpose of this course, to examine all angles, to explore all possibilities and to not reject or accept but to consider the material presented in this course as a starting point for your final project.

"To help you with that, we'll scrutinize a popular belief about how to alleviate poverty, the Robin Hood theory, and discount it. We'll also discuss why love can keep you in poverty. That class will make you uneasy, but that's what university classes like this one do; we enter into a negotiation of ideas that forces you to consider alternatives you normally would not.

"As St. Augustine said, 'People travel to wonder at the height of mountains, at the huge waves of the sea, at the long courses of rivers, at the vast compass of the ocean, at the circular motion of the stars; and they pass by themselves . . . without wondering.'

"By the end of this course, you will no longer be able to do that."

Lea shifted to the last slide that offered all the contact information as well as where the syllabus could be found. "Lea, Katya, Greg, and Howie—plus other graduate students who are helping me with this course—will be online, and should you have any questions, please let us know. See you next week." I waved goodbye.

Lea stood up, gave a relieved sigh, and said, "They'll love it."

My laugh was the last image on the television monitor in the back of the room. Then it too disappeared. I waited as she finished tinkering with the camera, and then asked before she busied herself with the next steps of production, "Who told you I was crazy, Lea?"

FIVE

L EA LOOKED BEWILDERED until she remembered what she'd said. She stopped smiling. I could tell she regretted that frustrated outburst, and that she'd hoped I'd forgotten. No matter how miserable this made her, I couldn't give up. Whoever fed my self-doubt kept me chained to a childhood I no longer wanted to live. "Your loyalty is to me, Lea."

"Prominent thought leaders haven't cracked these issues. A group of old women who call themselves The Raindrops can't either."

She almost diverted my intent with that comment, but again, I bit back my response. Reliance on fast and frugal heuristics stymies insight. How many times had I told her that? Lea had a first-class brain, but her failure to think around her biases disappointed me. Those green eyes turned defiant when I told her I expected her to recognize sloppy thinking, even her own.

"Older women can't solve our world's complex problems, Dr. Sommers. You should step aside and let younger, stronger women take up the challenge."

Her attack surprised me, but I didn't give her the satisfaction of responding to that diversion. She waited though, hoping that I would; then desperation overcame those expectations.

"You're foolish to think older women have an advantage," she said, "just because they've managed to live past sixty. They don't have the intellect for this kind of work."

Disdain now. How I hated disdain. The emotion made me feel less than, and I'd fought my entire life to conquer that.

"We're all biased," I told her.

"So what?" she said. "The Raindrops got a bit of publicity. That doesn't make them right." Now she was scrambling for any diversion to keep me off balance so she wouldn't have to answer the question.

Her response was a textbook example of how the brain, confronted with a rare probability, decides things aren't quite right and goes with the status quo. Since I'd formed The Raindrop Institute, I'd stumbled more than once over that belief. Nor had TRI's successes diminished its power. Did she believe that men alone could save the world? If so, they'd had centuries of male leadership to craft a better world, and it hadn't worked.

"Has my accuser read my books? Looked at the data? Attended my conference lectures?"

She shook her head and had the grace to look ashamed. I'd told her time and time again that sloppy thinking made humanity vulnerable.

"You believe older women don't have the capacity to think, and you won't question that belief despite evidence to the contrary. The Raindrops have made a difference in Brunswick County and in North Carolina. School leaders are taking new approaches, questioning old models, overturning silo thinking because of our influence."

Lea looked as if a pigeon flying overhead had dropped excrement on her blouse. Disgust is a strong negativity dominance in the brain—and infectious. I resisted the urge to look down at my own attire to see if any imaginative crap had landed on me.

"Who told you I was crazy, Lea?" My voice was soft enough that my demand was heard this time.

I didn't miss that I'd been trapped by my own belief that Lea should have been loyal to me. Sometimes, when I think about what the Raindrops and I are trying to accomplish, when I push aside my own beliefs and peek into the reality they hide, I'm so unsure we're doing the right thing that my insides quiver. Those moments when the beliefs subside, those are the moments when I know I don't have a chance at making a difference, because the Sentinel stumbles, searches, and sneaks away when pressed too hard for answers. But I can't back away from my quest. The stakes are too high.

When, after a long silence, she told me what I wanted to know, I wasn't surprised. My colleague Hendrix had been very busy, but then she'd had it in for me since she'd lobbied the dean to deny me tenure all those long years ago. But I was surprised when Lea's eyes telegraphed a rush of compassion for my involuntary wince.

"I shouldn't have told you," she said.

"Dr. Hendrix is always candid about colleagues."

Brutal is more apt. Hendrix had used emotional words, like crazy, to engage minds which are never indifferent to threats, including verbal ones. Reputations were everything in academe. You know that old rhyme, sticks and stones can break my bones but words will never hurt me—it's an outdated myth. Words hurt more than sticks and stones ever will. That's what made Hendrix so dangerous. She attacked reputations.

More troublesome was the implication for Lea that aligning

herself with me was a gamble. If I was wrong . . . Lea's career would stall, and all that time and money she'd spent would come to naught.

Research like mine challenged what was accepted, and that included Hendrix's legacy, her decades of research. Unfortunate, perhaps, but after reading Hendrix's work, I didn't think her findings stood up to scientific debate in light of advanced brain research. Maybe that was why she hated me. But that's how science works. Nothing is sacred.

"She didn't say you were *crazy*, Dr. Sommers, just that no one supported your research." More emotional words that translated to *unstable* and *beware*. Academic research into threats, even symbolic threats such as those emotionally laden words, went to an aversion to loss. Like disgust, loss aversion has a strong negativity dominance.

I should have protected Lea and dropped the subject, but Hendrix got away with audacious innuendo because no one questioned full professors. *No one.* Destroying another's reputation was a tactic in distraction to keep herself viable, because controversy kept the focus on others instead of her own lack of intellectual rigor. But badmouthing me to Lea was wrong. Students look up to professors as intellectual warriors. We shouldn't use them as minions for our own advancement.

"You'll let me know if Professor Hendrix mentions me again?"

Lea didn't meet my gaze. "I didn't want to tell you."

"If you and I are going to work together, we have to trust each other and look out for one another. I can't have a spy reporting back to the dean or to my colleagues."

"I won't tell anyone"—she looked up at me—"what happened this morning. Or that the Sentinel drove you to work."

I smiled. "The unconscious drives everyone to work. No one has a clue."

"And that's the problem, isn't it?"

More than she realized.

∼

Upstairs in my office, I set Brown Bear on top of the small round table I'd brought back with me from the farm. My father had made it, and I'd placed the table atop the antique silk Persian rug with muted threads of turquoise, aqua, and Santorini blue because those colors brought out the warmth of the cherrywood. I shouldn't have bought such an expensive rug because at the time I bought that rug in a shop in Turkey, I'd been an impoverished graduate student, at age forty-three, divorced, alone, without any spare cash.

Sometimes, like now, as I lost myself in the pattern of repetitive symbols and colors, I couldn't believe how naive and innocent I'd once been about higher education. Now I knew academics for what they were. When they patted you on the back, they were looking for a soft place to slide in the knife. But no, that was too caustic. Not everyone here was like Kathleen Hendrix.

Sitting down on one of the small chairs around the table, I pulled Brown Bear onto my lap. Kicking my shoes off, I relaxed as the plushness of the rug embraced my toes and the softness of fur against my fingertips soothed me, as Brown Bear always did.

Across the expanse of my desk, I looked out the window that framed the expansive sky. This had been a day for inconsistencies, I thought, as my fingers found comfort in Brown Bear's fur. I couldn't see the ocean from my third-floor window, but I knew the water was just a short distance away. Odd that something so powerful existed without evidence of its presence.

Like the Sentinel.

I did have a panoramic view of the roof of the library, which was located in the center of the campus. My writing cubicle was at the library. I should walk over and complete that article on how internships within the workplace don't work all that well despite the prominent belief that they do. Plus, I still had to do some research on conscientiousness and poverty. Then there was the research for the chapter Lea and I were writing.

Patterns shifted in my vision as I stared at the library. NCUW had renovated the place last year to include a cafe, snack bar, and lounge areas amidst the plethora of computers and stacks of books, both new and obsolete. I was disturbed by the new trend, although I couldn't articulate why eating while researching in a library didn't seem right.

The sky looked as if it might rain, which meant I'd get wet if I went outside, so I got up, retrieved a bottle of water from my small refrigerator that the dean didn't know about, and sat back down at the desk. I didn't want to talk to colleagues about the administration or editors about publications or folks who wanted me to speak about Raindrop . . . which left students.

Looking at all that brick and mortar, I couldn't fathom how something so permanent could be replaced by online learning. My father had had the same repugnance about no-till farming. He'd been the last holdout in Hawthorne County against what he called newfangled nonsense.

Beliefs again. No matter the erosion studies that indicated less topsoil was lost or the improved yield results with no-till, Dad had been a staunch defender of fall and spring plowing. Thinking about the amount of topsoil we'd lost from the Illinois farm because of his stubbornness made me nauseous.

Exposure to knowledge was supposed to produce as much growth as sunlight and rain, not the opposite. I was lost in thought, and, before I noted the time, and instead of what I thought had been minutes, an hour, two had gone by.

This wouldn't do.

I'd always been conscientious about my work. Several dissertations awaited my input, all of them in different phases, but I didn't have the energy for that tedious pursuit. At a press of the power button, the computer revved up, just like a car engine would, and the screen went blue, then black, and then two silhouettes appeared. Facing one another across a chasm of white space, the caption between them read: "Someone once told me the definition of Hell: The last day you have on earth, the person you became . . . will meet the person you could have become." My productivity as a professor had skyrocketed once I'd put that screen saver on my computer.

The Sentinel believed that silhouette watched me. That made him, and thus me, productive. Lea had escaped Cabrini–Green because the eyes that watched her as she grew up were nurturing of the woman she would become. As a result, at twenty-eight, she was a post doc student with an opportunity to become an assistant professor at a prestigious university.

On the other hand, Ellen's church family watched for evil and, when they found it, threw verbal stones. The result of their watchfulness was a woman who wasn't sure she should live.

Public shaming, humiliation, and condemnation break our will. We're hardwired to care about what others think of us. When my research on insight and civilization collapse stalled because of the usual emotional persuasions—ridicule, shame, and fear—passion for others' well-being kept me at my quest. I'm not a coward trapped by emotion. I don't stumble away from trouble.

Conscientiousness—more and more, I was beginning to think something was there.

My fingers tapped the keyboard. Inside my mind, the roiling, conflicting emotional storm I'd experienced that morning threatened to capture me once again.

Pay attention.

I straightened in my chair. My first idea, that insight could be used to think through complex messy problems, the idea that had started The Raindrop Institute, seemed puny when placed in conflict with this force within me that I couldn't see or hear. My second idea for TRI's rejuvenation, that conscientiousness could be the key that unraveled poverty, had the power to transform TRI, but conscientiousness no longer worked for me. A silent, powerful, deep, abiding fury resided within my brain. It threatened everything I thought I was. Like the gentle rustle of leaves we don't hear when we walk in the woods, we aren't aware of our inner turmoil.

Living all these years with the Sentinel made me think of him as something I could control or relinquish control to. *Not so.* The Sentinel isn't a gentle giant. He's a silent significant force, and he hadn't given me any choice this morning in the classroom or that weekend on the ladder.

System 2 had taken all day to process that data, and I still didn't want to face the conclusion. I had underestimated—no, that word is too insipid—I had never *fathomed* the power residing within me.

I'd been hijacked—my body moved without my permission

because the Sentinel believed me to be in danger when I wasn't. My mind raced through the facts in an effort to bring my fear under control. My fingers trembled, and my core went cold.

What other shouts from my Sentinel had I never heard but acted upon?

SIX

A KNOCK ON THE DOOR. Before I called out "come in," I had the presence of mind to open a desk drawer and shove Brown Bear inside.

Ash opened and then closed the door behind himself. That was the first indication I had that something was wrong. He never visited the third floor. He didn't believe in management by walking around. I liked the pin-striped suit. His broad shoulders made the suit jacket fall just right.

How many stripes were there in the fabric between his lapel and shoulder seam? Too many not to count, but I resisted and, this time, won.

"I thought you had left, Ash." That he hadn't was the second indication something was wrong. Something, or someone—and I had a sneaking suspicion it was me—had kept him on campus.

"I leave tonight." He ran his hand through his thick gray hair. "Dr. Hendrix was in my office just now, Dart. She's concerned you'll drive Lea Wilson away like you did Rosa, and we'll lose another professor of color."

"Rosa didn't leave because of me. If Hendrix has told you that Lea feels threatened, she's wrong about her also. Lea has no intention of leaving. She likes working here."

He didn't believe my denial. I could tell by the stern set of his lips that, despite everything we'd come to be to one another, he wasn't sure who was lying, Hendrix or me.

"Rosa Gonzales went to Harvard, Ash." He didn't look impressed. Everyone else had been impressed with Rosa's new position, but not Ash.

"Kathleen thinks she would have been happy to stay here except for your harassment."

"Much as I love NCUW, if Harvard called me up today, and said I had a job waiting for me, I'd leave. So would Hendrix. I was on sabbatical that semester Rosa was here. I hardly knew her at the time, though I've come to know her well since, but you've heard the rumors. I know you have." He looked pained. He'd heard the rumors and he ignored them, just as he was ignoring me. Easier and less political hassle to blame me than Hendrix, but I didn't let that stop me from trying to convince him. "Hendrix used Rosa to make herself look good. They wrote two research papers together. Rosa did all the work, and Hendrix took the credit because her name came first."

"You don't know that's true."

"I looked up both of those articles." And in the process found other discrepancies I would have to investigate further, but I couldn't mention that. Not now. "Hendrix's name is first on both publications," I said.

He looked surprised.

"Did you check out the fact that I was on sabbatical when Rosa was here?"

He shook his head.

"Hendrix has a reputation for complaining about her colleagues, did you take that into consideration?"

He didn't say anything.

"She's in your office talking about the rest of us more than any other professor you have on staff."

He didn't bother answering that one, and he didn't need to because we both know I was right.

"Hendrix's moral intuitions weigh more to her decision-making than factual accuracy. They always have, Ash. She's a master at the framing effect."

He frowned. "I don't know what you're talking about."

"Framing. A common psychological trap. First, she anchored your impression of me five years ago when I went up for promotion and tenure by advising you that I didn't deserve the honor. I've been fighting that initial impression she made on you since day one of our professional relationship. Then she built on that pernicious mental phenomenon by framing the problem of why Rosa left around racial discrimination, when the facts and the evidence indicate that's not why Rosa left. I'm not a racist and Rosa didn't feel discriminated against."

"I supported you for full professorship."

Only because I fought back. "The provost insisted."

He looked wounded. "You're ignoring all sorts of evidence that indicates I think highly of you."

"Then why are you in my office chastising me about Hendrix's accusations when they have no basis in fact?"

"I don't want her in my office complaining about you again."

What did that mean? He didn't want to be bothered.

"Whether Hendrix comes into your office is her choice, not mine." I didn't appreciate him treating me as if I were to blame. I'd brought more prestige and honor to this college than any other professor, but he always took someone else's opinion about me.

"Let me finish," I said as he started to interrupt. "She knows you're busy, she comes to you, complains, and you, being you, address the complaint without thinking it through. Action is a great management tool, but she's using you because you're too busy to question what her motive is. You yank the accused into your office and chew them out."

"What would you have me do?" he asked in that cold voice I heard only when he realized he'd acted hastily.

"I want you to ask me if I bullied and chased Rosa away because of the color of her skin."

"Well, did you?"

"No."

"So, what does that prove? It's your word against Kathleen's."

"Now I want you to ask me if I've had any further interactions with Rosa since she's left NCUW."

Awareness and embarrassment and that *oh crap* look sent spots of color high on his cheeks.

"I'll need proof."

I went to my bookshelf, grabbed several journals from my published works shelves, and threw them down on the desk in front of him. Flipping one after the other open, the headlines and the authorship in black and white made quite a statement.

"Rosa and I have written together, a series of articles for businesses on the hidden traps of decision-making. By the way, in case you're wondering, this conversation between you and me has tapped all of them—the anchoring trap, the status-quo trap—all of them. You should read some of our work. It's getting international acclaim, and you'll notice," I tapped one of the articles I'd opened and then another, "that Rosa and I alternate first authorship between those articles. We threw a coin for the first article and then alternated our names on subsequent publications."

And if I get the Salzburg gig, Rosa will be the first colleague I call.

"So what's with Lea?"

I threw my arms wide. "You're ignoring everything I said."

"Kathleen is delusional about Rosa and you. You've made that clear. We've laid Rosa to rest. She's your best friend."

"She's a wonderful colleague. I wish she were still here and Hendrix had left."

"What about Lea?"

I drew a deep breath. "She's scared to death. She doesn't like Hendrix, doesn't trust her, and she feels vulnerable because Kathleen has put her in the middle between the two of us."

"What are you going to do about that?"

"Continue to mentor Lea and protect her as best I can. I asked Lea to write with me. Hendrix also asked her to write. Lea doesn't have to choose, she can write two chapters, but my advice to her was to write with me. I can take her farther than Hendrix."

"Does Kathleen know about Rosa?" He gestured toward the journals.

"Everyone who reads my work knows I write with Rosa. Lea knew. *I'm* why Lea came here. I courted Lea, brought her here, hired her, and I'm mentoring her to the best of my ability. This university has one of the most racially sensitive environments I know. We use racial preferences to admit minority students. You tell me that Lea has been in your office complaining about encountering hate, and I'll resign. Has she?"

He shook his head. "Just watch yourself, Dart."

Threat? Or did he care?

"I don't want you hurt," he said, and the stiffness went out of his shoulders. "You should stay away from Kathleen. She has no filter where you are concerned. All this stress will aggravate your health issues."

"I don't have health issues, Ash. I'm just tired and overworked, and I have this dean who won't let any of us rest."

He didn't return my smile, but instead sat down at the table I used for student conferences and beckoned me to join him.

Now what? Had he seen me counting the stripes in his suit jacket? I couldn't help myself.

I pushed the pattern compulsion from my mind, stood up, and went to him with a brief touch to his shoulder. "I know you're doing your job, and addressing complaints is what makes you a strong administrator. But Ash, Hendrix is the only one on staff who's complaining about me." He nodded as I pulled out a chair from the table. "And Hendrix is the only one who's complained to you about Lea and me, isn't she?" He nodded again. "Doesn't that make you wonder about her perspective, because if there was something to her story, you would have had others in your office, especially the minority professors. And they haven't been in your office, have they, Ash?" He shook his head as I sat down beside him.

Up close, the compulsion to count the stripes overwhelmed me.

"Kathleen said you had that scruffy brown bear with you. Where is he?"

"In the desk drawer."

He looked so sad, I felt bad, but that couldn't be on my account. In this relationship, I took care of Ash, not the other way around, and I liked it that way. It couldn't change. I wouldn't let it change.

Now who's falling into a psychological trap?

"I've seen you carrying him myself." He drew a deep breath and

I sensed his nervousness and determination. "Dr. McCloud is the physician who referred Jennifer to a specialist. I want you to see him."

"I don't need to see a doctor. This is just stress, and overwork. That's all it is."

"You were counting the stripes in my suit coat, weren't you? Jennifer used to do that."

"It was nothing, a momentary thing. Nothing to worry about, Ash. See, I'm over it," I said, and wrenched my eyes from the silver threads that fascinated me to stare into his eyes so that he had the proof he needed.

"Then one day Jennifer stopped counting threads and asked if I was married."

I didn't know why she'd ask that, until after a bit, I did. Ash suspected I had what his wife had died from, frontotemporal dementia. Talk about falling into confirmation bias. That's when I looked away from that possibility and focused on something else, anything else.

"I won't go see Jennifer's doctor."

I couldn't face what I feared, not this time.

He knew my resolve because he stood up when I shook my head. I turned away hoping—no, dreading—that he would leave me alone, give up on me since his ploy hadn't worked, and then he turned back. Cupping my chin with his hand, that gentle strong hand, he lifted my face to his.

Relief rushed through me. I looked into his eyes and then closed my own at what I saw there. Those blue eyes looked sad, defeated, and scared. The brief touch of his lips on mine, the gentleness of that caress, I didn't know what to do but endure and savor what I couldn't have.

That brief touch ended all too soon. "I made an appointment for you at nine in the morning. I'd go with you, but I have to leave for China. I'm trusting that you'll be there, Dart."

I waited until the door nicked shut, then folded my arms on the table and laid my head down. My lips still felt his. He was confusing me with his dead wife because—and I had to face this—I might be as sick as she had been.

Widowers who sought female companionship wanted someone close to their own age and someone they knew. I was that person for Ash, and he wouldn't turn away from me if I were sick. He wasn't that kind of man. What I also knew was that some widowers sought women who reminded them of their wives. Those men felt secure and comforted in the role of caregiver.

He'd made me a promise with that kiss, but I didn't want that either. I wanted him to love me for who I was, even as sick as I was—if I *was* sick because, most of the time, I felt as if my mind functioned perfectly. I didn't want to be his second chance to get it right. I wanted more.

.ᔕ.

"We don't have a simple test for Alzheimer's, Dart. That's a problem."

Dr. McCloud had me seated on the examining table. He had very kind eyes, and they were as gray as his name. My mother's eyes had been blue, like the North Carolina sky when the sun was hot and high. For a cool color, Dr. McCloud's eyes burned hot just like my mom's had when she was upset or frustrated with something, which in retrospect wasn't that often, although most of the time when that happened, Dad was involved.

Why was I wanting both of them with me in this examining room?

That was so freaking crazy because they'd never coddled me or comforted me. No, their expectations had been that I would face and conquer whatever life threw at me. Which is why when Dr. McCloud put his stethoscope on my back and asked me to breathe deeply, I said, "I have frontotemporal dementia. My behaviors fit the criteria for behavioral variant FTD, the same disease that had killed Jennifer Wright."

"We don't have a simple test for that disease either. Or, for that matter, anything that remotely resembles either one of those diseases."

"So, what do you have tests for?"

"Occupational hazarditis," the doctor said as he sat down on the rolling stool beside the table.

"I have no idea what you're talking about." I found nothing funny about this situation.

He smiled and reached for my hand. "Professors who are stuck on themselves are prone to it."

"I have all the signs."

"Of course, you believe you do because you've been on the internet and remembered all the data points that agreed with your belief. They call that confirmation bias."

"I know what confirmation bias is. I teach the subject."

"Grip my hand."

I gripped his hand, and he nodded, then tapped that little hammer he had on my knee joints. My leg went up, then the other one jerked in response to a tap. "You're a dedicated professional. Normal people don't spend this much time trying to think. Half this campus displays the same symptoms you have. Professors are all a little demented, you know that, Dart."

"Not all of us." I sighed. "We keep the ones who are borderline on the third floor."

"Which is where you have your office."

Funny guy.

"Are you taking showers every day?"

Hygiene became a problem for people who had this disease. "I was sane when I woke up this morning, and I showered and I ate breakfast. I had an egg, toast, and a banana." Forgetting to eat, to shower, all those hygiene routine disruptions can be symptomatic of FTD, although the disease presents differently in each individual.

"Working in academe is hazardous to your mental and emotional health. I told you that the first time we met." He looked inside one ear and then the other.

"No, you didn't. You said I was lucky to get the job."

He'd been old even then, and so respected across the campus that all of the professors wanted him as their primary health care physician. I'd been lucky. He'd had a cancelation, and I'd managed somehow to get an appointment. I stuck out my tongue when he asked me to and tried not to blink when he shone a light in my eyes.

Doc had prescribed a statin for me when my cholesterol skyrocketed in my late forties then took me off the statin when my arms started aching so badly I thought I was having a heart attack. That had been in my late fifties. He was up on everything current and had such a wealth of knowledge and experience that all of NCU's faculty adored him.

Maybe he's right. Maybe you have been taking yourself too seriously.

"Your motor skills seem fine and your memory is excellent. You have anyone studying FTD?"

"Lea," I said, knowing where he was going with that. Her research documented the three types of the disease, the symptoms for each type, and how changes in the brain manifested themselves in behaviors that required twenty-four-hour care.

"Do you know what I have?" No call to be blunt, but sarcastic wouldn't cut it either. He was one of those men, the kind that had to make up their own minds. Surely, he'd see the error of his ways. I'd been clear in my narrative as to those odd quirks I'd developed.

"Repeat after me, please. Apple, Stone. Pasta. Building. Bugs."

While he stepped out of intimacy range, leaving behind a feeling of space where he'd once been close, I repeated the words while he opened cabinet door after cabinet door.

"I can make a pretty good guess," he said.

"And that would be?"

"Let's make certain first." He took down a jar of peanut butter from the last cabinet he opened.

I eyed that and said, "I'm not hungry."

He laughed and opened the jar, smelled the contents, and hunted for a knife to dig out a scoop. Then he turned back to me, peanut butter laden knife in hand. It went rather well with the white coat.

"I want you to close your left nostril."

I did.

He held the knife under my right nostril. Was that a surgical knife? "Can you smell that?" he asked.

I nodded.

"Then hold your right nostril shut." He held the peanut butter a little further away this time. "Can you smell it now?"

"The smell is stronger this time."

He lowered the knife a bit.

"Still smell it?" He held up the peanut-butter-laden knife.

"Yes."

He withdrew and, at the sink, cleaned the knife, then capped the peanut butter jar, putting it back in the cabinet.

"What were those words I had you repeat to me?"

My mind went blank and terror surfaced because I hadn't committed them to short term memory, then I recalled the mental trick I'd used to remember them the first time, ASP Brown Bear, and ticked them off for him.

"What did that tell you?"

He looked confused.

"The peanut butter." I indicated the cupboard he'd closed.

"Alzheimer's strikes the left occipital lobe and that's where your sense of smell is located. Patients who have Alzheimer's wouldn't have been able to smell the peanut butter. Your olfactory sense is quite sensitive."

I almost wilted with relief. Everything grew lighter.

"And the bad news?"

"The test doesn't work to diagnose other forms of dementia."

I may not have Alzheimer's, but I could have FTD, Lewy body, other types. FTD fit my pattern of early symptoms because patients demonstrate unusual and antisocial behaviors. That's because the frontal and temporal lobes are associated with personality, behavior, and language and when they shrink . . .

He patted my hand. "But I think you're just overworked and stressed. Stress does very odd things to humans. I'll tell Ash to back off."

That scared me. I didn't want him doing that. "You can't share my information with him."

"You're right, but I can share without naming names that I've had three professors from his college in my office this week and every one of you is overworked and exhausted."

Relief felt so good. Maybe I'd been worrying for nothing. "Don't forget underpaid."

He laughed. "Of course not. Go home, Dart, put your feet up, read a good novel, and forget about your troubles this week. Go sailing with Ash."

"He sails?" I hadn't known that.

"Has since he was a kid. We grew up on the same street here in Wilmington. Of course, I'm fifteen years older, but our parents knew each other."

That night on the way home, I stopped by the grocery store. There, I bought a jar of peanut butter and, on impulse, picked up a romance novel set in Elizabethan times about a mad duke inventor who kidnaps a governess. Maybe Dr. McCloud was right. Maybe I should relax more. When I got home, I ignored the computer, fixed myself a peanut butter sandwich, and read my novel.

～

"I worried about you, Dart. The whole trip, I worried about you."

Every syllable etched in exhaustion, Ash's voice had me sitting up in bed, the cell phone cool against my ear. Pushing my hair out of my eyes, swinging my feet over the side of the bed, and searching for my slippers, I realized I didn't know what to do next. What time was it? My clock radio said it was midnight.

"What's wrong?"

"I can't sleep."

"Ash." I sighed and reached for my robe. This wasn't the first time he'd woken me from a sound sleep. Some tension that I couldn't understand came across in his quickened breathing, the huskiness of his voice. Something was different about tonight's inability to sleep. Exhaustion perhaps. He'd just gotten back from his trip to China.

Maybe this was just jet lag. I hoped so, because if it wasn't, that meant the old nightmares were back and I'd thought him long healed from those wounds. But then, when a wife of thirty-eight years dies, for men like Ash—committed, conscientious, loving – learning to live without her might take longer. If that were the case, nothing could be more than it was between Asher and me.

"Jennifer died two years ago. You don't need to take care of her anymore. She's not there."

"I know she's gone, but you need me and I can't fall asleep because I don't know how you are."

This sounded neither like jet lag nor loss of sleep. This sounded like hallucinations, and he had never had those, or confusion. Perhaps he was confusing me with Jennifer, although that wasn't like Ash. He'd never confused me with Jennifer even when I woke him from his office couch at three in the morning

"When did you sleep last?"

"Doesn't matter. I can't sleep . . . I remember all the times she needed me and I wasn't there."

Of course, I didn't agree. He'd always been there for Jennifer. "When did you last sleep, Asher?"

"Three, maybe four nights ago. In China." Silence. "Nothing works, Dart, not alcohol, drugs, music, nothing works to help me sleep."

I heard the clink of ice cubes. He'd be slouched in the arm-chair next to the fireplace, his face unshaven, his eyes heavy, his skin pasty, his shirt rumpled, and the glass of whatever drink he'd tried caught negligently in one elegant hand.

And that's how I found him when I let myself into his house in Spring Haven an hour later. The female faculty always commented on how good-looking he was, with those broad shoulders, abundant iron-gray hair, piercing blue eyes, those even chiseled features.

I could look at him all night, but I told myself no, that he didn't want that kind of relationship with me, despite that kiss in my office. Nothing had worked, not talking, not silence, not calling him back; nothing had worked because Ash didn't want it to work. He wanted me there, so I'd thrown a coat over my tattered old sleep shirt, slipped on some shoes, and grabbed my purse on the way out to the Volvo. Traffic had been light and I'd made good time at midnight on a Monday evening. My imagination had invented all sorts of scenarios for how I would find him.

"You're here." His voice was slurred, and I removed the empty glass dangling from his fingertips and put it on the coffee table before he forgot and dropped it.

"You had another drink while you were waiting for me."

"Several drinks. Didn't work. Nothing works." He shoved his hand through his hair, combing the silky unruly thickness back from his forehead, but the slight curls wouldn't stay in place. They tumbled back when he leaned toward me so that I could see. "You won't go away."

"Come on," I said as I bent down to help him up. "Let's put you to bed."

We'd been in this situation before, not often, but enough that I knew the routine. He'd let me take him into the bedroom, I'd pull back the sheets, he'd fall on the bed, I'd take off his shoes and pull the sheets and blankets over him. Then I'd sit for a while beside the bed and read aloud until he fell asleep. That had always worked, and I had no reason to doubt that things had changed.

"No use," he said, but he got to his feet and, one arm around my shoulder and my arm around his waist, we walked into the hallway. When I got to the master bedroom door, I stabilized him with my hip, the hot, heavy imprint of him against my side, and shoved it open. I swept back the covers of the queen-sized bed and eased him down. He lay back with a sigh, as I unbuckled his belt, slipped off his shoes, and lifted his legs under the covers.

When I straightened, though, and went to step back, he grasped my hand. Blue eyes snared any movement. "Don't go. Please don't go."

I sat down on the edge of the bed. "I'll stay right here until you go to sleep." That's what I'd done the first time I'd put him to bed. Awkward then, but I'd done it several times since and knew what to expect.

"No." His head was restless against the pillow.

"You need sleep, Asher. You've driven yourself crazy, that's what you've done, thinking about all you didn't do when you did more than any one man should have done."

"I need more tonight."

"You're in no condition to do more, Asher."

He'd been concerned as a friend, and he wasn't ready for any type of relationship. He was still in love with Jennifer.

"Lie next to me and hold my hand. That's what she did. She held my hand or I held hers, but we both slept when I did that." Blue eyes stared into mine as he held on to me and wouldn't let go. "Please, Dart. You've come all this way, please come a little farther."

My gaze went to the bare expanse of the sheet next to

him—where Jennifer used to sleep. He wanted me to lie next to his warmth; did he expect me to share pillow talk, to be intimate with him?

As if he'd read my thoughts, he said, "Just lie next to me and hold my hand. That's all. Just hold my hand, and maybe I'll sleep."

I'd hold his hand and he'd pretend I was Jennifer. And what did I pretend? But Ash looked so exhausted, his head on the pillow, his haunted eyes leaving my gaze to search the corners of the room, as if he expected Jennifer to be there, hiding or unconscious, drowning in her mind's rebellion.

"Close your eyes, Ash."

He refused, his eyes heavy with drink, pain, and anguish, so tired that he couldn't sleep.

"Close your eyes, Ash. You need to sleep. It will be better in the morning, I promise."

When I let go of his hand, his eyes snapped open and he grabbed for my hand, again anchoring me in place. "Don't leave me."

"If you don't let go, I can't get into bed with you."

"I'll move over."

And I panicked. If he moved, the bed would be warm from his body heat, and that intimacy would leave me aching for more than I could ever have.

"No, no," I said, and my hand reached out to stay his shoulder, the warmth of that sending heat down my arm into my heart. "Don't move. I'll lie down. I promise."

He watched me; every movement I made, his eyes followed, his head turning on the pillow toward me as I swept back the covers, the crisp sheets heavy in my hand. The expanse of sheet lay exposed—long, wide, and smooth. I couldn't do this. But Asher watched and his gaze wouldn't let me go.

My fingers trembled as I untied my coat and let it slip from my shoulders to the floor. Before I lost my nerve, I slipped into the bed, hoping his night vision hadn't noticed that I wore an old, tattered sleep shirt, soft, worn, and faded from red to pink from so many washings.

It had been a long time since I'd lain beside a man, and this wasn't just any man, this was Ash. I hadn't come for seduction, not that it would have worked if I had. If I could bring him comfort for a bit and find it myself, what did it hurt as long as I remembered that he would never love me as he did her. My hand slid across the cold sheet into the dark vastness between us. His hand grasping mine, I lay still beside him, unable to look at him, my eyes on the ceiling.

"Close your eyes, Ash, and sleep. I won't leave. I promise."

He sighed and relaxed, then shifted in my direction, just enough that I could feel the faint heat of his body. His breathing evened out, the tenseness in his grip relaxed, and Ash slipped into sleep, my hand in his. But not deeply asleep, not yet at least, for when I went to pull my hand from his, his grip tightened and his murmur of "no" faded into quiet when I froze, held in place by his need.

Eventually his breathing evened out and, when it did, I found myself relaxing to the cadence of his sleep. That's when I too closed my eyes and pretended I was there beside him because he loved me.

Those dangerous dreams must have followed me into sleep, for I awoke to find his hand, still clasped in mine, under my cheek. I savored his touch, my eyes still closed, thinking I was dreaming, for I dreamt of him often. When I realized someone lay beside me, I stiffened with awareness.

"Don't," Ash said when I went to pull my hand out of his grip.

My fingers were numb. Given the lightness of the night, dawn wasn't far away. We'd slept for three or four hours, not enough for Ash. I hadn't meant to fall asleep, but our pillows were close, our lips even closer. I rolled away from him to lie stiff and straight on my side of the bed, my eyes closed, hoping that he would fall back asleep and let me go.

When he didn't after a while, I found enough courage or curiosity to turn my head on the pillow to find blue eyes staring into mine. He had been watching me sleep. For how long? And what had he thought? What had he decided? For he'd come to some decision. I knew him well enough to know that. I just didn't know what decision. I went to turn away, self-conscious again, and he sighed and turned onto his back, releasing me from his tormented eyes.

"That better?" he asked, but he didn't release my hand. Our clasped fingers formed the bottom V of the heat that lay between us, a link across the wide expanse of bed that wasn't wide enough.

I couldn't believe I'd fallen asleep. I'd meant to lie there, holding his hand, but I must have been more tired than I thought. Or more comfortable. Maybe that's why I hadn't leapt out of bed, when that was the first thing I should have done.

"This doesn't change anything."

"Is this the part where you tell me we're still friends?"

"I fell asleep, but I didn't mean to."

"This changes everything." His hand gripped mine a little tighter.

"We didn't do anything, Ash. This doesn't change a thing."

"I won't forget waking up to find you holding my hand under your cheek, your legs tangled with mine."

"They are not tangled with yours." Oh, they were and he felt so good. He moved his leg away and the coolness between us had me moving after him before I could stop myself.

"I didn't mean for that to happen."

I felt rather than saw his smile, and when he raised our joined hands to kiss my knuckles I almost did jump out of bed. I would have but my legs and weakened muscles wouldn't have supported me, and he and I both knew it.

"What did Dr. McCloud tell you, Dart?"

I hesitated, considering. When and if Asher Wright and I became a couple, I wanted it to be because he loved me, not because I had no one else to take care of me. But I didn't want to lie so I told him, "He thinks I'm overworked and underpaid and that my boss should give me a raise." That was the truth, just not all of it.

"Your boss does as well." He nuzzled my hand again, and I felt the soft caress that said he cared, that he knew what a relief the doctor's diagnosis must have been.

"Come for dinner this weekend, Dart. We'll have drinks on my boat and have dinner at a little restaurant I like on the wharf."

"I didn't know you sailed until Dr. McCloud told me you did."

He sighed.

"I don't relate well to men," I said. "I have two failed relationships behind me, my father and my ex-husband. You'd be better off with someone else."

"Then we have a date to go sailing," he said as if I hadn't spoken. "It's time I got back on the *Jennifer* again."

That must be the name of his boat. He let go of my hand, and turned onto his side, his back to me as if having settled the matter, he no longer cared whether I would go or stay. What had I done to make him that confident? "Do me a favor, Dart, stop thinking and don't leave until I'm asleep again. Okay? Just stay a little longer until I fall asleep."

"I'll stay." As soon as I committed, Asher's breathing slowed and his body relaxed while I counted the patterns dawn etched on the ceiling. I left him in that bed he and Jennifer had shared, to shrug into my coat, slip into my shoes, and close the front door behind me, resisting the temptation to stay.

SEVEN

THE NEXT MORNING, a text from Ellen stopped my headlong dash down the stairs from my office. By the time I reversed my steps and got to back inside to safety, she'd texted again.

Impatience in a person who had decided to die was a good thing. All last week, I'd pick up the phone and start to text her, then put it down again. Better to give her the time she needed than to ease my own panic. Better to let her come to terms with this on her own. Better to let her husband and family rally around her than a cousin. Yet, that had been hard, the times I'd thought about her. I was so glad to hear from her.

You willing to talk to me now?

I'm better. Forgive me?

Of course I would forgive her. We had more important things to worry about than my hurt feelings. Ellen was going to be okay. We'd see this thing through. I'd be with her every step of the way. She knew she could count on me. The first time the cancer had struck, I'd been there for her. I'd be there this time too.

When can I come see you?

Too late for that.

Too late? What did that mean?

I'm on my way to Mexico.

She couldn't go to Mexico. She was sick. She needed to stay here where people she loved could care for her. Now she was off to Mexico? On the spur of the moment? So much for giving her the time she needed. She'd run out on me.

I had to do something, Dart. And I knew that you would try to stop me.

I thought we loved one another.

I don't want to hurt you.

Does Bill know?

Of course. He's glad to have me gone.

Ellen, he loves you.

Have plane to catch.

What is going on?

Call Bill, he will explain.

Don't go, Ellen.

Love you.

Ellen?

My fingers hurt, that's how tightly I'd been gripping the phone.

Talk to me.

Nothing. Nothing in response. I couldn't believe she'd done this to me, to him. What was going on in her tangled mind?

When I came back from my thoughts, I was stroking Brown Bear's fur while I looked out the window, doing what, I had no idea, watching for what, again no idea. My frantic texts still showed on the phone, and the time stamp of the last one was 11:10 a.m. I must have gotten up to get Brown Bear but, other than that, I'd lost the past hour staring out the window seeing patterns in the clouds.

And I hadn't been thinking about Ellen. I didn't know what I'd been thinking about.

I turned Brown Bear to face me, and in those glass eyes, I

imagined I saw my own frightened reflection. I let the bear fall to my lap. I had to rely on the Sentinel to take care of me when I had these moments where I lost myself and didn't remember. But for how long could the Sentinel fight against the enemy within? I folded my arms around Brown Bear and held him safe, while I imagined another cell dying from the fury consuming my mind.

∼

Bill's and Ellen's house in Southport was another older home like mine, and it too had been built to last by shipbuilders. I climbed out of the Volvo, breathed in the sea salt air that made Southport a city of healing, and decided that I'd been wrong, I should have pressed the issue and broken past Ellen's denial.

The front door opened. "Come in, Dart. I've been expecting you." Bill's welcome surprised me. Blue eyes weary and swollen, he looked as if he'd spent the day crying. Understandable. Despite what Ellen believed, this man loved her; I'd stake my sanity on the depth of his feeling.

"She went to Mexico to consult a faith healer," he said as I walked past him into the house. "Other than that, I don't have any information. She said she'd call and give me the name of the place in a few days, but I don't know where she is or who she's with."

"And you let her go?" Ash wouldn't have let Jennifer go.

"She didn't give me a choice."

"She thinks you don't love her anymore." As I stepped into the foyer, I expected to find evidence of the chaos that had erupted in Ellen's body, but the house was as clean and relaxing as usual. Some women had a talent for making a home, and Ellen was one of them.

"I've been taking care of her for thirty years. You've forgotten; she left me, Dart."

Ash might have been right about Bill. He did love Ellen. Oh, he hadn't come out and said so, but thirty years was a long time to take care of someone you didn't care for. And Ellen had left me, and I loved her like a sister.

"The picture over the mantel," I said as I looked around, feeling the tension build within me at his sadness and frustration. "Is that new?"

"Ellen found that in a thrift store last month. Said the painting would be perfect over the mantel."

"She's right," I said, studying the portrait of the black grand piano in a lovely nineteenth-century drawing room. A beautiful girl, her flame-colored hair pulled back into a braid, sat on the piano bench, her delicate hands poised on the keyboard. Dressed in a long, check-patterned, cotton house dress with a white pinafore to protect her clothes as she cleaned, she must have just sat down to play because her feather duster lay on the top of the piano.

I noted a new rug in the living room. Swirls of color in the nubby texture, greens and blues, highlighted the cream couch and the blue-and-green accent pillows that Ellen had placed on the couch and chairs. "She thought she'd beaten it, didn't she?" I said, my voice low with concern.

"We both did." Bill shoved his hand through his wings of hair, which he still wore long, then rubbed his jaw as if his jaw bones hurt something fierce. And maybe they did, if the tension of the last week had centered there. He was always at the dentist getting something done. That used to drive Ellen crazy, but not so anymore, I thought.

"What happened, Bill?"

Without looking at me, he gestured toward the wing-backed chairs flanking the fireplace. He took one and I took the other. The small patterned rug in blues and greens swirled between us. Bill reached for the soda he'd set down on the small, glass-topped coffee table between us and rolled the coldness back and forth in his hands. Something to do, I supposed, as he thought about how to start.

"She tricked me. Told me that we were to pick up her friend—you remember Diane, don't you?—at the Raleigh airport, and I believed her. Then when we got there, she got out of the truck, told me that the friend request was a ruse, and she had a ticket for Mexico and that she was catching that flight, then she disappeared into the terminal. By the time I'd gathered enough sense to go after her, after I parked the car because the policeman didn't believe me and wouldn't let me leave it at the departure curb, she'd vanished." He looked around the room as if he were dazed, and I knew how he felt. This wasn't at all like Ellen.

"I don't know how long she's going to be gone. I don't know where she is," he said and put his hand to his eyes to hide the tears.

"Why a faith healer?"

"She went to him to convince those old biddies at church that God does love her." Despite the North Carolina hillbilly talk that Bill slipped into in moments of stress like this one, he had a first-rate brain. "Doesn't make any sense at all. You don't get cancer because you're evil. You get cancer because your immune system collapses, or your cells grow wrong . . . stuff like that. Not because God is punishing you." I saw the tears gathering in his eyes. "Why would they tell her that?" he asked.

"I don't know why they would be that cruel to someone whose cancer had returned." But I also knew that beliefs are the strongest forces within people. "She thought you might leave her when she enrolled in the master's program in psychology at NCUW."

"She told you that?" He frowned. "Why would she think . . . You mean because I have a high school diploma, and she's working on her master's, I would feel threatened by that?" He looked surprised. "Ellen and I are renovating this house," he gestured to the surroundings we were in. "We have a life together that is the strength for what we do. I love Ellen. To me she's just as pretty and plump as she was the day I married her."

Ash was right. Bill did love his wife.

"Couldn't you talk her out of going?"

"Didn't you hear me? She didn't give me the chance." He looked down at the soda he held and took a swallow or two before he answered. "I thought she'd beaten the cancer, Dart. I thought she wouldn't have to go through this again. And this time, although the doctor said they could try chemo again, he doubted the treatment would work. I'm willing to do anything, sell the house, the car, anything to let her have this chance if she thinks it will work. It took all I had in me to let her walk away from me. Ask Sandy if you don't believe me. He recognized the car and pulled in behind me in the driveway, and I was too emotional to talk. Why wouldn't she let me go with her?" His eyes teared up as he looked up at me, pleading with me to help him understand.

"Did you ask if you could go?"

"She wouldn't have liked that. She'd made up her mind, Dart. You know how Ellen is when she makes up her mind. Nothing sways her."

"Buy a ticket, Bill, and go after her. Find out the flight she was on, where it was going, and go after her."

"I can't do that. She doesn't want me there. She believes that God sent this healer to her so that she could be well."

We sat there in silence for a while. Me trying to figure out when my cousin had lost her mind, and Bill . . . I doubted that Bill was thinking much at all. He knew cancer was just as violent to the human body as planes laden with fuel were to towers believed indestructible. "If I interfere," Bill said in a low, soft voice, "bring her back, and she dies, I won't be able to live with myself. She wants this chance, and I have to abide by her wishes."

We talked for a while, and I wanted to tell him that Ellen wasn't thinking right, that he had to be reasonable, that he had to go get her, but I didn't say any of those things. Instead, I stayed with him until the silence became awkward between us. Bill saw me to the door with an expression of relief on his face.

"I still think you should go after her and bring her home. They can't help her in Mexico. If she calls, you'll call me?" If Ash had believed Jennifer was harming herself, he wouldn't have abided by his wife's wishes. He would have brought her home and kept her there where she was safe.

He glanced at his watch. "Let's give her some time to see if this faith healer can work miracles."

"She doesn't have much time, Bill. Not if what the doctor says is true."

"We'll try something different if this doesn't work."

"That's what I'm saying."

He looked at me in confusion.

"There won't be time to go back and try again. This decision negates other opportunities."

"There's always time, Dart. Ellen's a fighter. She'll lick this." He knew the truth, but he wanted to believe something different because his brain anchored that deception in another emotion. "She took LamyPie with her." His wide smile was meant to tell me I was wrong about Ellen, and my heart stuttered.

"She wanted something she could touch, other than her memories," I murmured because that's the way I felt about Brown Bear. "I thought that stuffed animal went into the trash. She said it couldn't be repaired after your cat tore out the stuffing."

"I didn't think Ellen would ever forgive me for that. I found a toy surgeon. You may know her, Sally Winey, lives on Oak Island. She fixed him right up."

"I do know her." Someone had recommended the toy surgeon to me. Sally had returned Brown Bear with a Band-Aid over his scar where she'd stitched him up. She'd also reattached his arm and re-glued his original bronzy-gold eyes. The bear had been in bad shape living on the farm. Too bad the toy surgeon couldn't fix Ellen or Bill . . . or me, I thought as I walked to my car in the sharp wind of that fall afternoon.

Bill knew, and he was just making the best of it. Or Ellen was right. He'd used up all the love he'd once had for her. What was that term? Compassion fatigue? Whatever it was, it was real. Or—I paused in the middle of opening the car door—Ellen loved him, her family, and me enough to try for the impossible. And that, I decided, was what I had to do with my relationship to Ash. I would try for the impossible, and if that didn't materialize, I'd cut myself loose from Ash, like Ellen had done with Bill and with me.

～

On campus that Monday morning, student voices and movement animated the landscape of grass, trees, and old brick buildings.

I'd spent the weekend binge-watching television on Netflix with an occasional jaunt over to a love story on The Hallmark Channel. I'd also spent time walking the beach, thinking about Ash, about Ellen, about Bill. I didn't want to be here. For the first time since I'd taken this job, I didn't want to go to work.

I walked from the parking deck to the psychology building, and at one point, I stepped off the sidewalk to let a group of students pass. They were so absorbed in the conversation that they didn't see me. Something tickled my brain as they passed. Something said this is what TRI should be.

And that got me to thinking.

A common goal brought students to this campus, and to campuses like it across the country. Campuses channeled energy and thought toward education. What would it take to make insight as essential as education to the human fabric?

I knew the accepted memes the think tank was up against. Our society has been slow to endorse female leadership. We've made women the engine for our economic well-being, but we've limited their initiative because women have long been conditioned to accept what society offers them. Like my mother, who sold farm eggs for whatever the townspeople were willing to pay. What would it take to persuade women to step into uncertainty and to go against the accepted memes that dictate their behavior?

Something here on this campus would take TRI to the next level. Barriers of location fell beneath technology's sweeping reform. Opening this brick-and-mortar campus to the internet and online learning had made it less vulnerable to the demands of state politics, budget restraints, and the culture itself. Technology could enable TRI to reach more of women's collective intelligence and localize insight around local problems. Certainly, increasing the number of members would make the think tank less vulnerable. I'd lost Classy to love, and my Ellen to cancer, and if I lost even *one* more of my renters, TRI would cease to exist.

When I next noticed my surroundings, I realized I'd walked to Stratton without thinking how I'd gotten there. The Sentinel again, he'd kept me safe and on time for my destination, despite my wandering thoughts.

Lea would be ticked I was late, so I consoled myself that if this problem simmered for a bit, if I stopped thinking about the situation, the answer would come to me—it always did. As I opened my office door, I thought about canceling the taping. I'd had good intentions over the weekend, but there had never been enough time to prepare for class.

"Morning," I said to Lea as I put my briefcase down on the desk and perched Brown Bear on top of the dreaded camera. He looked right at home there.

Lea frowned. "You're late, Professor."

Wait until she heard the haphazard lecture I'd put together. I set up my notes—or rather the half page I had jotted some notes on—and asked her what it felt like to fall in love.

"We don't have time to talk of love this morning."

Now that was just rude. "I can reschedule . . . or we can make time."

"What do you want to know?" Lea folded her arms across her chest and leaned back against the table behind her, one foot crossed over the other. She didn't appear at all relaxed despite the pose. She looked surprised that I'd been so adamant.

I was as well, but I wanted her insights. How I felt about Ash didn't follow the typical romantic heuristics. I didn't need his money, thanks to my father, and I'd made my own way, had always made my own way. I couldn't have his children. He didn't want children. While I found Ash attractive, most of the women across the campus did as well. He looked like a tall, lean Cary Grant—his facial features a little thinner, more ascetic—but while they appreciated the view, they weren't lining up to marry him.

"Have you ever been in love?"

"What does that have to do with poverty?"

I sighed and picked up my half page of notes.

She sighed and said, "Of course I've been in love."

"How did you know he was the one?"

"Love shackles your intelligence, makes you high, and because you care, you're more aggressive in defense of your mate. I've seen males in love protect females when someone makes them sad and vice versa. Couple that with the research that links the love bug to feeling invincible, and you've got potent stuff," Lea said, "I wouldn't fool around with love, Dr. Sommers, not if I were you."

Too late. I thought of how I'd left Ash sleeping. He felt safe with me there, and I felt safe with him. How did I explain that to myself?

"I still don't understand," said Lea, "what this has to do with poverty, with this class."

Maybe she was thinking I had lost my mind. I looked at Brown Bear perched on the camera and thought that I couldn't blame her. "I think love, or rather the romantic notion of love, keeps people in poverty."

"Now that's a reach." Once again, she folded her arms and leaned back. "That makes no sense unless"—she thought for a moment—"I never connected the dots, but the same area of your brain that lights up when you take cocaine, lights up when you fall in love."

"Falling in love is the heuristic—"

"Hold that thought." Lea got behind the camera and turned it on, waving at me to continue. "Now repeat what you just said and go on. Go on," she insisted. "Tell me why love keeps people impoverished because I don't understand how love could when so many say it's the only thing that makes being poor bearable."

The camera's warning light came on, and I was live. "Welcome everyone," I said with a smile as I scrambled to reiterate what I'd just said. "Today we're going to talk about love and Robin Hood and poverty. As the song goes, 'We'd do anything for love.' Sounds romantic, doesn't it? Nothing is further from fact when love keeps you impoverished.

"Falling in love is the heuristic your brain uses when you decide to marry. Consider this scenario. James and Ted want to marry you. Ted has money, but you're in love with James. You're young, idealistic, and impoverished. So is James. Both of you want out, and as that bond strengthens, you become united against the world. Your brain lights up. His lights up. You do stupid things like think you can change him, which is romanticized by society as the acceptable, preferred reform effort rather than incarceration because when James hits you, and when the kids come along, and he hits them, he's always sorry.

"You tell yourself, you're one woman trying her hardest. What's one woman in the greater scheme of things? You believe the love of a good woman does reform a mean man, and James isn't mean, he's angry and stressed because nothing he does puts more food on the table, and he loves his kids, or says he does, as much as he loves you.

"That's how you console yourself, but you know, deep inside,

Ted might have been a better choice. Wham . . . twenty years go by and you're saddled with kids, debt, and insurmountable circumstances, but sharing the same bed with James makes you feel safe because at least there's someone else there in this horrible spot with you. You're not alone, and at night, you reach out and touch him and that brings comfort, despite the fact that your kids can't sleep because they're hungry.

"Touch is one of the reasons women in poverty suffer their fate rather than change their environments. Loneliness is another because being lonely puts you at the edge of society, and that's where prey are found, around the edges, not in the middle of the pack. Women are taught in so many ways to value love and family, and even when the relationship is ensconced in poverty, those values keep women chained.

"And one more thing. As a wife and mother, women have value. That emotional belief anchored through biology allows women to surf waves of shame and despair that keep the impoverished unbalanced.

"That altruism has advanced civilization, which is not a small thing." I consulted my notes, turned to face the camera again, and pretended to talk to Brown Bear. "Before I turn to Robin Hood, which we've discussed more than once in this class, let me make it clear I believe what we have in place—income taxes, food stamps, earned income tax credit, and Medicaid—are helpful because they address the suffering, and that's a good thing. But suffering is a symptom, it's not the cause of poverty. So let's examine an idea that some individuals think might be a solution.

"Taking from the rich and giving to the poor, the story of Robin Hood, still lives for a reason. The idea has deep roots in altruism, which always zings our value system. The story is also theologically based.

"But the question remains: would poverty disappear if we gave the poor money? Maybe, for a moment, but that gesture is not a happy-ever-after solution." I paused, and Lea's eyes grew concerned.

Now her eyes narrowed—because she did not believe me or because she was considering what I'd said? Brown Bear smiled, or it seemed to me that he smiled, because he knew the logic.

"The gesture relies on the belief that money itself can solve the problem. Better homes, better health care, more food, fancier cars, all of that could bring an improved standard of living to the impoverished, which is what happens through taxes, food stamps, all of the aids I mentioned earlier, but that alone will not solve poverty. Once the money is disbursed, the impoverished and the rich are both at ground zero but with one significant difference." I went on to reiterate the conversation I'd had with the Raindrops regarding the production of items of value.

"The key to abolishing poverty is to recognize that a symptom, a lack of money, is not the underlying cause of poverty. For your team project, you might ask yourself, what is? What makes poverty impossible to solve? You'll find a clue in the discussion earlier about what falling in love does to your brain. You'll find another clue in thinking about wealth versus value and money as a simple technology that measures value."

Lea indicated I'd run out of time, so I concluded, "Beliefs are not facts. They become harmful when the balance between opinion and fact is disrupted. The Sentinel, what you know as System 1, is also at fault here because System 1 uses heuristics better suited to attack by saber-tooth tigers than to cope with poverty.

"The Mayans, you remember, we've talked about them before"—I smiled because I knew that the students watching this video would smile—"they sacrificed virgins in the belief that the sacrifice would make rain and end the drought. When rain didn't come, they sacrificed more virgins.

"Taking from the rich and giving to the poor is a belief, like the ones the Mayans had about virgins and drought, and if we implement that belief, which is gaining momentum in this country, we will be as blind to the facts as the Mayans. This particular belief, as altruistic and romantic as it sounds on the surface, won't work because it doesn't address the underlying problem.

"Now for some housekeeping that Lea has brought to my attention. This course is structured to help you think about things differently. That can be uncomfortable because exposure leaves our egos vulnerable to damage. This course is also structured for you to take action—that end-of-course project we've asked you to complete with the help of team members. Taking action equates to taking responsibility, which opens you to criticism and, sometimes, regret. We've put you at psychological risk, that's what education does. If you take one thing from this course, take this. Beliefs are not facts. Facts must balance beliefs because if they don't, we'll be like the Mayans. And on that cheery note, I'll see you all again soon."

Lea slipped out from behind the camera. While she did a quick check of the video, I breathed a sigh of relief that things had gone as well as they had. These segments were nerve wracking.

Brown Bear made my anxiety a little better, but not much. I gathered him up along with my briefcase and thought with delight of the hours that stretched ahead of me. I could do anything I wanted to with them. I'd go to the library, I decided, and do research for that chapter Lea and I were writing.

"I think," Lea said, "that if I follow through on the chat site with reassurances that the final project will be graded on identification of the societal barriers that contribute to poverty, careful evaluation of pluses and minuses of any and all suggestions they make for solving poverty, and their reasons for choosing the one alternative insight that challenges the status quo based on the evaluation of whether or not that plan will provide a future, we might live to see another taping."

"Too much?" I asked.

"I don't know if they—or, for that matter, I—see the connection between falling in love and poverty, but you've given them food for thought, and that's what good teaching is all about. You're not asking them to agree with you. You're asking them to consider whether love does keep people impoverished, and some of these students are going to agree, and some of them are not.

"Plus, I'm not sure we have a choice. Nature wants us to procreate, and love helps us do that." At the look of dismay on my face, she explained. "You told them truth, and you've said this before and it bears repeating again: *ideas, beliefs, assumptions, and emotion* control human behavior. But none of what you knew about the power of love stopped you from tumbling head first into it, did it, Dr. Sommers?"

Maybe she was right. Loving Ash chained me to a life of emotional loneliness because he couldn't love me back, and I'd be wanting what I couldn't have for the rest of my life. I'd be as trapped as those women in poverty, mired in emotion that kept me from living a fulfilling life, always regretting what I couldn't have. I had all these degrees, fame, fortune, but at heart, like them, like women everywhere, I yearned for love. I would change that weakness about myself, if I could.

"Are you and Dean Wright dating, Dr. Sommers? You spend a lot of time together."

Was it that obvious? "He's still in love with his wife, Lea. I think he always will be."

"You deserve better than that, Dr. Sommers."

She was right. I did, but I was learning that that didn't seem to matter. I didn't need Ash to take care of me if I was sick. I had enough money to hire caretakers if I needed care, and Robbie would be there for me. I could count on my nephew, and if I made him my sole heir, he would get the farm and the house for his troubles, although I knew that he would care for me even if I had nothing.

I didn't need Ash for anything, but I did want him. I had a feeling I always would.

EIGHT

ELLEN'S TEXT CAUGHT UP with me as I climbed the next to the last flight of stairs in the building. Exercise cleared my thinking. More than most in this university, I knew the importance of a healthy body for a healthy mind. And with the momentum that was TRI, plus the MOOC, I'd lost myself in the mental challenges and neglected my physical self.

My labored breathing eased somewhat once the majority of the stairs were behind me, but I still had a long way to go before I could climb four flights from the basement to the third floor without hitching breaths during the final sprint.

Mexico wonderful. Feeling much better. Bill says worried. Don't worry about me. I'm fine.

Her text made me smile and pause, my extended foot retreating from taking the next step up. I leaned against the wall so others could pass me although there was no one around, reading and rereading that text, savoring the honesty of her positive emotion. The relief—that she'd reached out to me, that things might be normal between us, like they used to be before the cancer had caused her to question and then run—made me mellow and happy enough to respond.

Miss you. Where are you?

Tepozteco. Mountains in central Mexico. Beautiful here.

Far away, I thought, trying to imagine what the terrain was like there. Steep hills covered in brush and thorns, and deep ravines that plunged into nothingness. I couldn't reach her if I tried, although I'd noted she was careful not to share the exact location. My guess was she hadn't told Bill either. Maybe she'd listen this time, and so I tried yet again to reason with her.

Come home.

Soon. I'm healing. I can feel the energies erasing the cancer.

Oh, that was troubling. *Doesn't work that way, Ellen.*

Dart, if you believe . . . It does.

Images of dark caves, overgrown trails, sliding, slithering rocks that rolled out from underfoot.

Mountains dangerous. Stay away.

Not so. Beautiful. Hiking tomorrow. Part of my spiritual journey, the great one says.

What great one?

No answer.

Don't do this.

No answer.

Come home.

No answer.

Come home.

She was gone. I leaned my head back against the cool tile of the stairwell. Once again, I'd lost her. This was what my life had become, waiting for what happened next. I had always made my own opportunities. I'd started TRI. I'd changed the world, made it a better place for so many people, but I couldn't control what I feared was already in motion both inside me and inside my cousin's lungs, heart, and head.

I slid the phone inside my pocket and climbed the stairs, fighting the pain in my aching leg muscles and my heart. Then I turned around, went down all four flights, and climbed the stairs again, and again.

~

"It's almost impossible to burn pot roast," Lynn said, drawing my attention back to the task at hand, "but you did it."

We had finished dinner, and the four of us were gathered at the dining table for our weekly Raindrop meeting, the one we'd kept postponing because we hadn't wanted to face how ineffectual we were at solving society's problems.

"Have another glass of wine," I told her, filling her glass with the merlot I'd bought on the way home from work.

"The potatoes were good," Susan said. "Those yellow-gold ones are the best though. How come you didn't use those?"

"This," I said, slipping into my chair at the head of the table and picking up my own glass of wine, "is what the Raindrops have disintegrated into—boring discussions of burnt pot roast and mediocre potatoes. We're supposed to be solving complex messy problems."

Mary Beth sighed and picked up her own wine glass. "I don't feel like solving others' problems."

"I'm with her," Lynn said. "We couldn't prevent Ellen from going off to Mexico to consult a faith healer, and she's not a stranger like these folks." She gestured toward the closed folders.

"Poor Bill," Mary Beth said.

Susan hadn't weighed in. She always had an opinion, but she sat there, toying with her wine glass, swirling the red liquid around and around, looking pensive and sad and refusing to meet anyone's gaze. That troubled me.

"It's classic, isn't it?" I said, as I too stared at my wine glass. "The cancer returned, she's desperate, and she turned to beliefs."

"She's put facts and knowledge aside for an unproven remedy." Susan spun her wineglass around and added, "That she believes will cure her, and instead, it's going to kill her." Susan spun her wineglass around yet again. Outside a gust of wind rattled the dining room windows.

"That's why Dart started The Raindrop Institute," Mary Beth said, with a smile in my direction. "Dart Sommers, rule number one. Substitute belief for fact, abandon empirical evidence, and you set the stage for collapse."

I hadn't done that with Ash, at least not yet. I was still together enough that I hadn't substituted beliefs for facts about our relationship. But the fury in my mind had started to erode other relationships because when Lynn said Ellen must be frightened beyond belief, I said, as if I didn't care my cousin was dying, "As are some of us who see the signs that poverty is edging this country closer to collapse."

The room got quiet for a while after that, then Susan straightened as if she'd made a decision. "Maybe we should face some harsh truths about The Raindrop Institute, Dart." She considered what she was about to add. "It's not the same without Classy. The three of us have been talking. We don't think we have enough brain power to keep TRI functioning."

Finally. But my cousin Ellen's act of desperation had pushed them to the realization, not my reasoned logic or facts.

"It's not as bleak as that," I said. Susan looked surprised. "We've solved some big issues in Brunswick County, North Carolina, and parts of the Deep South. Our business model has kept us from realizing our potential. TRI needs to make the leap to a peer-driven mode, as TED did."

Then I waited while they considered.

"Susan, do you know what TED did to keep power and give it away at the same time?" Susan was my researcher, and I loved watching her think.

"TED is bigger than ever, so they must be doing something right," Lynn said.

"They decided that real power was in ideas worth spreading," Susan said. "I read something recently about that organization, but it's slow coming back to me. Something about how TED started selling ideas and then switched to giving ideas away."

"That's what you've been trying to tell us TRI can do," Lynn said. She took a sip of her wine and considered what Susan had just said.

"Ideas aren't just for those who have privileged access to them. Ideas are as common and numerous as blades of grass in a yard."

"And if power becomes a current instead of a currency, ideas can be spread around," Susan said. "We're moving into what some call a maker culture. That's what you're doing with TRI, Dart, but the Raindrops have let you down."

"No, you haven't let me down. We've been doing this for five years, and we've reached a T in the road."

"TED still has the conference model, the old power"—Susan indicated the folders in front of us—"but alongside is the new power structure. They cloned baby TEDs. TEDx are local franchises that have popped up all over, and because of that, TED's reach expanded."

"You're saying that's what we need to do with TRI." Mary Beth leaned forward, interested now.

"That's right," I said. "Instead of shutting TRI down, or trying to keep TRI small and elite, we need to open the think tank up, set up a content structure that others can follow, and let the power flow."

"But how?" Lynn asked. "TRI isn't TED."

"It could be more. The trick is in teaching women how to see around corners and to give them permission to do so in a culture that restricts their adventures."

"Trouble there," Susan said. "No one has used this platform to solve complex messy problems. It's been used to generate economic returns, but you're not after that, and to spread ideas, but you're not after that either. You want to start a movement and challenge the power structures that have kept poverty in place."

"Someone has to. They're not paying attention." The clock sounded loud in the living room. It startled me. My grandmother's antique cuckoo clock. Somebody must have wound it. "Which one of you started the old clock?"

"I didn't."

"Neither did I."

"Do you think we have a ghost?" Lynn grinned.

"Maybe . . . maybe not. Could be a spring let loose. Or could be that the old clock thinks this is a capital idea."

"That's the problem," Susan said. "It will mess with capital. That's one thing this new power shift hasn't figured out yet. When power as currency goes by the wayside, so do the dollars."

"Is TED in trouble?" Mary Beth asked.

"No, baby TEDs have made TED more popular, and people continue to pay for those events."

"Baby TRIs can funnel interest into TRI, open a wider audience to our reach."

Once I had made that happen, I would feel as if I deserved my inheritance. This house, I thought, looking around me, this could be TRI's headquarters. My mother would have liked that.

"We need a way to train older women who are on the scene," I said, "but I haven't found how to make that happen."

"Difficult problem," Susan mused. "What do all of those women who live in all those forgotten towns have in common? What do women who live in urban poverty have in common?"

"We've been here before," I said. "Next you'll be asking me why we should focus on women." Before Susan could ask that question, I said, "Women and children are the ones who suffer. We should give women opportunities to solve their own problems, not dictate our solutions."

"Churches?" Lynn offered. "They all have churches."

"Won't work. Religion is a philosophy of powerlessness," Susan said.

"Lots of religious fundamentalism in the Old South. Exploded during the Reconstruction," I added. "Too bad because we could reach older women through churches."

"If not churches, where?"

"Schools?"

"Grandparents come to the games and the open houses, but little else." I was beginning to think this would be impossible.

"Quilting clubs, knitting groups, library groups?" Lynn said.

"Some of these little towns don't have a library, but libraries have books and people who read books like to think, to discuss, to explore . . . what about book clubs?"

Susan's question caught me by surprise. "Maybe I should contact those clubs at Anchor's Pointe"—one of the more populated communities between Southport and Wilmington—"and talk to a few of those groups. Get feedback from those women and see if it would work. It might just be what we need to take TRI to the next level."

That's where we left the discussion. When the cuckoo clock chimed again at midnight, I was still up, but I hadn't been working. I missed Classy. If she were here, she'd say if the clock chimed eleven times and I was still behind my desk in the living room, I was to go to bed. The clock had chimed twelve times, and time was running out. I hadn't devised a plan to make baby TRIs, even though I'd been sitting here thinking about what needed to happen. Nor had I devised a plan to save Ellen.

My mind wouldn't cooperate. Working with Anchor's Pointe book clubs would be too much work. Nothing would come of it, and I'd be wasting my time because those women wouldn't want to solve other people's problems. I went to bed, prepared to forget all about expanding TRI.

∼

"Again? You don't have anything prepared again?" Lea was furious.

"It's inexcusable, but I didn't have time this weekend." That was a lie. I hadn't felt like working, and so I didn't. I hadn't felt like working for a long time now. Nothing about my current behavior made sense to me. With everything on my mind, this MOOC lecture was not a high priority. More importantly, it had never been my priority. Putting my briefcase on the desktop inside the small room Lea and I used to film the MOOC lectures, I found myself not caring that she was upset.

That too wasn't like the old me. "We can tape this afternoon, Lea. It's not the end of the world."

"The students expect your lecture to be online by noon today at the latest. This schedule with Stanford leaves very little room for error. You assured me that wouldn't be a problem." She paused for breath. If her hair hadn't been so tightly braided, she'd have been tearing it out by the roots. That she wanted to showed in a quick touch to the braid and then a little moue of frustration.

"Postdoc students exist to make full professors look good, Lea." I was kidding, but I shouldn't have because she wasn't amused.

"What do you suggest I do?" I could tell she thought both my hands raised in exasperation—that universal gesture that said I'd done my best, and if it wasn't good enough, then too bad—to be an exaggeration.

"This isn't like you." Lea narrowed her eyes.

"Can't be conscientious all the time." I started to gather up my things.

"You can't go. This tape has to be on the website later this morning."

"Should I read my latest research?"

"You can read mine if you like. That would make you look good."

What did she mean by that?

"Isn't that what you just told me? Postdoc students exist to publish research that makes their professor look good—"

I held up one hand to stop the tirade. "You know I didn't mean it. What's wrong?"

"Nothing."

"Something. My guess—" I paused to consider then said, "Aha, Hendrix."

"She says you're using me to make yourself look good."

"I chose the most competent person I knew to make sure this MOOC was done right. We make each other look good." Or we would if I could get past the reluctance to prepare for this class. This weekend illustrated a pattern I didn't like to see.

Maybe just tiredness.

Maybe not.

"She said—" I shook my head to stop her, and Lea stared at me, the words dying in her throat.

"Let me guess. She wants you to work with her, not me." If Hendrix could get Lea to desert me, she'd use that to make me look bad.

"She said," Lea exaggerated the words with great patience, "that you didn't care about the graduate students, or any students," and I winced because my behavior this morning substantiated that.

"She implied that postdocs like me would be tainted if they worked with you."

Translation: they wouldn't be able to find a job. Professors traded on status, reputation, and credibility to establish trust as an expert—social proof, if you will, that one's expertise is of value and said value can then be marketed into power and currency. Lea knew what she was risking in telling me what had transpired between them. Students didn't take sides in fights between professors. She'd risked her career to protect me.

I should feel ashamed of myself, but I didn't feel anything at all.

"I'm not a hero, Dr. Sommers. But this course"—she waved her hand at the camera that stood silent in front of me—"can make a difference in people's lives. You needed to know so you can stop her."

Although I had nothing, I opened my briefcase. With any kind of luck, those notes I'd made on some current research would still be there. I'd stuffed them into the briefcase for safekeeping when I did another interview like the Oprah one, and hadn't removed them. That had been four months ago, and the notes were still there—another clue that I wasn't tracking quite right—tucked behind the textbook, Kahneman's classic work.

I took the notes and the book out as well, as a prop for this impromptu lecture. Smoothing out the papers, I smiled at Lea. "Get behind the camera, Lea. Let's do this," I said and hoped my confidence hid my despair because this wasn't me. I was always prepared. Conscientiousness had made me successful.

When she cued me up, I pasted a smile on my face and began. "In today's lecture, we're going deeper into the issue of Southern poverty and some of the beliefs that have kept it alive. As you've learned, beliefs capture us, keep us frozen, keep us comfortable, but not safe. We believe that poverty is normal, especially poverty in the Deep South, as it has been persistent across generations. We think it's part of the culture. We're wrong.

"Some believe the Civil War plunged the South into this abyss. Recent research points to something different.

"The first demographic of what Southern poverty looks like includes the homeless, single moms, widows, Hispanics, and African-Americans. No surprise there, right? And by the way, those demographics pretty much inform pockets of poverty in the United States. Four of those five groups grab headlines. But one group, other than Caucasians which should also be on the list, is overlooked by media, politicians, and advocate groups.

"Think for a minute. Take a guess." I paused for the briefest time of silence. "Some of you are right. It's a little-known fact that forty percent of older women, primarily widows, live in poverty. Odd, isn't it, that older women don't make the headlines. We hear about the homeless, about single moms, about Hispanics and African-Americans, but not older women. Says something about how we see older women in the South and across the USA.

"What differentiates the South's poor is the persistence of poverty here. Eight trends have kept poverty alive and well in the South." My thoughts went to Hendrix. Hendrix had grown up poor, and that's the tie she'd used to pull Lea closer. That she had talked to Lea made me so mad—who else had she invited to confide the least little indiscretion? At least I was trying to do something about the situation while she criticized others to protect herself.

"Professor?"

Lea's inquiry brought me back to the task at hand. She'd stopped the camera because I'd stopped talking.

"I'm sorry, Lea, I was thinking about something else. Start the camera. I'll continue."

I gathered my thoughts and went on. "Poverty damages the psyche, and that's helped to keep the South's poor entrenched in poverty. Add the lack of a minimum wage in five of the states, a lack of organized labor, low household incomes, lowest per capita spending by state and local governments, and a deficiency in preventative health care, and it's hard to climb out of this situation.

"I've been in the South now for a little over ten years, and I've grown to love Southern cooking. Hush puppies are my favorite." I smiled at Lea's expression. She didn't consider my taste in Southern cooking to be pertinent. "I've eaten that gourmet delight at numerous restaurants across the Carolinas. You see, hush puppies are comfort food. Popping those little balls of fried dough in their mouths helps people cope with the challenges of being poor. It doesn't take much money to whip up a batch of hush puppies, and the fat content alone satisfies, although there's very little nutrition in that food item. But go to any restaurant on the coast, and you can't help yourself when they put that basket of hot, melt-in-your-mouth goodness on the table. And if you add the honey butter—"

"Dr. Sommers, stop," Lea mouthed from behind the camera.

"—it doesn't matter what the research says, hush puppies have to be good for you." I laughed as she meant me to, and said, "And the crew filming this lecture are going to abandon me and find hush puppies if I don't move on."

That got a smile from Lea. I consulted my notes and said, "Southern food is a belief system that keeps Southerners content with their way of life. The research indicates that in their efforts to cope with the challenges of being poor, Southerners soothe themselves with food, cigarettes, guns, and religion, specifically the idea that Paradise awaits elsewhere but not here."

Lea's eyes grew rounder with the mention of religion and her hand movements urged me to be careful. Religion was fundamental to Southerners' psyches. I took ten minutes to point out how many of the South's poor pray for the strength to endure until they can return to the Promised Land.

"My brother, David, who lives on the family farm in southern Illinois and is not poor, is a very religious man. When I talk to him, he's always in a hurry to get to Paradise. He believes Paradise awaits him in the hereafter. It's that looking backward—or is it forward?—to the Garden of Eden, seeking a return to plenty, that keeps the poor unwilling to do something about their circumstances. Praying for the strength to endure anchors the poor to their life here on earth. If all one has the energy for is to endure, then the status quo psychological trap kicks in to keep you comfortable."

Halfway into that explanation I realized that Brown Bear wasn't staring at me. I'd left him in the office.

Maybe I was getting better.

Maybe worse things are happening to you than Brown Bear.

I hadn't thought of Ellen for a while, the apathy, avoiding work, none of that was like who I was. Maybe Hendrix had worn me down. If so, I should do something about that. As the cuckoo clock chimed last night, time was running out.

Lea's frantic motions meant I should talk . . . not think.

"Beliefs are tricky things. Each of the four culprits I've mentioned—food, guns, cigarettes, and religion—provides the comfort needed to dampen awareness of how close the poor live to chaos. Research has identified all of them as crutches that keep people comfortable. Although *comfortable* is the wrong word. These four things make it *bearable* to be poor in the South."

Ten minutes later, I wrapped up the lecture with Nuland's concept of the human spirit as an evolutionary enrichment. "For too long, we've allowed social class to differentiate them from us, but the poor are no different than you or me," I said. "Social class is a constructed, accounting device that cannot diminish the psychosexual universality that makes all of us human, nor does it dampen our need for mutuality. Some of you in this class grew up in poverty. Some of you are still impoverished. We've provided fee waivers for those in financial need because of generous donors who believe in what equality can be. We know poverty is not contagious. We believe poverty can be eradicated.

"The first misbelief we must address in our search for a solution to this persistent, messy problem of poverty in the South is the belief that the poor are different. Poverty could happen to any one of us. Once that misbelief is gone, we can harness insight to address the underlying problem and not the symptoms most of us focus on."

I smiled into the camera and paused to let them know that I was about to wind up the class. "For this week, Lea and her crew have set up chat rooms to monitor your discussions about today's lecture, the eight trends that keep persistent poverty alive and well in the South and the belief that the poor are different from you and me. Read Kahneman's book *Thinking Fast and Slow* and listen to any and all interviews that you can find with Sherwin Nuland. His thoughts on the human spirit—which is not to be confused with the soul or consciousness—as an evolutionary enrichment, a biological underpinning that maintains equilibrium, will jumpstart your thinking down paths that might lead to insight about poverty.

"I look forward to reading your thoughts from today's lecture, and I'll see you online."

Lea twisted some knobs, backed the camera away from me, and stepped out from behind it to hug me before I could stop her. "Thank you. Thank you. Thank you. You nailed it, Dr. Sommers." She released me but didn't stop grinning. "That lecture was totally awesome. I don't care what Dr. Hendrix says about you, she's wrong. Sincerity like yours can't be faked."

I backed out of her embrace to conceal the awkwardness I felt. For a lesson I hadn't prepared, I'd hit upon some insights, and I felt good about that. I'd always believed that science forced people to examine accepted beliefs, and that's where leaps of insight could originate, in the thinking and questioning, using both logic and emotion to provoke new thoughts toward solutions. It sure as heck beat paddling around the same whirlpool of accepted biases.

I picked up Kahneman's book, and some more papers fell out as I slid the book back inside the briefcase, trying and failing to think of something appropriate to say. That feeling was back—that none of this mattered—while another part of my brain protested that Lea was right.

When I picked up the papers, I realized what they were, when I'd written them, and that I'd forgotten about what I'd discovered. I couldn't believe I'd done that. *I couldn't believe it.*

"I'll see you next Monday, Lea," I said, gathering up the rest of my stuff, eager to get to my office so I could think about what was happening to me.

Lea stopped smiling and looked at me as if she saw me, not the me who could advance her career, but the real me.

"What's wrong, Dr. Sommers?"

The papers that I'd stuffed in the back of Kahneman's book were notes on Hendrix's publications and the discrepancies I'd found in her publishing records when I went searching for the articles she'd published with Rosa. The inconsistencies I found within a few publications led me to cross-reference all of Hendrix's listed pubs on her vita with the original journal articles. The notes I had taken documented the differences between the originals and what Hendrix had put on her vita.

I should not involve Lea in this, but I needed a second opinion on what I'd found. Professors were a means to an end for graduate students and postdocs, the established route they had to walk toward expertise so they too could become worthy of trust. Our brains were technological tools they used to make themselves appear more competent, successful, and capable. Rarely did the relationship become one of caring. Educators and physicians were odd that way, so very intimate, one with the mind and the other with the body, yet distant from one another because of the professional barrier that protected and isolated student from teacher, patient from doctor.

And something else occurred to me. If I did this, if I confided in Lea, this could be the end of my relationship with Ash, especially if I was right, but that's why I needed Lea. She would double-check what I suspected and make sure I was right before I went to Ash and destroyed Hendrix.

"Lea."

That inquiring, hopeful expression she turned toward me twanged my guilt again. If Hendrix ever found out she was involved, Lea's career would be over. But I had to do it. I had to know that I wasn't wrong, and I could trust Lea to find the truth.

I steeled myself and said, "I want you to do an internet search and see if you can find these publications." I gave her the list of publications from Hendrix's vita that I had concerns about, but I kept my notes about the discrepancies to myself. If she found what I found, then I would know I was still tracking right. If she didn't, I would go to the farm and talk to Robbie. He would know why my mind betrayed me. He always knew.

"I want you to find the original journals and check the details against these documents in the folder. Specifically, I want you to check that the titles are the same, that the authors are the same, that the sequence of authors is the same." At her confused look, I said, "First author, second author, third author, etcetera," and I saw that now she understood. "Plus, I want you to read the conclusions in the published document and the conclusions in the documents I've printed for you and see if they match as well. Can you do that for me?"

Lea nodded. If Lea did as I asked, and nothing else, she'd be safe from any harm, but I feared that she wouldn't because as she leafed through the publications, I saw comprehension dawn and something worse: satisfaction.

NINE

"**D**ART, HAVE YOU HEARD from Bill? Has he found Ellen?" Lynn asked as she, Mary Beth, Susan, and I sat down for our Sunday night meal. Classy had always served hot dogs and potato chips on Sunday evening and since she'd left, nothing had changed. Since we'd agreed that wine didn't seem the appropriate complement for hot dogs, Susan poured water for all of us.

I looked at Susan. "While I appreciate that you put the chips in my mother's crystal bowl, I thought with Classy gone, our meals might improve," I said, thinking of my pledge to eat more vegetables, more grains. Even as I spoke the words, I couldn't take my eyes off the scrumptious half of a New York cheesecake that Susan had set in the center of the table for dessert.

Susan defended herself. "I did add the carrots, but I couldn't resist dessert." The cheesecake did look good—with a lighter top layer, a creamy thick middle layer, and a golden graham cracker crust that looked sweet and crunchy.

"Dart, Ellen?" Lynn reminded me.

I wondered why I hadn't answered her question, because I was worried about my cousin, but that cheesecake looked delicious. Susan poked me and nodded at Lynn who sat across from me. I tried to forget about dessert. "I heard from Ellen, not Bill. She's still in Mexico, but she said she's happy and healing."

"Bill should have gone after her," Susan said as she passed the hot dogs.

"She didn't want him there," Lynn said.

"Doesn't matter, he should have gone after her." Susan shoved the potato chips toward Lynn to emphasize her point.

"Anyone know how Classy's doing?" Mary Beth had changed the subject just in time. Lynn passed the carrots to me.

"She isn't in Southport," I said as I fished a carrot out and passed the rest to Mary Beth. "We haven't heard the Seneca Guns lately." My home was one block from downtown Southport, and if Classy had been in town with Sandy, we would have heard the noise.

"Seneca Guns?" Mary Beth asked.

"You know, that big bang, the windows rattling, that would have been Classy detonating," Lynn said as she munched on a carrot, her mind on something else.

"I've always wondered, what causes the noise?" Mary Beth asked.

"No one's ever figured out that out," Susan said. "Lots of people experienced the phenomenon, but no one knows, or will admit to knowing, if they are sonic booms, earthquakes out in the ocean, or some phenomenon we haven't heard of. Blaming Classy has more probability though than tectonic plates jamming together offshore," Susan said as she picked up her hot dog, looked at it for a moment, shrugged her shoulders, and bit down.

I had already finished mine, or at least I thought I had; there wasn't anything on my plate but a pile of chips. I picked up a chip and said, "Sandy's going to be lucky if he survives her cooking."

"She thinks he's going to get healthier eating like this?" Susan indicated the crumbs of the hot dog she'd finished.

I pulled the cheesecake closer, took a slice, and put it on my plate. I knew these three women. If I didn't grab it now, I wouldn't get any. The first bite tasted so good, I took another, and another.

My phone rang in the living room.

"Might be Ash," Susan said.

"No, he's at a conference in London," I said, taking another forkful of creamy goodness that melted in my mouth. "He won't be back until late tonight. I'll be glad to see him. It's been a week since he left." The last thing he'd said to me was that I was to relax, and take it easy. As if I could manage that with my workload.

The phone rang again, and again.

"You going to answer that?"

I got up and went into the living room. "Dart here," I said.

"I'd like to speak to Mary Beth."

"Mary Beth who?"

"I believe she goes by the name Shaker since she's been living in your house."

"Who is this?" I frowned at the phone.

"Her daughter."

Now that was interesting. I didn't know Mary Beth had a daughter. I returned to the table. "Mary Beth," I said, holding the phone out to her.

Mary Beth raised an eyebrow, asking me who the caller was, while Susan took the largest slice of cheesecake and put it on her plate. Lynn took her own slice and Mary Beth shook her head when she was offered a slice. The cheesecake looked very appetizing and I hoped they'd leave some for me.

"This person says she's your daughter."

Susan and Lynn stopped eating. Good. Maybe I did have a chance at dessert. The hot dog hadn't filled me up.

Mary Beth went white, got up without touching the phone, and turned toward the doorway.

I put the phone back to my ear. "Tell her not to run away again," her daughter said.

I let the phone drop and said, "Mary Beth, she says don't run away."

Mary Beth stopped, turned, and I held out the phone again, hoping she would take it. That cheesecake was almost gone. I should grab a piece while I could.

Mary Beth shook her head. I turned on the speaker phone so that everyone in the room could hear. "Mom?" said the disembodied voice. I set the phone in the middle of the table and reached for my share of desert. Only two slices left. Graham cracker crust crumbs littered a plate in front of me, so I exchanged the dirty plate, someone else's plate since I didn't remember eating dessert, for a clean one and took a slice.

"Come home, Mom. Dad's gone, he can't hurt you anymore."

"He's gone? I don't believe you." Mary Beth stepped closer to the phone.

I ate more cheesecake.

"He died in his sleep a week ago, just as he wanted. And he never pressed charges, Mom. I talked him out of that plan. I heard him ask you for the pills. You did what he wanted you to do, and you didn't know they would put him in a coma. He woke up two days after you ran, and I've been taking care of him ever since."

Mary Beth looked close to tears. "I never wanted that burden for you."

"Then come home, Mom."

I ate another bite as I listened to their conversation. The creamy smoothness coated my tongue and stimulated my taste buds. Experts said nothing tasted as good as the first bite, that taste buds became saturated with flavor after that introduction, but they hadn't eaten this cheesecake. As Mary Beth's daughter explained how she'd found her mother two years ago, and that the little girl she'd played with on the beach was actually her grand-daughter, Mary Beth started crying. Lynn and Susan were dabbing at their own tears.

While they were distracted, I noticed the last slice of cheese-cake on the plate and grabbed it for myself because they would eat it all if I didn't, and that cheesecake looked good.

"Hey," said Lynn as I cut into the piece I'd taken. "You already had your share."

"No I haven't." I ate my first bite of cheesecake.

Mary Beth was promising her daughter that she'd be on the next bus home, and that meant that the Raindrops were down to two. "You're going to desert me just like Classy did," I said to Mary Beth after she disconnected from the call. She had a pleased smile on her face. I pushed away the last remaining bite.

Susan and Lynn stared at me as if they couldn't believe what I'd said.

"What's wrong? She's going to leave and the think tank is dead if she does. First Classy left and now Mary Beth's going. Which one of you will be next?"

"You ate the last piece of cheesecake," Susan said.

"I had one slice." I started to gather up our plates, feeling sorry for myself. I didn't have kids. All I had was my job, The Raindrop Institute, which was dying, and Ash, who was in love with his dead wife.

"Dart," Susan's voice had me looking up from my task, "you ate three slices."

"No, I didn't." I couldn't have eaten three pieces. "I had one, and I was lucky to get that. You and Lynn could hardly wait to get at that cheesecake."

"Lynn, back me up here," said Susan, giving up on convincing me and turning to Lynn for support. Her dreadlocks swung about her face. My palm itched to touch the patterns that the movement revealed.

"Doesn't matter, Susan," said Lynn. "There was enough for all of us to take what we wanted."

"You saw me take three slices?" I couldn't believe she'd been counting.

"I wasn't counting, Dart," Lynn said, "but I know you had two."

"She had three. I saw her take three."

But despite what Susan believed, I didn't remember taking three.

"I might have had two slices, Susan," I said, masking my confusion with something plausible because I didn't remember eating that third slice or for that matter the second one, "but not even I could eat three slices of cheesecake. You know how sick I get when I eat too many sweets."

"I thought I saw you take three." I heard the doubt in Susan's voice.

Lynn said, "It doesn't matter. We had plenty."

Susan bit her lip and shook her head. The movement of her hair, so enticing. The intricate patterns begged for my touch. Susan's dreadlocks swung about her face as she nodded her head in response to something Mary Beth said. I almost reached across the table, but I didn't understand this *new* compulsion. I knew what black people's hair felt like. I'd touched kinky hair a lot when, as a new college graduate, I started teaching a kindergarten class. I'd even braided Susan's hair a time or two in the six years she'd been my renter.

Mary Beth came over and hugged me. "I know that you think I'm deserting the Institute, but Dart, I've missed two years of my granddaughter's life. I won't miss any more."

First Classy had left; then Ellen, who had always been eager to discuss TRI's possibilities and options, wouldn't talk to me; and now Mary Beth was leaving. They'd all walked away from making a difference as if that opportunity didn't matter, leaving me to animate the think tank's carcass without its heart. How was I to fulfill my promise to my father if the think tank disintegrated? Three of us weren't enough, we needed more brainpower, and when Lynn went to distribute the folders waiting for us on the sideboard for our weekly meeting of The Raindrop Institute, I waved her away.

"Go and help her pack. I know you want to."

"Are you coming?"

I shook my head. "I feel kind of sick." They would too if someone had ripped the heart out of their life's work. How would I present TRI at Salzburg if the think tank no longer existed?

"You shouldn't have eaten three pieces of cheesecake," Susan said before she followed them upstairs.

I looked at the empty dessert plate. I didn't remember eating even one slice of cheesecake, much less three. Susan had to be mistaken. No one could eat three slices of cheesecake. She'd miscounted. Normally, I never had more than half of a helping of dessert as I didn't like sweets that much. Eating one slice would have been unusual, two slices definitely out of character, but three, that would have been unbelievable. She had to have miscounted, but Susan was a whiz with math.

She hadn't miscounted, which meant this symptom was something new . . . or maybe not. Stress eating happened all of the time, and tonight had certainly been stressful. With Mary Beth's departure—and she was upstairs right now packing to go home—The Raindrop Institute was doomed. Unless. . . .

And I knew what I had to do. After tonight, there would be two Raindrops left and myself. I had to have a plan to recruit more Raindrops or the Institute would collapse.

~

The note from Ash was in my work email. He wanted to see me in his office whenever I had a moment and could stop by. He'd returned from London just yesterday so maybe, my heart sped up a bit faster, he wanted to talk about our plans for this weekend.

Or maybe Hendrix had complained. Or maybe he'd heard about Mary Beth leaving. Or maybe Lea had talked to him about my MOOC and my disinterest in doing the job. There were all sorts of reasons why Ash might want to talk to me. Most of them were not good.

Undecided, I thought about not going, then decided I might as well get this done. I put Brown Bear back up on the highest book shelf in the office and walked downstairs. As usual, the waiting room remained open, but the door to Ash's office was closed. So much for the open-door policy the dean said he advocated. That closed door was such a common occurrence, professors and staff started joking about waiting five minutes rather than fifteen made you a person of importance.

The dean made me wait for five, which qualified me as an important person, before he opened the door and gestured for me to come in. Ash looked better than he had before he'd left for London. He looked rested, and I liked the pin-striped suit. The same suit he'd worn when he came up to my office and kissed me. The suit jacket still fell just right. I wanted to count the faint stripes of light gray on the dark gray suit jacket that echoed the lighter threads among the darker strands of his hair. But now, as with Susan's hair, I had the compulsion to touch, to trace with my fingertips as if touching the pattern would make it come alive for me.

I sat down at the familiar round table. He sat down beside me. That wasn't normal. He usually fussed with papers at his desk first while he marshaled his thoughts, then he would acknowledge my presence with a smile that begged my forgiveness for how busy he was, before he would pull out a chair—across from me, not beside me—and the meeting would begin.

He'd broken his pattern. My breath hitched. Hendrix then. I should have known.

"How are you?" Since I feared antagonizing him, given that Hendrix had already made up his mind for him, politeness seemed a safe enough opening for me to take.

Ash didn't look happy with me. "You've been avoiding me. When you didn't call Sunday or answer my calls, I knew I'd said something wrong."

Not Hendrix at all, and I felt relief until indecision as to how to handle this new twist in our relationship emerged. He never brought our personal relationship to the office. I looked down at my lap, at the tabletop, out the window as the students walked to class. Outside, the day remained bright and blue without a hint of fall.

"Aren't we good friends, Dart? I know I've made you uneasy, but our relationship is important to me."

"The young call it 'friends with benefits.'"

He smiled at that. "I do sleep better when you're beside me."

"It was just the one time, and we can't be doing that again, Ash."

He rested his hand on top of mine and squeezed it to reassure me. "I'm your friend, Dart, but I want to be more."

"Maybe you should start dating again, Ash. Find someone you like who doesn't remind you of Jennifer."

He gave me that deep blue glance that broke my heart. This time I squeezed his hand. "I care about you, you know I do, but I want someone to love me for myself, and you're in love with your wife. You always will be."

"Jennifer has a special place in my heart but she's gone, and I'm not. When I'm with you I'm not so sad, and with your health issues you need me, Dart. We need each other."

I didn't want to be desired because of my health issues. "Are you here this weekend? Maybe we can talk then."

When he drew his hand away, I was surprised. "I can't make that work, as much as I want to. Roger," and I knew he meant NCU's president, "put together an impromptu trip to California to meet with Stanford regarding the MOOC collaboration. We've got an opportunity to engage in more collaborative educational efforts with their university system than the class you've been doing. I don't know the details, but he's asked several deans to drop everything and go. I wanted to stay here, but he thinks it's necessary I travel because this college has been so successful with the initial course. I couldn't leave without seeing you again, though. I want to move beyond the babysitter relationship the faculty thought I needed."

"I think we got past that the night we slept together."

He didn't understand, but when his administrative assistant opened the door and said the president was on line one, I took my reprieve. I told Ash I'd talk with him when he got back from California. I would tell him then that I wanted to be loved for myself, not because my health issues made him pity me. I wasn't as alone in the world as he thought, and he didn't have to take care of me because I had taken care of him when he plunged into grief after Jennifer's death.

～

I buried my thoughts about Ash in work and put together the MOOC lecture for the following Monday. Two hours later, I was ready for a break. That meant walking down and up four flights of stairs, twice. The hallway on the third floor was quiet, except for the squeak of my shoes on the high-gloss floor. It looked smooth and shiny, and I almost bent down to touch it, thinking the surface would feel good, smooth and liquid against my fingertips as if I had dipped them in a lake.

Would it ripple? Would it be as cool as the water in the water fountain? What would that feel like if I let the water splash against my fingertips? Then reason caught up to my strange musings. The floor was dirty and who knew how many students had used the fountain for something other than getting a drink. Striding by a colleague's open doorway, I waved in passing, but the response back was a half salute minus the smile.

Now that was odd. Paula Schafer hadn't invited me to stop and chat. In fact, she'd ducked her head as I went by, pretending to be focused on reading a paper, maybe something on depression, which was her research area. Despite the gloomy research, Paula was the friendliest professor we had on staff.

Another open office door. Mark Stevens also at his desk. Mark was an assistant professor who would be entering his third year at NCU when classes began next fall. The third year was when the administration would decide whether to let the assistant prof go or stay and move further into the uncomfortable thorns of expectations regarding promotion and tenure. I put a little English on the finger spin this time when I waved, but the result was the same, that return half wave and a no smile before breaking eye contact.

The signs were clear, don't come in.

What was going on? These professors weren't that busy. Hendrix?

She'd been talking to more people than just Lea. I descended the first flight of steps to the second floor. Ignoring her poison had been a bad tactical decision. People always believed the worst of others as well as themselves because the brain had a built-in negativity bias. Ash had told me long ago that the best way to handle Hendrix was to let him deal with her, but he'd been gone a lot lately, he was leaving again soon, and that left me vulnerable to her rumor and innuendo.

Lea's door on the second floor was half open. On impulse, I knocked and pushed the door open with a smile. Seated behind her desk, Lea gave me a startled glance that was not the greeting I'd expected. She didn't look happy to see me.

"Good afternoon, Dr. Sommers." She straightened her shoulders. Blond braids this morning tumbled about her face—she'd changed her hair, again. Those braids made her green eyes pop, and I clenched my fists against the itch to trace the patterns in those fat braids of glossy hair. That urge to straighten out the corkscrews was almost overpowering because I had to feel them, had to touch them.

To quell the impulse, I grabbed for the armrest of the wooden chair that sat in front of her desk, folded my tingling fingers around the hard substantial wooden structure, and almost sighed in relief as the urgency lessened.

"What's going on? I walk by colleagues' offices, and they duck their heads and pretend to be busy. You don't seem that happy to see me either."

"I've been warned again to keep my distance from you, Dr. Sommers." She looked scared, and she wouldn't look at me. Her eyes were focused beyond my left shoulder, on something or someone out in the hall.

"By whom?" I sat on the edge of my chair, my hands clasped together in my lap because the itch had become a demand to touch her hair, and maybe that's why I missed what she was trying to tell me.

"One person thinks it's time for you to retire."

"Retire?" I tried to get her to laugh that off, but she never smiled or blinked or showed any compassion for my confusion.

"Older professors like yourself who delay retirement hamper our enrollments, destabilizing cutting-edge research, and until you retire, nothing will change."

That stung. My reputation was stellar. "No one on this faculty is doing what I'm doing."

"Perhaps you're right, but you do have to admit that older pro-fessors who hang on past their prime prevent the administration from hiring younger professionals." Again, her gaze went to the hall.

"That's a leap in logic. You're equating youth with better teaching, better research, better everything."

"Not at all. It's a simple matter of making way for the next generation."

"My students don't think so."

"Your students have grandparents your age. Some professors tell me the students tolerate you."

Once retired, old professors were forgotten seconds after they stepped away from the building. That was a jolt to those of us used to thinking ourselves irreplaceable. For the lucky ones—myself included I hoped—the work lived on, but unless I could launch this new revised version of TRI that focused on poverty, even that might be gone.

"You're resentful that older professors are hanging onto their jobs?" I couldn't believe this conversation was happening. And she kept looking at the doorway, and I didn't understand that either.

"Jobs are scarce in academe, and it's my turn. You've had yours."

Anger had me standing, unable to sit any longer. Lea also stood, meeting my gaze without blinking, but she nodded, a slight nod only I could see, toward the open doorway behind me.

Something wrong here.

She wants what you have.

No, something else going on.

She'll take what she wants and she wants what you have.

Another slight nod toward the door.

"Hendrix," I whispered.

"The students feel sorry for you," Lea said, her focus on me, willing me to understand.

Hendrix is older than I am.

Don't believe this, said that other rational voice that knew Lea was on my side.

Don't you dare criticize me.

The ferocity of the fight inside my mind left me confused. I didn't know which voice spoke the truth.

"My teaching evaluations are excellent." I put both of my hands on her desk and leaned closer to make my point. "The students don't think I'm obsolete."

"They feel sorry for you." Her eyes again went to the doorway.

She was wrong. The students didn't feel sorry for me. "Lea, you and I are writing a chapter together. Every week in class, you're behind that camera, and I couldn't teach that MOOC without you. And as young as you are, there's gray in your hair as well."

Her hand went up to a fat, glossy braid and my attention centered there on the pattern she'd revealed. The conflicting conversation in my head, the strain of talking about one thing without forgetting the other deeper message, loosened the control I had on my compulsions and, without my being aware I was touching her, guiding her fingers to the tantalizing pattern, tracing the silkiness of her hair, and following the single strand of gray hair in one blond plait.

Lea's eyes went wide. Her hand pushed mine away.

"What are you doing?" Hendrix asked from the doorway.

Why did you do that, what were you thinking?

"She saw us, Dr. Sommers," Lea whispered. Her eyes were on the open doorway, but when I turned around to look, no one was there. Hendrix was gone, straight to Ash's office was my best guess.

"Hendrix?"

Lea nodded. "She was there all along. I tried to warn you."

I stepped away from her, away from the temptation to touch her hair again.

"You should leave, because if you don't, she'll make my life hell."

"Of course." She was right. Hendrix could run her off like she ran Rosa off, like she was trying to run me off.

Beautiful patterns.

Tell her you're sorry, that you couldn't help yourself.

Touch her hair.

Protect her from Hendrix.

Leave.

I made myself listen to the rational voice and left Lea's office. Lea stood still, her hand to her hair and that single, glossy, satiny strand of beautiful gray I'd inappropriately touched.

TEN

ENDRIX'S EMAIL about the incident crossed my desk within the half hour. She hadn't wasted any time reporting the incident.

From: Kathleen Hendrix, PhD

Sent: Monday, 4:15 p.m.

To: Dart Sommers, Lea Wilson

Subject: Sexual Harassment

Your behavior is inexcusable, Dr. Sommers. Had you treated me with the disrespect you showed Dr. Wilson, I would have called the police and had them arrest you.

Once again, you are creating a hostile environment for junior faculty. This time, though, I will not stand by. I know what you are, and I will not let you destroy another young woman's promising career.

I suggested Dr. Wilson file a grievance and document this incident as sexual harassment. Dr. Wilson chose not to follow my advice. While I applaud her restraint and good will, I know she is afraid of you and feels threatened by you, and you are undeserving of any courtesy from her.

Kathleen Hendrix, PhD

I hit reply all and responded.

From: Dart Sommers

Sent: Monday, 5:00 p.m.

To: Lea Wilson, Kathleen Hendrix

Subject: RE: Sexual Harassment Misunderstanding

Dr. Wilson accepted my apology for invading her personal space. If my behavior was perceived as sexual harassment, Dr. Wilson did not share that insight with me. And I am troubled that you feel she intimated as much to you. Perhaps, in response to your misunderstanding of what transpired between Dr. Wilson and myself, we should meet to discuss these accusations in person.

I look forward to the conversation at a place and time of your choosing.

Kindly,

Dart

From: Kathleen Hendrix

Sent: Monday, 5:15 p.m.

To: Lea Wilson, Dart Sommers,

Subject: RE: Sexual Harassment Misunderstanding HA!

You and I do not need to meet, because I have no misunderstanding of what transpired between you and Dr. Wilson. Such behavior, sad though true, is typical in individuals who do not respect diversity.

Kathleen Hendrix, PhD

From: Dart Sommers

Sent: Monday, 5:30 p.m.

To: Lea Wilson, Kathleen Hendrix

Subject: Zero Tolerance

Are you calling me a racist?

Dart Sommers

From: Jarvis Asher Wright, PhD, Dean of Psychology

Sent: Monday, 5:45 p.m.

To: Dart Sommers, Kathleen Hendrix

CC: Lea Wilson

Subject: Meeting requested

Dr. Sommers and Dr. Hendrix,

Please be in my office tomorrow morning at 9:30 to discuss what has transpired.

I have cleared my calendar to accommodate you both. I
have not invited Dr. Wilson to this meeting because she
has responded to me by email and indicated her prefer-
ence to not to be involved in the disagreement between
the two of you.

Sincerely,

Dean Wright

I hit reply all and typed I look forward to the confrontation. Then
I read and reread, changed "confrontation" to "meeting," read and
reread, and then deleted everything. I typed three words *I'll be there.*

~

Lea met me in my office early the next morning before my meeting with Ash and Hendrix. When she came in, I glanced up, said,
"Close the door behind you," and went back to pondering how I
could protect her in the upcoming meeting.

Since you were stupid enough to drag her into the mess.

I hadn't meant to.

When Lea put the file folder she'd brought with her on top of
my desk, she said, "Dr. Hendrix is a liar." She pushed the folder
toward me, and my eyes went there, hoping it contained the evidence I needed, and yet, paradoxically, dismayed that she'd vali-
dated Hendrix's stupidity.

"I printed the documents on my home computer, as you
requested. I did not use any of the equipment here at the college."

"That's good."

Her eyes grew wide as she caught the nervousness in my voice. "She's dangerous, Lea."

With a swirl of black skirt, Lea sat down in the chair opposite my desk and crossed her legs, combat boots without socks on her feet, a bomber jacket over her skimpy T shirt as she waited for me to open the folder.

"Only three?" My surprise made her stiffen. I'd asked that she check on sixteen articles because I suspected that Hendrix had falsified those publications. Just enough to make a difference but scattered across forty years of a career, not enough to draw unwarranted attention.

"Those three are fine. It took some digging but I found those to be as she noted them on the vita. The other thirteen articles you asked me to find didn't have her name on them, so I put them in this folder." She dug into her briefcase and brought out a very thick folder. "These are all the articles that didn't have her name listed on the original publication." She put the file on my desk. "But she has put her name on those same articles when she listed them in her vita."

She's a year from retirement.

Another foray into the briefcase and, this time, Lea withdrew Hendrix's vita, almost eighty pages in length.

"She's been lying for a long time, Dr. Sommers." Lea shoved the vita, opened to the publication pages, across the desk. The red ink that circled Hendrix's name on thirteen of those listed pubs matched the thirteen publications without Hendrix's name in the folder. "Looks like she made associate professor through her own efforts, but she added her name as last author to one article, a very minor pub, but it counted, right before she went up for full, and she included the others over the next twenty or so years.

"She's been at NCU her entire career, and once she reached full, it appears no one in administration checked to see if she was telling the truth," Lea said. "We can't let her get away with this."

I looked up from the vita and across the desk at her. "I promise you, I will not drop my investigation or ignore the results, but I want you to forget what I had you do. I should never have involved you."

"How could she do this?"

I reached across the desk and took her hand.

She raised startled eyes to mine. "I know. Professors aren't supposed to touch postdocs, but I need you to listen to me." I continued to hold her hand in both of mine. "Don't talk to anyone about this." She started to protest, but I gripped her hand tighter, and she slumped in defeat. "I want you to forget that we talked. Promise me?"

"She was listening outside my door yesterday, Dart. That's why I pretended to be mean to you. Everything I said, that's what the students are telling me about her. They want her gone. Lies like this"—she indicated the vita—"hurt the university."

"Yes, they do, which is why administration may not act on the evidence, assuming there is evidence."

"But of course there is. I found it." She tapped the papers on my desk.

"No," I told her, "you didn't find it. I did, and it may be nothing. There are places that research can hide, and I need to be certain of the evidence before I act. You don't know anything about Dr. Hendrix's publications. Rumors will start flying once I take this to the dean, and that will make Hendrix angrier."

"But I want to help."

"I won't let her hurt you."

And if what I had in mind worked, Hendrix would be gone from NCUW long before Lea needed her support for securing the assistant professor position. I sat there trying to figure out what I should do, how I should proceed. If I turned Hendrix in, the administration wouldn't be happy. Ash would be furious, and he was already mad at me. I released Lea's hand and pushed myself away from the desk a bit. Then I spun the chair around to look out the window and considered the impossible, not using the evidence I had to bring Hendrix down. I shouldn't be thinking like this, but if my mental health issues grew worse, I wouldn't have the stamina to push The Raindrop Institute where it needed to go.

Hendrix had the need burning inside her, or she wouldn't have falsified her vita. She'd been smart about it, a little lie here, another there, but the fact remained that she wanted glory and fame, and she'd cheated to get it. Dad always said mud stuck, but I had watched mud dry, turn to dust and blow away. If I worked with Hendrix, she would provide the fire to move TRI to greater heights.

She lied to get where she is.

Ideas survived despite people, not because of them. So what if she stood beside me on the podium at Salzburg?

Do the right thing.

I couldn't die without leaving something of myself behind. And that's what this decision came down to. What was I willing to give up to ensure that The Raindrop Institute survived when I was gone? I spun the chair back to face Lea.

"Are you still researching frontotemporal dementia?"

Her eyes lit up. "My most recent study indicated subtle signs of change in humor might be an early sign."

"The methodology?"

"Interviews with forty-eight friends and caregivers of people with FTD. I found changes in humor displayed as a symptom of dementia nine years before actual symptoms. One woman laughed when her husband scalded his hand. Another guy laughed at a barking dog who was scaring children. Both of them went on to display frontotemporal dementia."

I frowned, trying to understand. "Laughing at actions that one normally didn't find funny happened many years before the actual diagnosis?"

"They theorized that humor puts demands on many aspects of brain function, like emotion, puzzle solving, social awareness. That's why it could be a canary-in-the-coal-mine warning for people. If this behavioral change displays nine years or more ahead of other mild symptoms, like apathy, then that would allow for planning, saving, marshaling resources, education, participation in research trials, all sorts of things."

"Including diet and exercising," I said. "The researchers think that a Mediterranean diet and daily exercise can help stabilize mild symptoms."

"It can. Wicked disease, Dr. Sommers, but by studying FTD, we can find where moral character is located in the brain, and that's key to your conscientiousness theory about poverty."

Ah, more familiar territory for my brain. I caught both of us up in that pattern. "That debate's been going on for centuries among philosophers and psychologists." I'd read all of those great arguments and still wasn't enlightened. "Morals used to be thought of as outside us, like the Ten Commandments. Then ethics research shifted the origin to the individual and virtue theory, then shifted again to thinking of the community as ethics, and now researchers are rejecting all that and speculating that maybe values—doing what's right—have been hardwired into our minds and generational experiences, and are what make us different from succeeding generations. Which is interesting and helps explain differences in religion, because there are some who think that those differences are memes that have been adopted as heuristics by the brain."

"I'd rather lose my memories than my values," Lea said.

So would I, but I was beginning to think I might not have a choice. I dragged myself back from the void where no morals existed and collected my thoughts. "I don't know much about frontotemporal dementia or other dementias. I'm interested in reading your research and learning more."

"You found yourself unable to resist touching my hair yesterday, didn't you, Dr. Sommers?"

I hadn't fooled her, but she wasn't running from me. My gaze went again to the single braid and that strand of gray. This morning it didn't interest me in the slightest, but Lea was right, yesterday the chemical compulsion in my brain made it impossible for me to resist. I'd been compelled to touch her hair and feel its silkiness.

"It fits, Dr. Sommers, with your other strange behavior. Once I saw, once I recalled all of the episodes, the incidents where you've acted out of the ordinary. I saw the pattern. I hope I'm wrong, I really do."

I almost didn't share with her, but she deserved to know. She worked more intimately with me than anyone else. "I went to see Dr. McCloud. He said I didn't have Alzheimer's and my odd behavior is a manifestation of stress and overwork. But he didn't test for other types of dementias."

"There's no cure for any of them, Dart."

I dropped my eyes from the pity in hers.

"Dr. Hendrix isn't making it easy, is she?"

I nodded because that was all I could manage to do.

~

Later that morning in Ash's office, Hendrix didn't say hello. When I sat down beside her, she got up and moved to the next empty seat.

"Sun in your eyes?" I asked.

"The perfume you're wearing is giving me a headache."

"I don't wear perfume."

She raised one eyebrow and shrugged. Anger at her contempt had me contemplating retaliation, but before I could act, Ash looked up and frowned. He tapped the table top with his index finger for emphasis. "Both of you are professionals, and I expect you to act as such."

"There's no need for me to sit here and be insulted," I said. "I sent Dr. Wilson an email this morning apologizing for my impulsive behavior."

"What happened, Dart?" Ash asked, and his quiet but steady voice calmed my emotions. Some people have that ability to emphasize what's important.

"Lea is frustrated with her career path at NCU and someone has told her, swayed her into thinking, that the old professors like Dr. Hendrix and me are standing in her way." I hoped I had phrased that right to protect Lea. "Perhaps someone promised her something and then didn't deliver." I looked down at the table for a moment gathering my courage and my thoughts, then raised my head to again look Ash in the eye. "Emotions escalated. Both of us were angry. We said things we shouldn't have said. Did things we never would have done had we not been angry, but I was wrong to make my point in the manner I did, by touching a gray hair in her braid, to point out that she herself was getting older."

"You put her in her place."

Hendrix's comment squeezed my weak resolve to be professional. I'd always had a hard time admitting that I'd messed up. Hendrix knew that about me. She'd sensed what made me squirm, and she'd poured scorn into the wounds I was trying to heal from so long ago, when my father used to accuse me of mistakes I'd never made.

"You know," I said the words as slowly and precisely as I could, "I think I did."

The dean sat back in his chair. "That's a different motive than sexual harassment. It almost makes you human, Dr. Sommers."

Was there a faint smile on his face? Must have been my imagination, but I relaxed. Maybe this was going to turn out okay after all.

"You're going to let her get away with this blatant display of sexual harassment, arrogance, and jealousy?" Hendrix's mouth twisted with disgust as she leaned across the table trying to intimidate Ash.

Her invasion of his professional space didn't intimidate Ash. "She's apologized."

Hendrix's face twisted into ugliness.

"Dr. Sommers's actions were not professional, I agree with her on that, but we're all human. If Lea had complained about her treatment, that would be another matter, but she didn't, Kathleen, and I asked her twice about the incident."

Hendrix sat back in her chair. "If you had given Lea the MOOC as was her right, then Dart's load wouldn't be so heavy."

Wait. What did she mean? Give Lea the MOOC? She wanted me, a full professor, to step aside from the most prestigious course on the campus, the single course we shared with Stanford, and give it to an untried postdoc? That didn't make sense.

"Lea is younger," Hendrix said, her hand gestures more expansive now as she tried to persuade Ash to share her point of view. "She has more energy, more insight, and her research base is more extensive in the area of Southern poverty . . . as is mine."

"I suppose you think Lea should take over The Raindrop Institute as well?"

"No," Hendrix turned her hard gaze in my direction, "that belongs to *me*."

Now we were getting to her real agenda. I could feel my eyes widen, my heart stutter with astonishment. I'd misjudged Hendrix. This was more than smugness and confidence. This was the arrogance that motivated humans to overthrow governments, to take no hostages, and to kill off the insurgents.

"What makes you think The Raindrop Institute belongs to you?"

"Dean Wright."

"Ash?" That betrayal stung. I turned to look him.

"He promised me when you got tenure five years ago that The Raindrop Institute would be mine if you failed to develop its potential."

"Why?" I managed to ask.

Ash said, "The Raindrop Institute, in my opinion, is a reflection on this university. If you can't make it work, then we need to put someone into play who can. After the Oprah interview, the Institute should have fast forwarded into fame and status. Instead, you've lost two members, and momentum. You're floundering, Dart."

I hadn't told him about the defections of Mary Beth and Classy, about the pleas for help I couldn't answer. How did he know?

"Kathleen is more than willing to help you out."

"Not help. I never said I would help. You know the ideas I have for the Institute will make it a household name, Dean Wright. That's what this university needs to make NCUW the shining academic star of the East Coast."

"Aren't the two of you forgetting something?" Both of them saw me as insignificant; I could see that in their expressions, as they stared at me. "TRI doesn't belong to the university."

"Of course, it does," Ash said. "You dreamt it up while you were working for the university. We've given you the leave time you needed to make it happen, and we've funded it."

"No, you haven't. You turned down my request for funding."

"An oversight on my part. I'm willing to put significant resources toward the effort so Kathleen can make it what it should be."

He'd give the money to Kathleen, but not to me.

"It's already what it should be," I said.

"What?" Hendrix almost spit the word out. "Give it up, Dart. You can't take it any further. I can."

I pushed my chair away from the table. "TRI belongs to me. It's not a university initiative. The university has no claim on that work."

"Don't be so sure of that," said Hendrix. "We can make it very difficult for you."

I ignored her and looked at Ash. "I thought you cared about me." I knew the minute I said the words that I shouldn't have. But at least I hadn't reached out and patted his hair. Nor did I feel any compulsion to do so. "TRI belongs to me, and I have the documentation to prove it. I have not received any funding from the university or the college, nor have I used materials, support staff, or university public relations material to promote TRI." Except for Lea; she was working with me on the website and the MOOC, but the research I was doing for the institute informed the class, so that didn't count.

"Wrong again, Dart. Bless your heart." Hendrix smiled, and I hated her for thinking of me as less than. "Hadn't noticed before how that rhymes. Rather sweet, don't you think?"

"No, your words aren't sweet. They're condescending. And I'm not wrong."

"The dean has given you release time for TRI."

"In exchange for promoting the university."

"But that also establishes TRI as a university initiative."

"Free advertising doesn't indicate ownership." I pushed the chair against the table. "Dean Wright has no authority to take TRI from me or to involve you, Dr. Hendrix, in the day-to-day running of the initiative. He knows that, and if either of you try to take this away from me, I will find a way to stop you. TRI belongs to me."

"Dart, think twice before you alienate NCU. We can help you move TRI to an international scale," Ash said.

Be careful. You can't be sure that he knows, and if you mention Salzburg, then he will find a way to take TRI from you. Ash would give his entire career to share my moment at Salzburg. *No that's wrong thinking.* But I'd seen the pattern I wanted to see and the logic didn't matter. It would be best to play these two along until I had Salzburg wrapped up and done.

"I'll think about it," I said.

"That's all I can ask for at this moment."

Again, that quiet, steady voice comforted me even when I

suspected he'd used me to get what he wanted. But was that the disease talking or reality? Ash wouldn't use me to get what he wanted, would he?

Hendrix grew restive, but Ash quelled her with a glance. "You can afford to give Dr. Sommers a little more time to get used to this idea, can't you, Kathleen?"

Now I really was confused. Whose side was he on?

ELEVEN

"**L**YNN, I'M A SCHOLAR, not an artist."

I should never have let her talk me into this. She'd been at the dining room table painting, and I'd sat down while I waited for Ash. Then he'd texted he'd be an hour late picking me up, and I'd made the mistake of telling Lynn. The next thing I knew, she'd had an apron over my good clothes, an easel propped in front of me, and a brush in my hand.

"Honey, this is art therapy."

This was woo-woo, and the scientist within me was appalled. Therapy wouldn't help me. I solved my own problems. And then I realized the brush in my hand was trembling. Lynn patted my shoulder. She had a streak of blue paint on her jeans and a blotch of red that had spread into the faint lines around her mouth—or maybe that was red lipstick. It was hard to tell with Lynn because she was a serious painter. And she meant well, I knew she did.

"Nothing else has reduced the stress in your life, Dart." Lynn put the canvas she'd prepared on the easel. "I've wanted you to try this for the longest time."

She'd been pestering me since I'd almost fallen off the ladder painting the trim.

Lynn held up the picture I'd selected last week when

she badgered me to get started. I hadn't told her I'd picked it because I liked the title, *Sliding into the Deep*. The artist had painted a simple two-dimensional shed with a pitched roof about to topple into the ocean but still upright, for the moment at least, against a turquoise blue sky. Never mind that skies never went that color nor were oceans black, the image called to me. And it was simple, two sides and a roof. Anyone could paint that.

"You sure?"

I nodded, relieved she hadn't called me out for not trying hard enough.

Lynn handed me a pencil and a sheet of paper, and proceeded to show me how to transfer the image onto the blank canvas, one dot at a time. Fifteen minutes later, I connected the dots with straight lines, and the shed emerged.

Perfect, except as Lynn pointed out, the building wasn't centered. But I'd copied it. Just to be certain I looked away, looked at the picture, looked back at the canvas, and I could see it now.

Still not centered.

I erased the dots and the lines and tried again. Lynn encouraged me to keep trying. That's what I liked about her, she always encouraged me.

Nothing changed this time either, because although it looked right, the simple structure wasn't centered when I measured the space around the shed yet again.

Lynn didn't say a word, and I loved her for that. She had to see what I was doing, had to wonder why my brain couldn't process what I'd done wrong, but she was patient, and she let me keep trying until I positioned the shed in the middle of the canvas where it was supposed to be.

The measurements said I'd gotten it right, and so did Lynn's smile. That grin erased the worry that had come into her eyes.

That's when I knew I would be engaging with Lynn in woo-woo at least once a week. Her art therapy would be my tire gauge against mental deterioration. But that meant I'd know every week I painted if the disease had progressed.

How could I face that?

How can you not?

That voice again. Maybe I should listen because that voice was why I was waiting for Ash.

~

Cool evening air wafted over the pier. The day had been unseasonably warm, and the diners took advantage of the warmth to eat outside in the ocean breezes. Ash and I watched the sun set on the water as we finished our meal, the fresh catch of the day for me and a steak for Ash. The conversation hadn't been as bad as I'd anticipated. We'd talked about his trip, the implications for the university, and nothing about our personal lives. We were back to being friends, Ash and Dart, instead of the deeper relationship that Ash wanted.

"You've been quiet all evening," he said.

That's because I'd tried to pretend I wasn't scared out of my mind. I didn't understand why it had taken my brain four attempts to center that shed. I'd tried to put it out of my mind and enjoy the food, the company, and the breezes, but the distress hadn't gone away. Something wasn't right, and as I toyed with the stem of my wine glass, I wondered if I should confide in the one man who might make a difference for me.

"Why don't you tell me what's troubling you?"

If things between us weren't so complex, maybe I would—but no, that wasn't a viable excuse for avoiding the truth. Ash had nursed Jennifer through frontotemporal dementia, and he knew what to say, how to reassure me and tell me I was just having a bad day. That made my mouth quirk up in a slight smile, and he caught that.

"I was just thinking that I could count on you to tell me the truth." And I could. I could count on the man, but my boss was another matter, which is why neither of us had brought up TRI this evening. Discussions of TRI belonged in the office, not on this perfect evening.

He covered my hand with his. "You can," he said, and his own small smile delighted me so much I relaxed for the first time all evening. "You can count on me, Dart. That's what I've wanted you to know for the longest time. I want you to count on me."

Maybe telling him, instead of keeping it to myself, would lessen my distress because I was scared now. Very scared. The data were clear—something was amiss when I couldn't center a simple two-sided structure in the middle of a canvas.

He looked so solid, so dependable sitting there, the afternoon sun highlighting his blue eyes, that glisten of white in his gray hair—no doubt about it, Ash was devastatingly beautiful in a totally masculine way. Why I was pushing him away when I could have him closer didn't make sense anymore. He was still in love with his late wife, but she wasn't here; I was here, and he wanted me. I took a sip of wine, fixed my eyes on the colorful swaths of pink, orange, red, and gold that covered the darkening sky, and I told him about *Sliding into the Deep* and how I'd made four attempts to get the shed centered on the canvas.

"But the fourth attempt, that one worked?"

"Lynn was quite happy and so was I. Now, though, she wants me to paint the darn thing."

"And you're afraid that you'll paint outside the lines, make the sky blood orange, and the structure a shed in shambles from a hurricane?"

I glanced down to where our clasped hands rested on the white tablecloth. He hadn't let me feel alone, not once. Nor had he mocked me. My dad would have said, "Buck up, face what you fear, and stop being a baby." Emory would have said, "You'll be all right, babe," and turned the conversation to his job, but not Ash. He clasped my hand tighter. That's why I was able to admit my deepest fear.

"Sometimes that's how I feel, Ash, when I can't control what's happening to me. My brain feels like scrambled eggs in a hurricane, and in the next minute, I come back to myself and I'm okay again."

His hand tightened on mine as if he would never let me go. "You'll be fine, Dart. This is just overwork and stress. Dr. McCloud is the best in the business, and if he didn't find anything out of the ordinary, then believe that this too will pass."

"But he asked me to come back in six months." I hadn't told Ash that part of the conversation. "Is this how it went for Jennifer?"

"No," and now his gaze went to the horizon and the setting sun. "Every person is unique in this disease. Until the end, and then Alzheimer's, FTD, Lewy body dementia—they all result in the same thing. The brain dies." Despite his sad voice, his words were steady.

"While the heart lives." My quavering voice wasn't sad.

"You read too much, honey." His deliberate attempt to lighten the conversation steadied me. "I prescribe no internet for the rest of the weekend."

I looked at him, and that glisten of white in his hair distracted me, and my fingers ached to trace the pattern those threads made against the iron gray.

"What arc we going to do, Ash?"

"You're coming home with me."

"I am?"

"You are." He paid the bill and then pulled out my chair. Together we walked from the restaurant along the pier to the car. "We're going to sleep in the same bed, so that each of us gets a good night's sleep. We'll hold hands, I'll kiss you good night, and I expect you to be there, warm and snug against my side when I wake up. Since Jennifer's been gone, I don't sleep well by myself, and I suspect that you don't either, Dart." He looked at me. "Do you?"

I thought of the nights I woke at two a.m., again at three a.m., thinking what I would do if I were sick, and the fear I felt at what lay ahead of me wouldn't let me go back to sleep, even though I desperately needed the rest.

"We'll go sailing tomorrow. No one can have worries on the ocean. Not allowed, Dart."

"Then I'll leave them behind on shore."

"Where the tide will take them out until there's nothing left to worry about."

"Will I be okay, Ash?"

He turned me toward him, took me by the shoulders, drew me closer there in the twilight of darkness, and pressed a soft, tender kiss upon my lips. "I've been trying to tell you, babe." I smiled despite myself because he knew how much I hated that word.

"What happens next won't be your fault. Both of us will be okay as long as we have each other."

I leaned back to look at him. "Tell me the truth"—*before the light goes and I can no longer tell if you are lying to me or not.* "Do you miss her?"

"Every day, but she told me to live and, with you, I want to."

～

After a few weeks, Ash scheduled another meeting between Hendrix and me. Reluctant, I found all sorts of excuses, but these past few weeks of trying to keep up with my normal job responsibilities and TRI's work had convinced me that I needed help. My brain seemed more sluggish and slower every week. I found myself preoccupied with counting. How many bridges did I cross on the way to Wilmington? How many boats did I see on the Intracoastal Waterway? White Acuras? Black Mercedes?

Maybe Ash was right that a partnership between TRI and the university might work.

Susan and Lynn were helping me with the training manual I was writing for TRI's website; however, we had too many ideas. Obviously, TRI needed more members, but how to recruit them? That remained the question. What was becoming increasingly clear was that Susan and Lynn had very different ideas about how to do what needed to be done. The result was a mess of agendas that pulled us apart.

And Ellen promised me she'd call, yet Bill hadn't heard from her, nor had I, nor had her relatives and friends. Bill wanted to give her another week. She'd indicated her spiritual guide in Mexico had specified a blackout period, effectively isolating her from those who loved her. More and more this was beginning to feel like a cult, but Bill insisted she was happy there and not afraid.

When I entered the dean's suite, Ash understood why I put my phone on the conference table. Not so Hendrix.

"How rude to take a personal call during business meetings. Nothing, not even your cousin's minor health issues, can be more important that solving Southern poverty."

She was so good at making me look self-centered that I almost had to admire her for it. Odd, what one believes despite evidence to the contrary.

"This is the concession I'm willing to make." I turned off the ringer. I could still see texts that came through, and it would vibrate instead of ring.

"They'll call back if you miss the call, Dart." Hendrix's grimace seemed overdone to me, but Ash didn't say a word.

I left the phone alone and turned to her. "Ash wants us to work together, and I have to admit I'm overwhelmed with all I have on my plate. How do you see us working together?"

Hendrix wasn't pleased with my overture. She thought I was trying to make myself look better. Maybe it was the words "working together" that angered her. Those words didn't fit her mind-set of me as a self-centered know-it-all who didn't respect others because I had more experience and better credentials.

"TRI belongs here," her finger hit the table. "The intellects that can think through complex problems and solve them are here—not out there." She waved her hand toward the window of the dean's office and the poverty-stricken neighborhood that bordered the university campus. A developer had bought up all the properties there and would soon bring the wrecking ball in to demolish the homes that had sheltered the poor. I was one of the few faculty members who thought the poor shouldn't have been displaced, but Hendrix belonged to the other camp, the one that promoted growth and change no matter who was inconvenienced.

"Do you think those people"—and again she waved her hand toward the slum area—"can come up with ideas that might solve their plight? If so, wouldn't they would have done it by now? No one in their right mind wants to live as they do, to go to bed hungry at night and not know where their next meal is coming from."

"Most of them work two or three jobs," I said. "They try their best to provide food for their families, and sometimes they fail." I leaned toward her, willing her to understand. "All of us are one step away from where they are."

"The system isn't broken. The poor need to work smarter, but they don't have the intelligence to do that. This university does."

She hadn't read Lea's risk and decision-making research. I leaned away from her, wanting nothing to do with that outdated rationalization. "You envision TRI as a think tank of university professors?"

"Yes," she said, and her big contented smile made me pause. I still believed my grass roots movement, despite faltering at the moment, was the way to make a difference in the lives of the impoverished. University professors were too removed from the realities of being poor. We had a profession that offered us autonomy, not service jobs where we punched a clock or were at the mercy of quotas. Granted, some government officials and administrators wanted to bring that organizational pattern to the ivory tower, but ideas and truth, the quests we engaged in, didn't conform to that business model.

Hendrix continued to outline her plans for TRI. I had asked her how we might work together, but I had ceased to listen. Breaking into her monologue, I said, "Dr. Hendrix and I can't work together, Dean Wright. Her ideas about how she wants TRI to look are very different from what made my think tank the success it is today."

"You don't have a choice," Hendrix said before the dean could speak.

"Yes, I do," I said. "TRI is my idea, my work, my quest, *mine*. What you're proposing will lock its light in darkness. Universities are no longer the center of thought in this country."

"You've lost your mind."

"And we did it to ourselves, locking ourselves into an ivory tower, refusing to get our feet wet, our hands dirty. We have to work with the people, not hold them at bay."

"You want to teach the masses how to think?" Hendrix looked aghast at the very thought of that. "Dart," she said, edging closer, "they don't want to think. Edison said it best: five percent of the people think, ten percent of the people think they think, and the other eighty-five would rather die than think."

She pitied me, she did, and I hated it.

"I took a group of older women from all walks of life, some of them impoverished—"

"One of them a criminal," Kathleen interjected.

"Mary Beth didn't commit a crime."

Hendrix paid me no attention. "And the other a slut of a barmaid who can't keep her pants on."

"Classy's not a slut and she's happy with Sandy."

Had Bill's text not diverted my attention I might have hit her, she'd made me so angry with those false accusations against my friends.

Ellen missing.

Went for hike in mtns this morning and has not returned. I'm leaving for Mexico tonight. Will keep you posted.

He'd copied their kids and myself. I felt dizzy with dread and wondered why Bill hadn't let me know earlier. I would have gone with him. I must have looked devastated because Ash leaned nearer, and said, "You okay?"

"Ellen went for a hike in the mountains this morning, and she's missing."

"I'm sorry, Dart." He reached out to touch my hand, and if Hendrix hadn't been in the room, I knew he would have pulled me close. That's what I wanted him to do, for I wanted the touch of his hands on my shoulders, the warmth of his body against mine, to drive away the cold that had swept me up when I read about Ellen.

"Dart—" he started to say, but my phone pinged again, another message coming in. Maybe Bill had been wrong, and I turned my attention from Ash to the message. But it wasn't from Bill. This text was from the Salzburg Global Seminar.

Congratulations. We're pleased to announce that you are our choice to lead the Salzburg Global Institute symposium on world poverty.

"Now what?" Hendrix snarled the words because I wasn't paying attention to her. I was rereading the text because they wanted me to host, they really did.

I looked up from the text and told Ash, "The Salzburg Global Seminar has asked me to host a symposium on world poverty."

Hendrix started to smile in anticipation.

I ignored her and said, "I'm willing to work with the university, but Dr. Hendrix doesn't deserve the honor of being with me on the world's stage at Salzburg." I had Salzburg and I didn't need

Hendrix's fire or energy to keep me going. I would do whatever it took to keep the fury in check long enough to get me to Salzburg and to take TRI international.

Hendrix started to sputter, but Ash ignored her as well. "I understand," he said. "The university will support you in any way we can. Just tell us how."

"Now, wait a minute," Hendrix said.

She was still yelling at him when I told Ash we'd discuss details later and excused myself to contact Bill.

TWELVE

CLASSY AND SANDY were waiting for me when I got home that night. I pulled the old Volvo into the parking space on the street and walked up the steep flight of concrete stairs to where they sat on the porch swing. Seeing them there brought back memories of eating cookies with Emory, my ex-husband, on that swing while he told me he'd come home to die, of my sister-in-law, Sarah, buying those blue ceramic pots and filling them with red geraniums. Although she'd divorced my brother, David, I filled the pots every summer, and the blooms lasted deep into fall. Classy knew my memories tantalized me here, and she had plans to add yet another one.

I set my briefcase down and settled into my brown wicker rocking chair. Nice of them to leave me my favorite spot. Across the front yard, the street, and the park beyond, the Cape Fear River flowed into the Atlantic Ocean, and I could smell the salt and the sea and feel the wind in my hair.

Sandy grasped Classy's hand. She returned the squeeze and looked to him for help.

"What happened?" I asked, for I could tell that something had dimmed their expectations.

"The Southport police department downsized the force,"

Sandy said, his brown eyes resigned to the inevitable. "I'm on an unpaid leave of absence for a few months, and I'm not old enough, nor do I have enough money to retire." He looked out to the ocean. "The thing is, Classy and I don't have a place to go." The ocean breeze lifted his hair back from his high forehead. "Without my paycheck, all we've got is Classy's Social Security, and we can no longer afford the rent on the house we moved into."

My dad would have given them a few dollars for gas and kicked them down the road, but I wasn't my Dad.

"I can get my job back at the bar," Classy said. "I already talked to them about that. Don's happy to have me, but Sandy and I were hoping that if my old room wasn't taken, we could stay here for a bit, just until we get ourselves on our feet."

"We would love to have you back," said Susan. She and Lynn came up the steps, their arms wide open. Classy screamed, jumped up, and hugged them. Sandy seemed nervous, and when I nodded, he nodded his head as if to say, I owe you one, and went down to get his and Classy's suitcases from the car.

As the porch erupted into noise, I sat there, in my own world, stunned by how the fury within my mind had disrupted reality. *Classy's room was still empty.* So was Mary Beth's. Without that income, I'd be in the red in a matter of months.

I remembered I'd had the rooms cleaned, but I'd closed the door to each bedroom and forgotten about them. That I'd passed those closed doors every night on the way to bed and hadn't thought once about renting them out or fretted about the loss of income shocked me.

What else had I overlooked?

What else wasn't I paying attention to?

Dinner that night was noisy and loud with plenty of laughter. Classy kept reaching out to pat Sandy's shoulder or include him in the conversations with Susan and Lynn. The poor man couldn't find time to eat the meal Lynn had prepared.

When my phone rang, I recognized Bill's number and motioned for Sandy to bring his plate and fork, and together we went out on the porch so we could hear Bill's update on Ellen.

Outside, the night was as bright and full of silvery moonlight as if it were daylight. I put the phone on speaker and told Bill that Sandy was with me.

"You've got to come down here, Sandy," Bill said. Search and rescue had searched all afternoon he told us, found nothing, and would begin again in the morning. The frustration in his voice broke into demand. "They won't listen to me. You're a cop, Sandy, they'll listen to you."

"Bill, I'd be glad to help you out, but I don't know those fellas."

"They aren't out searching for her."

"Night falls quickly there. They'll find her in the morning."

"She's alone."

"Don't do anything stupid, Bill. They'll find her. She'll be okay."

"It may already be too late."

"Don't think like that. She'll be happy to see you in the morning. You stay put tonight. You hear me, Bill?"

"I need you, Sandy. Please, you have to come."

Sandy looked at me, and I nodded my head. The money I'd been saving for a new furnace would get him down to Mexico.

"Your friend Thomas, in Anchor's Pointe," Sandy asked, "should I contact him or catch a commercial flight out of Wilmington to Mexico in the morning?"

"Tom's ready and willing to fly anytime to help me out with

this. He'll bring you down. I'll call him tonight. Just be ready first thing in the morning."

"No sense you falling off a mountain in the dark between now and then," Sandy said. "Promise me you'll stay put in the motel."

"I've no choice. It's too dark to see anything."

"You won't be able to bring Ellen home if you're laid up."

"Just get here, man. I need you. They won't listen to me." He hung up on us.

Sandy started pacing the porch once I disconnected. "That little gal out in the wilderness. . . ."

"Ellen gets lost in Walmart," I said. "If she's stumbling around those mountains in the dark, her body weakened with cancer. . . ."

Sandy paced fasted. "Not to mention what that faith healer has her taking," he said. "Could be hallucinogenic weeds for all we know. She had to have been out of her mind to go into those mountains."

"She hates snakes," I said. "They have snakes down there, and spiders, and scorpions." I thought about her living room she'd redecorated, the painting she'd found for above the mantle, the rug on the floor that brought the colors into focus, those good decisions she'd made when she thought she'd been healing.

"We'll find her, Dart." Sandy laid his hand on my shoulder and looked me in the eye. "We'll find her and bring her home."

The desire to feel his arms around me, to hold me tight, to reassure me that everything would be okay made me stumble away from him. What was that? I didn't love Sandy, I didn't want him. I wanted Ash.

I clenched the porch's banister rails and looked for help in the silvery night. I wanted Ellen home, I told myself, that's why my emotions were over the top. Maybe if I told myself that enough times, this inappropriate yearning to feel Sandy's arms around me would go away, but it didn't and I turned toward the light in the house and went inside. Sandy followed.

"His buddy from Anchor's Pointe, Thomas. . . that's who'll take you down?" Susan asked after Sandy answered all their questions.

"Probably him . . . or the guy from Bald Head," Sandy said.

Classy told them about how Bill worked part-time at our little airport, and people offered him and Ellen rides to anywhere they were going.

"Good thing your passport's up to date," Susan said.

"Told you that honeymoon of ours was the best," Classy said to Sandy. Bill's friend had flown them to the Bahamas for their honeymoon, and they'd had to update their passports, which meant Sandy could go to Mexico without delay.

As I walked down the hallway to my room, I opened Mary Beth's door. The room was clean, empty, and ready for occupancy. Tomorrow, I thought. Tomorrow I'll put an ad in the paper and find another tenant. Why I hadn't rented out the bedrooms? It wasn't like me to let something like that drop. And why wasn't I more concerned about Ellen? I should be down there hunting for her, but I wasn't. I didn't want to get on a plane, but that wouldn't have stopped me in the past. Maybe I was too old for adventures, more concerned about my needs than Ellen's, my wishes than hers—but I'd given Sandy the money, I reassured myself. I'd done the right thing.

My lack of empathy didn't mean I had FTD. All humans were self-centered. I was exhausted; all of us who loved Ellen were, and I needed a good night's sleep. That would put me right, and I'd think about going with Sandy tomorrow.

~

The next morning, Sandy left for Mexico, and on the spur of the moment, Classy went with him. She'd never been to Mexico and, if I funded her trip, when they found Ellen, she'd convince her to give up the faith healer and come home. When Classy set her mind to something, that something happened. And I let her convince me because I felt guilty for desiring her husband's arms around me when my thoughts should have been on Ellen.

A text from Bill that night said they'd gotten there and that Ellen had not yet been found. Daily updates from Classy started with hope, then dwindled to defeat as the search and rescue became a search and recovery. Three weeks after their arrival in Mexico, Sandy and Classy came home and brought Bill with them.

He hadn't wanted to leave, not without Ellen's body.

We'd all gathered at his house, Sandy, Classy, Ellen and Bill's kids, and me. The consensus was Bill shouldn't be alone his first night back. He looked more exhausted than I had ever seen him. Ellen wouldn't have thought he wanted her dead if she could have seen him now.

"I want you and Sandy to move in with me," Bill said to Classy. "Sandy can help me coordinate with the Mexican authorities and it will be easier if he's here."

I tried to be positive when I was around Bill. Maybe Ellen had survived because of strangers' kindnesses, had kept herself alive somehow, been abducted and treated well, treated horribly—it didn't matter as long as she lived. What I knew was the tension no longer vibrated in the thread that connected my thoughts with hers. Or that's what I told myself. The truth was different.

Unless someone asked me about Ellen, I didn't think of her.

"What was it like where she disappeared?" Susan asked Classy.

Hope in my friend's voice built a vision in my mind of Ellen sitting beside a quiet stream in a bucolic meadow.

"Beautiful and deadly, all sharp edges and scrub brush." Classy brushed a cake crumb from her lap. Someone had brought chocolate cupcakes, Ellen's favorite. "Sandy and I are going back, once we bring Ellen home."

"You're doing what?" I asked.

"We're going to live there."

"Mexico?"

"Retirees live pretty cheap, and the people we stayed with want us to come back. It's beautiful with the mountains and the climate. Lots of retirees from the States live in the area. They let us into their homes once the community learned about Ellen."

"I never imagined." But I should have. Sandy and Classy would be happy anywhere, including Mexico. Ellen would have wanted them to be there with her. My cousin didn't like being alone. That's what made this so hard, knowing she was alone in those mountains.

"If Ellen's spirit is lost in those mountains, our being there might bring her peace."

A simple heuristic that comforted both of them. And was that so different from my useless hope that she was alive when everyone knew she couldn't have survived?

"She could still be wandering around out there. She didn't take her cell. Maybe she didn't want to be found," said Bill.

"Your wife," I said, "went to the faith healer because she was desperate. She felt her church family had turned against her."

"And she thought I was going to leave her," he said.

"Would you have?"

"Never. Ellen was, is, my life." Classy and Sandy both put their arms around him as he started to sob.

I didn't know what to think. Bill hadn't gone after Ellen. He'd let her stay in those mountains by herself. Maybe Ellen had been right about her husband. Maybe she'd known what the rest of us didn't want to see. But then I realized I hadn't gone after her either, and I professed to love Ellen like the sister I never had.

Back home, I sat down at the computer in the living room and turned it on. While it beeped and buzzed, I tried once again to pick up that mental thread that connected me to my cousin, but the thread lay limp and lifeless in my mind. The house was quiet. Lynn and Susan had returned with me and were already asleep. Outside, the night itself was still.

Going into my email, I started through all the unread mail that had accumulated, and there was a ton of it, evidence I hadn't been keeping up with the normal day-to-day duties of my job.

One more data entry for FTD.

I noticed the sender on a message buried about four unread messages down, The Salzburg Global Seminar. I opened it, eager to read what they had to say and what they said filled me with dismay. They hadn't heard from me, and unless I answered within the next twenty-four hours, they would assume I didn't want to host the summit on world poverty.

Nothing could be further from the truth.

I'd forgotten about the invitation.

They said they'd called.

I checked my phone. Voicemails. Lots of them. All unanswered.

I couldn't believe I'd done that. Here was another bit of data that my symptoms were worsening. I got up, went to the front window, and stared out into the dark night. How could I have forgotten what had been so important to me that I'd daydreamed about it and almost fallen off a ladder?

I turned away from the window and sat down before the computer. The screen glowed. My cousin Ellen had reached out for her last chance, knowing that she was risking everything to be healthy. Now it was my turn. I typed my acceptance, glad they contacted me, and apologized for not responding to their text. Then I hit send, waited for the message to disappear, shut down the computer, and was at peace.

Even if this invitation hastened my own fall into the fury that consumed my mind—a fury that I suspected to be frontotemporal dementia, the disease that had killed Jennifer Wright—I'd be strong enough to grasp my last chance, for TRI, for myself, for my father, for Ellen. FTD wouldn't take TRI from me until baby Raindrops were everywhere in the world.

~

That Monday, I sent an email to the dean, asking for release time and also for research assistance. That was the easy one because Ash and I had talked over the weekend and mapped out a plan of action that would conserve my energy and also allow me to focus on hosting the summit.

Then I composed a second email, the one I would send to the program faculty and the department chair and copy the dean. I rewrote it several times to find the right tone, for professors are competitive idealists. Perhaps just the right notes of excitement and joy as well as an undertone of "I couldn't have done it without you" would appease those on staff who considered themselves my equal or had more extensive research into issues of poverty than I.

Hendrix wasn't going to be happy no matter what I did, but if I did this right, I'd minimize her involvement when I asked for the university's help and for the faculty's assistance.

From: Dart Sommers

To: Chair, Psych Professors

CC: Dean Wright

Subject: Salzburg Honor

Colleagues and Dean Wright,

I have wonderful news to share. I've been invited to host a worldwide summit on poverty at the Salzburg Global Seminar in Austria, and I need your help. As several of you are also on the bleeding edge of the poverty revolution, please join me in Salzburg for this event that can and will make a difference in the lives of many across the world.

How gratifying it will be to have a table of NCUW professionals at the Schloss to showcase our university's efforts to extinguish poverty. Moreover, if you research poverty with other professors, please recommend that they contact me as well. We want the American representation to be on equal footing with that of other countries. I've already asked several prominent international researchers to provide the foundation for a platform of speakers around issues of, solutions to, beliefs about, and ongoing efforts to combat poverty.

This is a dream come true for me and an honor, but I can't

do this summit alone. Please mark your calendars. The summit will run for six days culminating in an evening gala and final wrap up.

Please also be aware that because of the extensive planning needed to hold the summit, I am requesting that Dean Wright release me from teaching duties during the coming spring semester.

Join me in this opportunity to make a difference.

Best,

Dart Sommers

The dean's email response came back almost immediately.

From: Dean Wright

To: Dart Sommers

CC: Chair, Psych Group

Subject: Teaching release granted

Dart, congratulations on this achievement. NCUW is happy to assist you in any way possible, including a teaching release from all classes during the spring semester of 2017.

You make us proud!

Sincerely,

Jasper Asher "Ash" Wright

Hendrix's email came a few hours later.

From: Kathleen Hendrix

To: Dart Sommers

CC: Dean Wright, Chair, Psych Group

Subject: Salzburg Summit

Colleagues,

I'm writing to share my thoughts about Dr. Sommers's request and the manner in which she imposed her needs upon us.

Upon discussion with Dean Wright, I've been told program faculty must take up the slack while Dr. Sommers is off having fun in Austria. However, my understanding is that we do not have to assist Dr. Sommers at Salzburg, although we can if we so desire.

Which brings me to my second, more important point. Salzburg is a city of wealth. The Schloss is a symbol of that wealth, a sprawling castle amidst beautiful grounds. How can she, we, use such a showplace to discuss issues of poverty when our meals will be prepared by renowned chefs; expensive, specialty foods will be brought in for our enjoyment; and our beds will be made in the morning by those paid to wait on us?

It strikes me as hypocritical and distasteful of Dr. Sommers to ask us, her colleagues, to afford ourselves such a privileged experience when around the world millions are going to bed hungry each night.

I do not need to associate myself with such an organization to continue my research into efforts that will eradicate poverty.

Sincerely,

Kathleen Hendrix, Professor

The mental accompaniment of a sword swishing from its scabbard and the resulting clash of steel resounding in my ears accompanied my third reread. I wanted to blast off a rebuttal but instead, I pushed away from the computer, paced my office for a bit, and remembered . . . what I had also forgotten.

Grabbing my desk chair, I spun it around, sat down, and brought up Hendrix's vita on the computer screen. There. Under presentations. Salzburg Global Seminar presentation on teaching autistic children. That had been ten years ago, and she'd gone back for a second presentation a year later because they'd liked her so much. Now I remembered the talk she'd given to the faculty on her return and her comment that Salzburg was an honorable event and everyone on faculty should experience it.

Something else, I thought, something more in that vita, and I scrolled past presentations through grants until I found affiliations, on page sixty. She belonged to the NCUW Club, a very special, posh restaurant on campus that the university had established to impress donors.

And she denounced me as hypocritical.

My response to her email was brief.

From: Dart Sommers

To: Kathleen Hendrix

CC: Dean Wright, Chair, Psych Group

Subject: Salzburg Summit

Dr. Hendrix,

Universities and professors seek grants, taxpayer dollars, and donations from the very wealthy to explore ideas. Perhaps the money that pays our salaries, keeps our offices heated in the winter and cooled in the summer, and sustains this university should be given to the poor.

You have presented twice at the Salzburg Global Seminar. You belong to the NCUW Club. I don't have to tell you that the Schloss is a symbol of endurance and an inspiration that the impossible can be achieved. Places like Salzburg and for that matter this university, secure our illusions that life is not chaotic, unpredictable, and brutal. However, our work in Salzburg won't tolerate that pacifier.

I hope you will join us in our efforts to address world poverty and to make a difference.

Sincerely,

Dart

But before I hit the send key, I paused. Perhaps if I didn't respond to her viciousness, ignoring her would extinguish the boorish behavior. No, I decided, extinction was the wrong tactic to take. I hit the send key.

That decision cost me, although at the time, when she didn't respond, I'd thought I'd won. A few hours later, I sent another email on a different topic to program faculty, this time a gentle reminder that the program had designated five p.m. tomorrow as the absolute deadline for all program faculty to review doctoral applications and submit any targeted questions they wished those applicants to answer.

Hendrix's response slapped me in the face.

From: Kathleen Hendrix

To: Dart Sommers

CC: Psych Group

Subject: Re Gentle Reminder

I will not be able to meet this deadline. *(Uh oh, she's saying she wasn't informed, didn't agree—my imagination whirled with possibilities. She's too wily to put in the specific reason. What is clear is that it's your fault.)* I will need more time for the task. *(And if she doesn't get it, that's harassment, discrimination . . . the legal system offered her plenty of refuge.)*

I have had MANY OTHER obligations that were previously scheduled to be completed. *(In other words, she's too important to be bothered.)* I will submit my evaluations next week. *(Interpretation: she'll do this when she damn well feels like it.)*

Kathleen

When I responded, with exaggerated politeness, that we had all agreed to the deadline, she accused me of singling her out.

And she didn't stop harassing me.

Whatever I sent out to the program or the chair and the dean on behalf of the program, Hendrix responded in a manner that made me look inept, addled, incompetent, or vicious. Her emails suggested I was singling her out, always a dangerous action in an academic setting.

As November wore on, she started to personalize every message as an attack on her. Finally, it occurred to me that I was in a duel with a skilled fencer of words and innuendo, and I had underestimated her. She'd perfected those bullying skills to stay alive in the competitive environment of academe. She'd also cheated and lied to stay here, but I had forgotten to bring her lies to the dean's attention.

Nothing would help, I told myself; Ash would ignore what I had found, so why bring it to his attention?

I felt as if someone had splashed Payne's gray over everything. Although my words about TRI and Salzburg painted colorful, vibrant word pictures, Hendrix's slow black jealousy and hatred dampened my passion. My paintings for Lynn grew grayer and grayer and the paintings themselves more abstract as that passion faded.

Or that's the lie I told myself. The brain always anchors deceptions in emotions. The frustration, anger, and fear that had made my childhood miserable had come back to life within me as the more complex emotions like conscientiousness faded.

That isn't who you are.

And that was another thing. Those whispers in my brain. As if two selves resided there, the one that spoke to me reminding me of what I should do, who I used to be, the dreams I had, and the other, still for the most part silent except for those demands, the sudden hijackings of my thoughts, my body.

All of it almost too much and crippling to productivity. Instead of arriving at the office at eight as I did during the semester and semester breaks, I'd stumbled in at ten in the morning, congratulating myself it wasn't one, reassuring myself that I got more work done at home than I could with the constant interruptions at the office.

That was a lie. At home, I stared out the window at the ocean, contemplating little, and letting my thoughts wander.

THIRTEEN

A S THE SEMESTER DWINDLED to an end, my research stopped, my preparations for Salzburg withered and died. Perhaps this was what burnout felt like.

Big difference.

This wasn't burnout. The toxic social environment I found myself in heightened the clash of values within myself. No one at the office took my side against Hendrix. My humiliation continued because administrators feared her and the turmoil she could stir up. Only Brown Bear stood beside me. He sat now, on my lap, unafraid. That's what I liked about Brown Bear. He didn't know fear.

The person I was becoming preferred to obsess about patterns, counting, textures, and Brown Bear. I would tape the last MOOC later this morning, and then the course would be over. The experiment had gone well, all things considered. Maybe I should act on that other idea I had, an e-book from the lecture notes that I could post on my website as a how-to book to see around poverty, to prevent generations from making decisions that trapped them in hunger, fear, and resentment.

Teaching the course had convinced me that poverty remained our biggest threat to stable civilizations, at least until the environmental violence went nuclear. Then there was my idea for TRI, the one that had once seemed too odd, too big, but that wouldn't go away. Who I used to be said write that e-book from the course as a primer for book clubs to use when they accessed insight.

But I only thought about it. I didn't do anything about it.

I taped the last MOOC with Lea. She was the only reason my teaching retained some semblance of normality. I summarized the high points of my lectures and also discussed the suggestions and rationales that students had come up with for ways that Southern poverty might be eradicated. I proposed that small things can make a difference and that those solutions originate with the individual, then I turned to a final insight, burnout as a metaphor for poverty.

Basically, the research defined burnout as a state of being, not as a physical or psychological or intellectual failing. Poverty could also be thought of as a state of being, I suggested. And if burnout as a state of being robbed the individual of the ability to pursue a productive professional life, then could poverty as a state of being wear one out to the point that they are exhausted with the effort to just be, thus investing less in their jobs, as a result accomplishing fewer things, becoming less effective?

That would increase the feelings of cynicism and inefficacy . . . and so I continued at that last lecture, highlighting how to look at poverty from the perspective of decades of research on the syndrome of burnout.

My commentary must have stirred something in Lea because after the taping she said, "That feeling of being unappreciated. Why is that so harmful to humans?"

"Brains are wired that way. To encounter evidence that you

are not of worth—be it a promotion you didn't get, resources you needed and didn't have, coupled with what seem like random events that affect promotions and awards or wealth and keeping food on the table—that feeling of being unappreciated depletes energy. One tipping point for burnout in the workplace is fairness in the environment. Anyone can see the implications of that for fighting poverty."

"Workplace civility?"

"Yes, that decreases burnout." And the self I'd started consulting said, *It's not that simple.*

"What's not that simple?" Lca looked confused.

I didn't realize I'd repeated the words aloud.

"It's more than civility," I said. "If we're kinder toward one another we would enjoy what we do and find value in it."

"Dr. Hendrix hasn't read the research. She's asking the doctoral students what it's like to work with you on dissertations or as research associates. She wants to know if you're overbearing, or distant, or mean, or unresponsive. . . . she copied about six of us in that email trying to get more information."

I looked at her and my heart sank. "You didn't stop at my request, did you?"

"*We* didn't stop, Dr. Sommers."

She'd involved others. *This is bad.*

"Her vita is a fake, and if you don't do something, we will."

"You can't. She'll destroy you like she's trying to destroy me. Credibility is everything. That's how women like Hendrix win in academe."

"Then help us out."

"None of you can be involved in this."

"Graduate students spend time and money to get a degree from this college. We deserve the best from those who teach us. No one wants to learn from a liar and a cheat. You can't let that happen, Dart. If you don't do the right thing, the toxicity will get worse."

Listen to her.

Graduate students deserved the best we could be. Their minds were as sharp as ours, sharper, and they deserved a helping hand, not a push off the ladder of success if they disagreed with Hendrix and her plans for them.

"Do something," Lea said.

Although I said I would, I could tell she didn't believe me.

Maybe Lea's disappointment spurred me to take Hendrix's vita home that afternoon, but the pattern I found kept me working through the night, making sure I hadn't missed anything. Those embedded lies, just enough to make a difference, not enough to scream *cheating*, were difficult to expose. Sneaky, hiding evidence in plain sight. And brilliant, no one would ever have looked if she'd behaved herself, if she'd been good, kind, and helpful.

But now that I knew, the pattern became obvious. The evidence had to be solid. She'd moved her name on some of the publications from fourth and fifth author to first or second. But at least she'd done the work, I thought as I flexed my cramping fingers. With other publications, most published in lesser known psychology journals, she'd added her name to the list of authors. That meant they'd done the work and she'd taken the credit. And then with some pubs, she'd added her name and removed the real authors' names.

Once I found those patterns, I hadn't been able to look away. And I was glad I did, for I found the presentations were padded as well: Hendrix hadn't been at Salzburg at all. She had either tried to get in twice and they wouldn't take her, or she'd fabricated both invitations. Lea was right. Hendrix had to be stopped.

The clock struck one in the morning when I put the marked-up vita in a folder. I put the file in my briefcase. I'd give the evidence to the dean when I went back to work on Monday.

~

Ash refused to see me.

He was busy.

He was out of town.

He had to eat, didn't he?

Lea texted later that week that unless I met with the dean, the students would request a meeting to discuss the matter. That's when I camped out in his waiting area with the hope that he might fit me in. I'd walk him out to his car when he left at five to go to some celebrity author event the university was hosting that evening if I had too, but I wasn't going away.

And I waited, the bright red folder on my lap, until Ash appeared at 4:50 p.m. and beckoned me into his inner sanctum. I hefted the red folder which was weighted with more than I wanted to bear of my own doubt and reluctance.

"What's on your mind, Dart?" He didn't even sit down at the table. Instead he started gathering papers and folders from its surface, shutting down the computer as well, in a hurry to make the event. He hadn't looked my way. Translation: I'm busy and this had better be good. Make this short.

If that's how you want this played. With a slow slide, I pushed the red folder toward him. The movement slowed my mind until that was all I could see and hear, that bright red folder slipping, sliding, scraping, gaining momentum, leaping over my reluctance, and breaking free of restraint. It was done now, I thought, watching the movement. That's how the worst catastrophes that come your way start, don't they? With something so ordinary, like standing on a ladder watching the paint brush you dropped spattered droplets of white paint on green leaves.

"What's this?" Ash looked up as the folder slid into his peripheral vision. He reached out.

I came back from counting that past pattern of dots. "Evidence."

"Of what?" His hand hovered but didn't touch the folder.

"Dr. Hendrix's lies and deceit."

He drew his hand back. "Dart, I don't want to get into the middle of this little argument with you and Kathleen. I've told you, don't respond to those emails. That will extinguish the behavior."

"This isn't about that."

"She's a whistling teakettle in the tornado that's your life. Ignore her."

"She lied."

"I know you think she's been disrespectful, but she'll get tired of the game. Kathleen is a respected professor, and she's justified in expressing her views." He stuffed some more papers into his briefcase and checked to see that he hadn't forgotten anything on the desktop. He picked up the red folder. "I'll look at your documentation, but there's little I can do."

"Don't blow this off, Ash. What you're holding is evidence."

"This isn't copies of the email exchanges you've been having?" Surprise, then distaste, flickered across his face, but awareness came too late. He'd already picked up the folder. "What's in here?"

"Evidence of a falsified vita."

He stood there, his thoughts suspended, his eyes glazed, holding the red folder he'd grabbed in his haste to get me out of the room. The folder fell back to the desk with a soft plop. Some of the papers slid out. My gaze and his tracked the fall, then the cascade of papers. No way to hide from her culpability now, not with all my red ink imploding the building blocks of her career.

"She's the most prolific writer we have in the college."

I showed him precisely how she'd cheated to become that prolific.

"This doesn't make sense."

It was inconceivable that a professor of Hendrix's standing would do such a thing. This was a forty-year career of a highly respected professor, who keynoted conferences, held positions of power in organizations, including administrative duties at the college. If anyone had positioned themselves to become a public intellectual it was Hendrix. Couple that with the fact that she was an inspiration to students of color, and no wonder he was confused. He'd believed in a false logic that professors who held positions of power, respect, and trust wouldn't lie to keep their jobs.

"Some of those falsifications," I indicated the folder, "started long ago, when she was an associate professor with a family to support and one paycheck coming in. People do crazy things when food and shelter are on the line. She probably promised herself each and every time that she wouldn't do it again. Except, she got away with it, and it was easy to slip in another falsified paper."

I hated to see his disappointment because he was the one who would have to clean this mess up. I watched as he thought through any number of scenarios. When he reached across his desk and picked up the phone, I felt nothing. After telling his assistant to cancel his event that night and make his apologies for other commitments, he asked her to call the provost's office for an appointment in the morning, then wished her a pleasant evening and said he'd see her tomorrow.

When he sat down, opened the folder and started to read the first of the notes I'd stuck to relevant pages of that eighty-page document that was Dr. Hendrix's professional life, I braced myself for the argument. He wouldn't take my accusations as truth unless he could prove them himself. And that was okay. The one thing I'd learned about Ash was that if he did this for Hendrix, he would do it for me, or Lea, or any of the faculty who served under his watch.

When he booted up the computer again, I knew we would be in his office for a while. A bit of tension uncurled itself in my stomach. I noticed his hands as he typed one of Kathleen's false titles into the computer. Then I watched the screen as the machine spun— although that was all in my mind because the screen remained blank then brought up the list I'd found. I relaxed because I hadn't screwed up.

All he needed was to go further, and that's just what he did, finding the journal's website, looking for any and all verification of the published article, and when the journal's website revealed nothing, he went to the library's search engines, and again nothing turned up. The title was there and the article had been published, but Hendrix's name was not on it, or on any of the sites that he searched. The facade would hold up through cursory glances, which would satisfy those of us in a hurry, because as Hendrix knew, reputations were shortcuts the brain used to categorize people.

An hour later, he closed the folder and said, "She's had a long and distinguished career. Do you want to end that for her?"

That wasn't fair. What would happen next wasn't my fault.

"It's not what I want. If you are looking for me to give you permission to pretend that neither of us know, I won't do that."

"This will hurt the college and the university."

"She might leave quietly."

"You know she's never done anything quietly. There might not be enough here to justify firing her, even if all the dirt you've dug up is correct."

"Have the lawyers double- and triple-check my investigative work. Do it yourself."

"That's why I made the appointment with the provost."

"Don't let them convince you to ignore this."

"I know that Kathleen has been unkind to you."

"Unkind?" I laughed out loud at that. "I let the Raindrops know that if something happened to me, they should inform the police that Hendrix pulled the trigger."

"It isn't as bad as that."

"What she did to me was humiliating and demoralizing. And it's been going on for years, and you allowed it."

"You wanted to pay her back."

No. I didn't falsify her vita. She did that. This isn't my fault. I brought this to your attention, I didn't create the mess. I hadn't ever wanted her destroyed. I just wanted her to shut up.

"You found a way to get even."

"I didn't falsify her vita, she did that."

"I'll be checking."

"You should check everyone's vita. They are posted online for the world to see. You should go further than I did." I tapped the folder. "I didn't read every publication to see if the conclusions she reached matched the data she collected."

"She wouldn't do that. You had motive to go after her."

"She intimidates people."

"Not you."

"I've known about this for several months now and couldn't bring myself to tell you."

"So why now?"

"The students know."

"Oh hell . . . How many?"

"Her doctoral students."

"She's been warned to treat them with more respect and courtesy. I've told her time and time again whenever complaints were lodged."

"Maybe she wanted to be caught."

"After all these years?"

"She can't claim a mistake. The lies have been in black and white for a long time. Lies get bigger and secrets get harder to hold the older one gets."

"And that's why you brought this to my attention?"

I stood up and gathered my things. He would do the right thing now. I could see it in his eyes. He didn't like it but he would see this through.

"Does it matter? The why of it?" I pushed my chair in against the table. "I don't think so at this point. You have a personnel issue that I've brought to your attention. I trust that you will take the appropriate action. Maybe I'm wrong."

"Whether she's fired or not, she's done as a professor. The students won't trust her, and the faculty will be wary of her," he said.

"I take no pleasure in this, Ash."

"If I were you, I would." He flipped the folder shut with one finger and shoved it away from him as if he wanted nothing to do with this. "And you're not wrong."

"She thought she was smarter than the rest of us," I said, as I stood up. But I wasn't thinking of Hendrix any more. I'd moved on to my own problems. The essential morality that was me was still there fighting back, but if what I suspected was true, that my brain was wasting away, Ash would have cause to *let me* go one of these days.

The thought didn't bear thinking about.

I was almost at the door when he said, "I'm still expecting you for dinner this weekend."

I looked back at him. Considering.

Maybe this is how Hendrix started. She put down that first small lie on her vita, adding her name to the list of authors on an obscure publication, to keep her present a reality. And when she got away with it, she lied again, to herself and to others, because there was so much at stake she didn't want to lose.

He smiled at me, as I left him sitting alone with the red folder. Before I shut the door behind me, I told him I'd have dinner with him this weekend. As I closed the door, I told myself I was all kinds of a fool, because I still had hope that I would always *know* that I loved this man.

And it was already too late for that.

Whatever was inside my brain had begun to erase the empathy I'd once felt for other humans. Within those last minutes of conversation, I'd realized that had this situation occurred a few years ago, I would have gone to Hendrix, not Ash, and told her, not him, I knew of her deceptions.

The reasons why that wasn't a good idea flooded my brain. The truth remained stable in the midst of that chaos. Maybe if she resigned, the university wouldn't bring other charges, like fraud, against her or revoke her pension. But to resign, she had to know that her duplicity had been uncovered. When I got home, before

I became distracted or changed my mind, I sat down at the computer to compose a message to Hendrix.

She doesn't deserve a warning.

I paused before I hit the send button because this felt like the right thing to do, yet a part of me wondered if this impulse might be the mixed up part of my brain talking. Regardless, the impulse was too strong to resist. I sent the email to Dr. Hendrix.

FOURTEEN

P UTTING THAT FOLDER in Ash's hands revived my work habits, or maybe with the semester concluded and with no more emails from Hendrix, my emotional barometer righted itself. I could think again. My motivation for work returned. I implemented the first step in the process Lea and I had put together for TRI, and a week later, I pulled up at the gatehouse of Anchor's Pointe to talk to the Busy Bookers book club.

They'd accepted my request to speak about The Raindrop Institute. Although hesitant at first because no connection is apparent between discussion of books, particularly novels, and eradicating poverty, once I explained they understood.

The guard at the gate, not armed but looking very official in his rent-an-authority uniform, waved me to a stop. As the window rolled down, I smiled to show how friendly I could be and said, "Dart Sommers to visit Stacy Adams." The tang of fresh salty air invaded the car as did the warmth of sunshine.

"Just one moment." He consulted the list and didn't smile.

What would he do if I punched the gas, busted through the flimsy one-arm restraint, and drove on through without being admitted? Then I noticed the stream of Mercedes, Volvos, Lexus, and BMWs from Anchor's Pointe gliding past me in the lane on the other side of the guard house at a sedate twenty-five miles an hour. This was an impressive place but nothing like I was used to. And wait, was that a Tesla? Those were California cars. Maybe I'd made a wrong turn and ended up in Silicon Valley. And why was I considering breaking the law? I didn't do that sort of thing.

The guard continued to consult his list for the day and gave a grave nod when he found my name. A slip of paper on my dashboard said I was legal, and I was through the checkpoint. This community was at the top of the list of wealthiest cities in North Carolina. Income data from the latest census placed most of the residents within the top quartile of richest Americans. Baby Boomers from New York, New Jersey, Connecticut, and other northeastern seaboard states had discovered they could enjoy four seasons plus the ocean in North Carolina. Nothing like this would have been possible without cars, local airports that could zip them home to see the kids and grandkids, and the money to make that happen. The big homes housed relatives whenever they visited for a bit of the salt life and, although school buses trundled up and down Anchor's Pointe roads, the average age in the community was late fifties to early sixties.

I'd done my homework for the visit. Those who had FTD wouldn't have bothered, but the rationalization felt false.

Lots of folks out on the golf course, I noted as I drove deeper into Anchor's Pointe, and because the December day was warm and sunny, bikers and walkers shared the road. Nice community, but as I drove past the crowded marina and boats that took crews to operate, I wondered if I'd made a mistake thinking that the Busy Bookers, the only book club to invite me to speak about TRI, might want to help me out.

This storybook town with its manicured lawns, beautiful homes, and Southern charm—all surrounded by endless real estate dedicated to playing a game called golf—could be the subject of the textbook on survivorship bias. The people who lived here carved out the life they wanted.

I parked the car in the driveway of 3362 Linkpin Drive and marveled at the Southern mansion with wide sweeping porches, bay windows, and manicured lawn that said "gracious living." This wouldn't be my retirement. I could never afford this on a professor's pension. Even among impressive homes, this one stood out. Locking the car seemed silly given where I was. So did my irreverent thoughts that moving white to blue to green described the best way to play golf.

Better not bring up that theory. I didn't want them to throw me out before they listened to what I had to say. Shutting the car door behind me, I walked up the brick sidewalk to the sweeping front porch that was decorated with masses of flowering plants, comfortable cushioned wicker rockers, and a glider like one we'd had on the farm. Yellow and white, just like the one my mom used to sit in to shell peas.

I hesitated before ringing the doorbell. They'd laugh me right out of this fancy place for suggesting they might be vulnerable to poverty. Brunswick County used to be the poorest county in North Carolina before the Baby Boomers started to move in. I would have to convince them they couldn't shut poverty out with gates that closed after their cars' exhaust.

I pressed the doorbell. The chime within sounded, a deep gong, then a whistle followed by the melody from the movie *The Good, the Bad, and the Ugly*. Things were looking up. That's what I had come to discuss with them.

Footsteps sounded in the hall. My stomach tightened. I remembered these were adventuresome, intelligent people. They'd all uprooted themselves in retirement and moved far away from the familiar. Older women understood the importance of social relationships. Most residents did volunteer work that kept Brunswick County afloat, and the dollars that came out of this place supported many, many local businesses. Maybe my idea wouldn't be a hard sell.

A shadow darkened the frosted glass from within. Then the door opened wide, the noise of conversations and laughter snatched my attention, and the hostess of the Busy Bookers, a tall beautiful blond woman who looked to be forty said, "Hi, I'm Stacy, welcome." She grabbed my hand and led me inside.

I had an impression of space, light, graceful elegant furniture, beautiful woodwork, and then Stacy introduced me to the women who'd come for the book club meeting. I could see the speculation in their eyes. I glanced around the room hoping for a sign they saw a normal human being, which is always somewhat in question when people interact with a university professor.

"So, why are you here?" asked one lady whose name I didn't know. I didn't know any of these folks other than Stacy who had let me in.

"She's here, Rachel, to discuss why men like to argue." Laughter burst from all corners of the room.

"Which is why romance novels sell," Rachel said. "You all are missing my point. Although I must tell you that I've often thought that preoccupation with the male member is to blame for most of our social problems."

"You can't blame everything on men, Rachel."

They'd forgotten I was in the room. I was wasting my time. These women didn't want to think, they wanted to have fun.

"Young women's hormones get in the way of common sense just as often as male hormones," said another. "Ten minutes in a man's arms can lead to a lifetime of poverty for both of them."

Wait a minute. Cloaked in humor and common sense, a bias could masquerade as wisdom when stated that way. And I was just about to comment on love, sex, and poverty, when someone else said, "It's not as simple as that."

"Of course, it is," another older woman said. Heads cloaked in different shades of gray nodded. The younger women in the room, I noticed, weren't taking sides. Interesting. They let their silence pretend for them. From a neurological perspective of my research, I had another example of the unconscious brain caring about what others thought.

"It's as easy to fall in love with a rich man as it is a poor one, that's what my mother always said." Rachel turned to me and demanded, "Don't you agree, Dr. Sommers?"

That was my cue. I could have told Rachel that humans are psychosexual beings, but I doubt she would have listened. Rachel was one of those who believed, and nothing I could say would sway that belief. Maybe if she knew how rare it was that rich men and poor women had access to one another, that fact might bend her belief. "Anyone here see *Pretty Woman*?" I asked.

That brought *oohs* and *ahs* and "I loved that movie" and "Of course it wouldn't happen in real life" and "Except it did, and it was just so romantic." Skeptical glances my way, and if I dared smash romance, they were going to make short work of my idea.

"Even I enjoyed that movie, but not all of us look like Julia Roberts," I said, "and social barriers aren't all that permeable." That earned me some smiles of understanding.

"Why are you here?" Rachel asked again.

"You might be wasting your time with us, Dr. Sommers," another Booker said. "We're not intellectuals. Some of us worked, but a lot of us stayed at home and took care of the kids. I followed my husband, and it was my job to make a home for us."

I nodded, thinking that's why they didn't understand. *Careful,* you have to be careful. She's right at the edge of being indignant if she even suspects you think yourself better than she is because you have that PhD. Although I never did understand that envy. How I lived my life didn't mean their choices were less valuable. I would have given anything to trade places with some of these women who'd had children and a love that lasted a lifetime.

"That didn't stop you from thinking," I said. The Booker still looked skeptical, but her indignation had gone to simmer. I looked around. "Intelligence doesn't disappear because you're standing at the kitchen sink instead of sitting in a boardroom."

No quips this time. A different kind of silence. They were considering. I could see it, then Stacy said, "No offense, but we can't help you if we don't know why you are here. Men who are much, much smarter than we are can't solve poverty."

Rachel's friend came to her aid. "It's too complex, too big, too messy."

Those were my words.

Yet another friend said, "It's a problem best left to intellectuals and politicians rather than women like us who are living our last years in the sun, or on the golf course, or caring for our kids and grandkids."

"I think what she means, dear," said the little old lady sitting in the most comfortable chair in the room, "is that we live in a gated community. We aren't poor. We have nothing in common with the impoverished. They made their beds, we made ours, and it's not our fault that ours is more comfortable."

"At that little school down the road, they have a washing machine and a dryer. They wash the kids' clothes because their impoverished parents won't do it," another Booker said. "Doesn't take much, to wash out a pair of pants and a shirt every night."

"Clothes don't dry overnight in this climate, Jenna. You know that," said another Booker.

"But they would during the day," said the unrepentant Jenna. "Some of those kids don't bathe. They have green mold growing on their scalp." She turned to the others for confirmation. "You all have seen it when we go in to volunteer. And the ringworm. They're sleeping with animals. It's disgusting."

Some of the women shifted. My guess was that their dogs or cat slept on the bed with them. As for ringworm, it was an infection that didn't care about the size of one's pocketbook. Jenna didn't believe me, so I said the facts again, pointing out that facts vie with beliefs for dominance. Jenna refused to give up her belief that ringworm affected the lower socioeconomic class and no other

"They have jackets and mittens there for those kids who don't have any warm clothes," said another Booker. "That's how kind those who have are in this area. The teachers have to take the tags off the new clothes and rumple them up a bit because if the kids go home with new clothes, their parents take the clothes back to where they were purchased, and the parents work the system to get cash, somehow, someway."

"Just goes to show, these people aren't dumb," said another Booker who hadn't spoken before.

The research bore that out. Low intelligence was not a prerequisite for being impoverished. I looked around the room. Everyone there was dressed nicely, they didn't smell, their hair was washed, fingernails painted, they weren't drooling, and they spoke proper English. Their clothes were from the nicer department stores, and the jewelry they wore, while not flashy, made a statement.

This generation of women had turned away from power before, during the woman's movement in the '60s and the '70s. Had I been stupid to think they would want another opportunity to speak for themselves, to take on the challenges of the world?

They invited you. Which meant I hadn't been wrong to come. I tried again to help them understand how they could help. "Current beliefs about the poor don't solve the problem."

"Their problem is not ours."

And there it was, the one belief about the poor I'd come to fear. This was the attitude that could stop The Raindrop Institute in its tracks.

"If you are unwilling to listen to what I have to say, why am I here?"

"It's what we do, dear. We listen, we process, and then we go out and play golf."

"We're just a group of women who gather once a month to discuss books, Dr. Sommers. We have a good time," explained another Booker. "It's important to keep the brain functioning."

"And there are no repercussions to our thinking if we're wrong," piped up another one.

"Beliefs among the poor are strengthening against people like you." My comment made the room grow quiet. "They will sacrifice rich people on the altar of utilitarianism, and it's going to be just as ineffectual as the Mayans sacrificing virgins to stop the drought. Older women like yourselves have a lot to offer this culture. In fact, we are the one demographic group that does."

I was one step away from seeing contempt in their eyes. Bearing witness to their disgust was bad enough. They weren't going to help me and, as I listened to the silence, I almost—almost —threw it all away. Then I caught what I had missed in the engagement with Rachel and her friends, the body language of the other Bookers who hadn't spoken, the pleating of a skirt, the flutter of hands rubbing a headache away, and eyes that winked . . . she winked at me, the woman in the corner, the one with the flashy nails, whose clothes screamed haute couture, and who looked like I had always yearned to look—classy, aloof, cool, and oh so composed.

She winked again.

Someone had swayed this club to give me a chance, and I wanted that someone on my side, voicing her thoughts with mine, or The Raindrop Institute initiative involving book clubs would falter and die. Because I didn't have the courage to do this twice. I'd forced myself to come here, to talk with these women. I hadn't piqued their interest, or provoked them, or riled them up—the methods I used to keep my student interested. I should turn the conversation so that Ms. Couture would feel safe standing beside me. I squinted and saw that her name tag read Carol Lee.

"Women of our age have been conditioned to think that wealth or education or being loved by others will keep us safe from life's chaos. None of that is true."

"Young lady," Rachel said, "I've been married for fifty years, and my Ralph is the best thing that ever happened to me."

In other words, you can't touch me. Didn't she realize that insulation worked both ways? It kept out the cold, but also the warmth.

"I began my research on poverty by studying civilization

collapse. That disaster happened six times, at least, in our human history, and we are at the cusp of another collapse. Marriage to Ralph isn't going to protect you when that happens."

"We're in an age of prosperity," said Rachel's friend. "The stock market is at an all-time high, jobs are improving, the economy is coming back, and Americans are breathing a sigh of relief that we escaped economic depression with a few scrapes and bruises. And Ralph has always taken care of Rachel. It's what he does."

"And when he dies? What will happen to Rachel then? How is she going to stand against what is coming our way if none of you," and I included everyone in the room with that glance, "will think for yourselves? Our indifference to the moral injustices around us caused the Civil War. Had we addressed slavery, instead of ignoring it, the Civil War would never have happened. Moral outrage is building again in this country because poverty exists. The resulting chaos will not stop at your gates."

"We can't do anything," Rachel said. "We're older women. The frailties of our bodies limit what we can do. And we've learned to endure, as women before us have done for centuries."

"Then, might I suggest that it's time women learned a different coping technique because enduring isn't working." She didn't like that, and I didn't like saying it. If lives across the globe weren't hanging in the balance, I would have been gentler, but I didn't have time to coddle her—I didn't have time to coddle any of them. "Poverty can be stopped, but we have to set aside our biases, our beliefs, and see around corners into the hearts of the problems and stop putting smiley faces on the symptoms."

"Intelligent men and women have tried and failed to solve this problem," Rachel said and others nodded. "It's God's punishment."

Another lull in the battle, and this time, I didn't have anything left to argue. God's punishment always stopped me, ever since beliefs had driven Ellen away.

They'd won. I'd lost. *Time to go home.* I reached for my briefcase.

"My Jenny died," said Carol Lee, Ms. Couture, and the room grew aware, as if a thunderstorm had appeared on the horizon, "but my husband and I believed we had given her everything that would protect her—wealth, education, and faith—and none of that kept her safe. She knew how to change the flat tire she'd had that night, her father had taught her how, but the young man who killed her wanted what she had. He didn't need to kill her to take the car, but he did."

The sudden inexplicable loss of a loved one made the room grow quiet again. Chaos had shown up again where they least expected it.

"You came here because of the beauty," Stacy said.

Carol smiled and nodded. "When the grief of losing Jenny becomes too much, the sunsets over the ocean remind me of how her smile brightened my cloudy thoughts, and how her beauty burst forth when she smiled. In that last burst of light before dark, I can be with her again."

The beauty of century trees and the ocean had helped me accept my father's passing. Beauty made chaos bearable. These women were as afraid as those in poverty. That's why they volunteered. They created beauty through gifts of food, money, diapers—and that was all well and good, but those impulses didn't provide a means of value that would bring those in poverty into a better way of life.

"Poverty makes young men sullen and angry, and I want no part of that," said Rachel.

Before I could speak, the woman seated next to Carol Lee said, "I am tired of living with your fear."

Rachel looked dumbfounded.

"Your fear of poverty keeps me a prisoner in my own home. The propaganda that news programs spiel about the poor places the blame with the poor instead of with the culture that accepts that human indignity. We place the blame on everyone else but ourselves. We've found the scapegoats, and as Dr. Sommers says, they are our beliefs."

She turned from the group to face me. "How can the Busy Bookers participate in The Raindrop Institute initiative, Dr. Sommers?"

"Keep your discussion groups small."

Research indicated small groups were most successful at problem-solving and generating new ideas. Groups like theirs, between five and twelve or fourteen members were large enough to provide insight and small enough to stay focused. The advantage was they were all women. That too was proven by research—that if you have women in brainstorming groups, the groups function better and come up with more cogent ideas.

"Dig deep to uncover your beliefs about poverty. Confront those beliefs and move them aside."

"Mud sticks to those who mess around in it," said Rachel as she struggled out of her chair.

"Mud dries to dust, Rachel, and it doesn't leave an open wound in your heart," said Carol Lee.

I liked Carol Lee. She was more than just fancy clothes and a pretty face. When Rachel left, no one else followed her out the door.

The ladies and I spent an hour talking about poverty and the biases our country held about it, and when I left, promising to return the next month with the e-book that would help guide their discussions of poverty, Carol Lee and her friend, Faye, plus Stacy, saw me to the door.

We talked about the first step in thinking outside the box: becoming aware of biases and how limiting they were. As they ruefully pointed out, they'd already uncovered some hefty biases that held them captive. And they agreed that by my next visit, they would ferret out more, and that they would be aware of confirmation bias and how powerful that was.

"I'm sorry about your daughter," I said to Carol Lee.

Carol Lee looked out the front door at the beauty surrounding the house. I don't think she saw that. "I have two other daughters," she said, "and I want to keep them safe. To do that, we must change the culture in which we live. Faye and I believe that young children shouldn't go to bed hungry every night, and young men shouldn't feel empowered to take what doesn't belong to them because they are angry."

"We know we have to go outside the gates, Dr. Sommers," said Faye. "Our values and work ethic got most of us here. I grew up in poverty. So did Carol Lee," she nodded toward her friend. "It took us a while, but we got out and we have no intentions of going back. We know that if we can do it, others can as well."

"Then we'll begin next month," I said. "I'll put that e-book together between now and then."

"Some of our members are afraid," Carol Lee said.

"They shouldn't be, not of what we are trying to do. Your courage will bring the others along. Thinking outside the box is fun, so the fear won't last."

"It's not that," said Carol Lee. "It's the responsibility. What if we do something wrong and someone gets hurt?"

"Good intentions have paved the way to our current problems. Our social programs have allowed people opportunity to consume products inefficiently. That's the way humans are wired. We had good intentions, but they haven't worked. Now costs are soaring, and the money isn't there to keep providing what was never wanted. If we do nothing, everyone will suffer."

I left Anchor's Pointe with the intention of going to the office and working on that e-book I'd promised them. If this worked out, I'd take Ms. Couture—it was hard to think of her as Carol Lee—and her friend with me to Salzburg.

Bill's text brought all those good intentions to a halt. *Ellen found. Flying to Mexico to bring her home.*

I was texting him back—*Where? Is she okay? How?* —when my phone rang. Classy.

"Is she okay?" I asked before Classy could talk. "Tell me she's okay."

"A hiker found her body, Dart. She'd tumbled into a ravine."

That picture snapped clear and sharp inside my mind . . . Ellen crumpled beside the small trickle of a stream . . . Ellen's brown eyes staring into nothing . . . a trickle of blood running down her smooth white cheek. None of my imaginings were real. She'd been out in the elements for too long, but beauty subdued chaos, and that's how the Sentinel chose to cope.

"How do they know it's her?"

"The swami or whoever in the hell he is identified her. She'd spoken to him right before she went for that walk, and he described what she was wearing, her hair, her sunglasses. She still had on her wedding ring. It's Ellen, Dart. Bill's friend flew him down. He'll be bringing her home soon. Sandy went with him."

"I should have gone after her."

"We should never have let her go," Classy said and hung up the phone.

～

We held Ellen's funeral at the gravesite because the body was not fit for viewing. She must have hiked a long way that first day and had maybe survived the second as well, going deeper and deeper into the mountain range, but she hadn't been alive to meet the dawn of the third day, or so the officials speculated. They said that she'd fallen, hit her head, and died. For that small gift, I was grateful.

The minister from her church finished his brief sermon, and we broke apart, the small group who had come to say goodbye. Lynn and Susan were there, as well as Classy and Sandy and several of Ellen's friends from the university. Ellen and Bill's kids stood with Bill. None of the women from her church showed up, and I hoped it was because they were ashamed of themselves.

None of us wanted to leave, and I was the last to go. After the funeral, when the sun set that night, I remembered Carol Lee's words and went up to the second-floor balcony of my home to watch the sunset. I never went there because it's too rickety, and I haven't had the rotted boards on the deck replaced, but that night I was careful. I stood and watched and remembered Ellen, who had brought so much beauty into my life in the moments we'd had together.

Then I went back to my computer and worked into the night.

FIFTEEN

I ALWAYS GO HOME to Illinois for Christmas; even that first Christmas after my dad died, I was on the road, like I was tonight, heading home. The Raindrops would prefer I fly, but I like driving through the night. After ten o'clock, the traffic dwindles and I have the highway to myself with moonlight leading the way accompanied by the white noise of the tires.

This was the first time Ash had come with me, and circumstances were a little different. If I'm by myself, I can drive for hours, thinking about nothing as the miles to Illinois flash by. The Sentinel gets me to where I am going without mishap. But when Ash is seated in the passenger seat, he tells me when to brake, to turn, to accelerate, and to watch out. As a result, the Sentinel thinks *why do double duty* and relies on Ash to guide me.

After I reached Asheville and escaped the mental ties to Southport and the university, driving with Ash got quieter, and memories of my father and thoughts of Robbie pulled me onward through the mountains and the hills of Tennessee. Ash and I kept driving through the rolling hills of Kentucky, Indiana, and Southern Illinois as darkness, then moonlight, settled over the land.

"Tell me about Robbie," Ash said. He was anxious because this would be the first time he'd met my family. Too bad he hadn't met my dad. My father would have liked Ash.

"At six he was my father's shadow," I said.

"But your dad didn't like him, right?"

"That's what we thought, but what Dad said and what he did were two different things. He taught Robbie everything he knew."

"After David came down with diabetes, I donated my farm rent for five years to help Robbie start farming organically." Now sixteen—no, he was seventeen—Robbie was the farmer that Dad always wanted David to be. He ran the hundred acres that we organically farmed and made money selling the produce, meat, eggs, and a thousand and one other things that kept the Illinois farm solvent. No, not just solvent, but successful.

"He and his father live at the farm place now," Ash said, and something in his voice had me looking over at his profile lit by the ambient light of the dashboard. Strong chin, high cheekbones, and that hair I loved to run my fingers through. I was glad he was with me.

"That's right," I said, turning back to the road and the separated white center line that whizzed by as one continuous thread. "We almost lost David to sepsis a year ago but the treatment worked—that time. Robbie said it won't work next time."

That's why I wanted to be there for Christmas Day, surrounded by all the farm experiences that had given me the stamina to make my way in the world. My father waited up for me. There'd been sleepy inquiries as to the drive and the night, and then he'd gone to bed knowing I was safe.

I couldn't expect Robbie to wait up, but David had told me they'd leave the front door open.

"Is he always right?" Ash asked.

"Who? Robbie? Mmmm . . . Almost always right about water. He's a water witch, a dowser, and to see that willow rod bend in his hands, it's amazing. He says the water pulls at his wrists and even if he wanted to, he couldn't hold that rod steady."

I smiled, remembering the water witches of my youth. They were mystical, mysterious people. Only one of them hit good clean water every time and plenty of it, and he made a decent living at his hobby. Robbie was ten times as good as that guy.

"And what about when people are going to die?" Ash turned his head and I felt that steady gaze upon me as firm as the steering wheel in my hands. "Is he right about that?"

"David doesn't have long. This time the doctors and Robbie are in agreement."

In the moonlight and my headlights, I saw the first large flakes of snow start to fall.

"We might have a white Christmas, Ash."

"Been a while," he said, considering the weather. "I'd forgotten how beautiful falling snow can be."

"Let's hope we can make it home before it gets too deep," I said, speeding up. My Volvo had new tires, but as the snow fell, the highway turned slick, then blurred into a white path instead of a two-lane highway that led up to Hawthorne. As the temperature fell, the car's interior grew colder, despite the heater.

Thoughts of the farmhouse warmed me. My old bed would have lots of quilts and comforters, and with Ash there beside me, I'd be warm. There might be some hot water in the kettle on the wood-burning stove. Dad used to keep that kettle full and Robbie did as well, for the humidity kept the house comfortable. We could have a hot toddy and let the snow fall into drifts.

When the snowflakes accumulated to several inches, I clenched the wheel a little tighter.

"Want me to drive?" Ash asked, but I shook my head, afraid that if I stopped, we wouldn't be able to continue. All-wheel drive kept me more or less on the road, and with snow crunching under my tires, I pulled up the short incline to the house on the hill that overlooked the valley my father loved. Trembling with fatigue and adrenaline, I switched the engine off and slumped in the seat. Ash relaxed too and took in the winter land before us.

"They won't be up," I said as I looked at the house. There was a light on in the living room though and another in the kitchen.

Home, I was home after more than sixteen hours on the road. Maybe I should just wrap my coat around me and sleep in the car, except I couldn't stop shivering. But that's what I was thinking of doing when Robbie, swathed in coat, hat, gloves and boots, opened the door to the house. The warm light fell on the falling snow and the path that would lead me to the warmth inside. He came out into the cold, opened the car door, and without anything other than, "Glad you're here, Uncle Dart," he scooped me into his arms and carried me into the house, settling me into the big chair by the fireplace.

Ash followed with our luggage

"You weren't this tall two years ago." I sipped the hot water, honey, and lemon that Robbie had fixed for me and stared up at him. He'd shrugged off the coat and the gloves. Where had the slender little boy gone? I'd been used to looking down and now I looked up. This giant was over six feet, and he had the shoulders and the muscle to match that escalated height.

He smiled and ducked his head. "All my teachers want me to go out for basketball." He kept glancing at Ash.

And I realized I hadn't introduced them. "He's a friend, Robbie."

"He's more than that, Uncle Dart," he said and reached out and shook Ash's hand with a gesture that was almost grateful.

"Why do you call her Uncle Dart?" Ash asked.

"Calling me Uncle Dart was Robbie's way of making me feel welcome in a family that valued boys." Something about that handshake between Ash and Robbie troubled me. What was it?

"I'm glad you're a girl," Ash said to me with a smile.

And I was glad he was here with me. Maybe Ash and I could make this work. But something odd about that handshake still troubled me. Robbie didn't like to touch people, but then I'd been on the road and was tired—maybe this was nothing more than polite courtesy. We'd raised the boy to be polite.

No, something else than politeness. More than good manners. Then I knew—by his gesture, I knew what I'd come home to learn. My hand clenched on the coffee cup. I must have held out some foolish hope or convinced myself with all the wrong data to feel as devastated as this. But maybe I'd read the situation wrong, maybe Robbie was wrong. He couldn't know. I hadn't told any of my family about my episodes.

The firelight warmed the knotty pine of my old home and my cold bones, and part of me expected Dad to wander into the living room from his study just down the hall. I glanced that way and Robbie said, "I work there now." I nodded. It seemed right that he would step into his grandfather's pattern. But I had a feeling Robbie would walk farther and faster toward success than my father had.

The firelight played on his handsome face. He had my mother's black hair. He'd inherited the waves and tousled curls, but on him they didn't look at all feminine. The boy I loved was as tall and broad-shouldered as a man, but he was still there, that little boy who'd been quiet and reserved and who didn't care at all for people. Yet he'd picked me up and carried me inside. And when I told him that he was getting better, he did not understand. I could tell by the way his shoulders tightened and that brief frown.

"You didn't like to be touched when you were little."

He relaxed. "Have to touch the animals. They don't understand if you don't."

"I'm different."

"Had to bring you in."

"All the animals bedded down?"

"I saw to it when the storm first hit."

"It'll be a white Christmas then." And a beautiful one and maybe I could talk him into considering college.

And as if he could read my thoughts, Robbie nodded.

"You'll go to college?" I couldn't believe it.

"Maybe." He looked into the fire. "Grandpa wants me to."

"He always wanted you to go to college? Don't you mean your father?" Ash's question hung in the long silence.

"No, I mean Grandpa. He, his ghost, visits, but doesn't stay long. He knows I want to stay here on the farm."

Ash didn't look convinced.

"He's interested in you," Robbie told him. "Grandpa thinks you're good for Uncle Dart."

I almost felt he'd said that to Ash so that I would listen.

Ash nodded his head and grinned. "So do I. Maybe between the three of us, we can convince her I have her best interests at heart."

"A college education is a good thing to have," I told Robbie. "Grandpa's right about that."

"I'll work something out," he said, before he yawned and said he was for bed.

Halfway across the living room, he turned and said, "I put in a bathroom next to the downstairs guest room. You might want to use that rather than your old room upstairs. We don't heat the upstairs anymore."

I let my head loll back against the comfortable chair. That drive had been a long one, and I was exhausted. But the pattern in the flames had me thinking of a former student. Dannie was a math savant, but he couldn't tie his shoes, wouldn't remember to eat, and had to have a caretaker to help him dress, bathe, and get to class. Yet he could do complex math inside his head. When I met Dannie, he was almost done with his PhD. The university had put together a math curriculum for him. He couldn't find the building, but he could do the work. When IQ operates in the tails of the Bell curve, as it did with Robbie and Dannie, certainties tumble aside.

When Robbie picked me up from the chair, a few hours later, the fire had burned low. He carried me and Brown Bear to bed, Ash not far behind us, for he'd fallen asleep as well. And when I woke up in the morning, warm underneath the covers that retained Ash's body heat and my own, I remembered what my nephew had whispered when he put me to bed: "Okay, Uncle Dart. You win. I'll try college if you'll hang on."

He'd known I was sick. That's why he'd put the bathroom in, so I'd not be afraid of what was to come because I wouldn't have to face whatever this was alone. Now he'd made this bargain with me. He knew, if I could, I'd keep myself stable so Robbie had his chance at college.

And somehow that gave me the courage I needed. I would go see Dr. McCloud when I returned home.

The night before we were to leave, Ash and I sat with David by that same fireplace and talked about Ellen. Robbie was there, but as quiet as he was, he didn't say much. We forgot about him except when he put another log on the fire, poured the hot water for more tea, or offered honey and lemon. He always made sure his father was comfortable, and toward the end of our conversation, he stirred something into David's tea that made my brother grimace, but he sipped without comment.

"The boy thinks he can keep me living longer than I should," David grumbled with an affectionate look toward Robbie's direction.

Ash grinned. He and Robbie had a lot in common.

"Drink your tea," came the gentle rebuke from the kitchen.

"Tell me about Ellen while I drink this stuff," David said. "I should make the boy drink it. Tastes terrible."

"Didn't Bill call? I'd just assumed—" I broke off when he shook his head. "Bill didn't have much information, but Ellen's body was found several miles from where they think she started walking."

"In a crevasse?"

"Yes, we were fortunate they could find her. People vanish in those mountains."

"The cancer had come back, you said?"

"She went there to consult with a spiritual healer. I can't decide if she was desperate or courageous, but I think she knew that the cancer would kill her this time."

"Did she really think Bill would leave her because she was taking too long to die?"

Ash's face went solemn.

"Ellen wasn't one to endure. She wouldn't let me help," I said and turned to confront David's judgment. He was like Dad. He would tell me I should have tried harder.

"Can understand that." His gaze was on the fire. "It wears you down, cancer does. Any illness does." He wasn't thinking of me at all, but of the disease that held his body hostage.

"I think she didn't know what to do, and no alternative pleased her. If she lived, she was convinced Bill would leave her and she'd be alone. If the church ladies were right, she got cancer because she was evil. And the graduate student side of her, the side based in logic and reason, said God's wrath was humanity's wishful thinking. Any way she looked at it, Ellen felt doomed. That's why she ran."

"Ellen didn't want anything to hurt any longer," Robbie said before he turned to his father. "Uncle Dart's sick, Dad."

David's eyes closed briefly as he were in pain, then went intent upon me.

"I'm fine. Just a little overworked with what I have to do for Salzburg."

"He's an empath, Dart." David's warning told me not to dismiss Robbie's insight.

I used to worry about Robbie. People like him either learned to control their ability or the gift drove them mad. When I felt the gentle touch inside my head, I turned to him. Robbie returned my gaze and the heat inside my brain subsided.

Trying to heal you.

How's it going?

And before he could answer, I shuttered the mental link between us because, like Ellen, I thought it better that I not know and still have hope than to be certain. Ash felt my withdrawal and reached for my hand. His warm fingers enclosed my trembling ones. I couldn't bear to know if the contagion was too established. Doctors called this reaction denial, and I guessed that's what I had. But I'd been raised to face what I feared. I couldn't keep up the pattern of facing it, then ignoring it, of acknowledging it, of discounting the stupid apathy, the complex pattern seeking, the withdrawal.

"Robbie is tuned into earth and human energies neither one of us nor most of humanity can access," David said to Ash. "Around Hawthorne, he's got a reputation for finding water."

"That's a good talent to have."

I met Robbie's gaze. His troubled eyes seemed lost, and he didn't understand why I had pushed him away. I didn't know how to explain.

"The healing is still a latent power, but we first noticed it several years ago when a calf came down sick. Robbie spent the night with the animal and in the morning, while Robbie here was sound asleep in front of this fireplace, that calf managed to pretty much destroy the place, he had so much energy."

Why won't you let me help, Uncle Dart?

"Dart has moments when she loses herself in patterns," Ash said, his hand still clasping mine. "She's had two or three episodes of that, of forgetting if she's eaten, and now, I've noticed, of apathy. She used to outwork every colleague, but now, the work is picking up and she's holding her own, not excelling.

"She's keynoting a prestigious summit in Salzburg. The semester is almost over, and I've done what I can for her next semester, given her a course release, a graduate student, but the workload will intensify as the summit draws near. She wants to hold on."

"You forgot Brown Bear," I said.

Ash frowned. I patted his hand and turned toward the fire. If I didn't have to look at anyone, that would make it easier.

"I'm sleeping with Brown Bear."

"Brown Bear?" David asked.

"Robbie's cast-off bear that I gave him when he was little."

"So that's how he's connected to you," David mused.

"Robbie?"

"It's the bear," David said. "He had that toy for a few days, carried the thing with him everywhere, kissed and hugged him, before I acted the fool and made you take Brown Bear back home with you."

"This bear?" I held up Brown Bear and Robbie smiled, reaching across his dad to smooth the fur.

"The little guy cried and cried," David said.

"Connection," Robbie said. "That's how I know that you're ill."

"It's not stress, is it?"

"It's better when you're calmer. Let me back in, Uncle Dart, I can help."

"It won't hurt you, being inside my head with whatever this is?"

He shook his head and his eyes grew distressed, then with hesitancy and intent, he leaned closer and one forefinger traced the path of destruction high across my forehead. I closed my eyes and leaned my head back against the chair.

"Can you take away the compulsion to touch other people's hair? It makes them very uncomfortable, especially those of African-American descent. My friends understand, but what if I do this do a complete stranger?"

David groaned.

"Yeah, I know, very inappropriate behavior. Nothing would get me in trouble faster in academe. The compulsion is real, and I've tried to control it." I remembered the time I'd touched Lea's hair and the numerous times I'd patted Susan's hair as I went by where she sat or stood. She'd accepted it as something a friend would do, the connection similar to touching one's arm, or shoulder to get their attention, but the impulse had been more frequent of late. Susan had begun to suspect that what she'd thought was just connection might be driven by something more.

"When my symptoms first presented, I thought it was Alzheimer's and, of course, I'm a researcher, so I read the research and the first-person accounts, and it became clear that my symptoms were different from those of people suffering from Alzheimer's. I wrote it off as stress. Then, as Ash told you, the compulsions got worse. I can feel my motivation ebbing, the joy I always had about my job disappearing. That other self within me, she's the one I try to listen to now, but the compulsions are too strong sometimes."

"But the very fact that you know and are capable of understanding what is happening to you, that would indicate that you don't have this disease."

David's denial was as strong as mine.

"Ash's first wife died of FTD. He can tell you FTD presents differently in each individual. I've used my brain all my life, trained it, and developed my intellect. Robbie knows, and now I know that the corruption is there. I'm compensating for the corruption, or at least I think I am, but FTD is killing my brain, David. I'm dying."

"Not for a while yet, Dart." Again, Ash reached for my hand. "With the proper diet, exercise,"—Robbie was nodding—"we'll beat this thing."

Ash was also in denial.

"You're talking yourself into this, Dart," David said. "Go see a doctor."

"I already know what this is, David."

"No, you don't. Robbie could be wrong."

I turned to my nephew. "Are you wrong when you dowse for water, Robbie?"

"Never."

"And he's not wrong about this or about your diabetes."

"If I go first, I'll save you a place." And there David was in my moment of need, the brother I'd missed my entire life.

"She'll go back to Dr. McCloud," Ash reassured David. "I'll see to it."

Robbie visited me in my dreams through Brown Bear that night and every night after that. He brought his healing magic with him.

SIXTEEN

AFTER WE RETURNED to North Carolina from Illinois, I went to see Dr. McCloud. He sat down and took my hands in his. "Dart, we've known one another for twenty years. Let me be frank. Research can be a pesky thing. Medical students are convinced they have the most god-awful diseases because they read and think, yes, I have that symptom, and that one, and oh my God, I have cancer."

"I don't have cancer, but I'm disappearing."

Not so much. Robbie's massaging your brain cells.

And that was true, I'd been feeling better since coming back from the farm, but according to my research, FTD could plateau as the brain compensated for its loss, then plummet, then plateau, sort of like descending stairs and resting every third step.

"Of course you don't. You think you have frontotemporal dementia." He considered for a bit. "Tell me about the different types of FTD."

And I began to regurgitate all the facts I'd gathered, when he cut me off and said, "Stand up while you're doing that, would you, and try to balance on one foot." I did as he requested and didn't pause when he started to time how long I could keep my balance. It stretched to twenty seconds before I started wobbling and then to twenty-five before I put my foot down, just as I finished up with, "Behavioral variant FTD is the type I think I'm developing."

"And why is that? And stand on the other foot, would you please?"

"Apathy, no drive, little emotion—anger and fear, yes, but not embarrassment or guilt. I ate three slices of cheesecake and didn't remember eating any of them, I find myself searching for patterns, and I have what you medical folks label a compulsive and ritualistic behavior—I have to pet Brown Bear and touch hair."

This time I managed ten seconds, not long enough, and he and I both knew it.

"What kind of hair?"

"Tabooed hair, the patterns of light get lost within the kinkiness but they lurk there. I have to find them."

"Ritualistic behavior is a symptom of FTD," he agreed. "The symptom is also related to aging, stress, and exhaustion. Sometimes it is the preparation stage for a career change, or a symptom of burnout, or, in highly productive people like you, contemplation of insight."

"In other words, my wanting to lie around all the time may be anxiety because I'm procrastinating about preparing for Salzburg? I'm surprised you have a job with that diagnosis."

"Didn't you just get back from Illinois?"

"Family."

"Creative spurts, or rebellion, or any number of things require contemplation and time to let things simmer."

"I don't feel like myself."

"Smithers in archeology is interested in the fall of Rome, and Hastings in biology could care less because his snails didn't have anything to do with the fall of Rome. Poverty's not that sexy, you know. People have to work themselves up to be indignant about it. But then you've noticed that, haven't you?"

"I don't find solving poverty to be a priority anymore. I'm coming to accept that poverty is too big for me to beat, too big for humanity to overcome."

"Professors can't do what they do without spending immense amounts of time alone and inside their heads trying to find the pattern of things."

"You think I'm exhausted, overwhelmed, and burned out on poverty?"

"FTD robs people of values, emotions—that's why it's sometimes called social dementia."

"My dad believed that hard work overcame any obstacle."

"But that's not true of poverty or frontotemporal dementia," he said. "Crap happens, and the resulting chaos takes away comfort, security, and hope. We like to pretend that chaos doesn't exist, but what we really don't like is looking at it."

"The ones who have it made, like me, say 'there but for the grace of God go I.' Rather smug to believe that, isn't it?" I looked at him, hoping he hadn't noticed my vulnerability. "Maybe I'm bipolar, schizophrenic. . . ." I stopped as he reached for my hand. He leaned closer to me.

"Tell me, is it wrong for a husband to cheat on his wife?"

"Of course it is."

"Do you laugh when someone falls down and hurts himself?"

"I don't like reality TV."

"Is it wrong to eat three pieces of cheesecake?"

"I didn't eat three pieces."

"You said you did."

"My friends said I did. I don't remember doing that."

"What about reaching out and touching someone inappropriately?"

"Lea is a friend." But I knew I hadn't been able to control that impulse. So had Lea.

"You were in a professional setting."

"Don't forget the compulsions to continue doing it."

"Well?"

"Yes, it's wrong . . . and I didn't care. I understand what is right and wrong, or at least I do now—who knows what I'll be like in the next five minutes." I looked at him and I know he saw the dismay on my face. "It just doesn't seem to matter. One of the case studies in Lea's research is about an FTD patient who liked to open mailboxes. She said 'federal offense' every time she opened one, and she'd been warned, many times, not to do it."

I didn't want to become like that.

"If I were to guess, Dart, I would say you might be in the very, very early stages of FTD."

"But you said—"

"I know." He took my hand. "No definitive test but based on the narrative and observation, maybe. We'll need to do more blood work and testing to measure how your brain is functioning."

"I failed, didn't I?" That troubled me as much as the diagnosis. I was an academic. We don't like to fail tests. "You tricked me." I had expected to be asked to remember my address, or relate the conversation we had at the beginning of this visit.

"No trick. A test. FTD displays with people in their early fifties, although the range is from forties to mid-sixties. You're showing very mild symptoms now, and you're in your early sixties. If you weren't so intelligent, my guess is you would never have noticed anything wrong. Certainly, the people around you haven't said anything. It's very unusual for the patient to pick up on the decline by themselves."

"I have no one else to look after me." Except for Robbie. I would always have Robbie, but my heart was breaking because if I accepted this diagnosis, I couldn't stay with Ash.

"FTD affects the part of the brain that regulates social behavior. Your reaching out to touch Lea's hair, to pat Susan's head when you pass by her sitting on the sofa in the living room, your compulsion to pet Brown Bear when you're around professionals, those actions trouble me. They indicate you are losing your self-restraint and self-control."

He's not wrong.

Dr. McCloud pushed back from me, the wheels of his stool creaking and grumbling on the tile floor, and clasped his hands together between his knees. "If this is FTD, you're compensating for it, and I would expect nothing less from a brain that is as competent and commanding as yours. The anomaly is that you spent fourteen hours finding the pattern in that vita." I'd told him what I'd done with Hendrix.

What I hadn't told him was that once I discovered the pattern, I wallowed around in the luxurious complexity, following the threads of inquiry to the bitter simplicity of her cheating, so I explained what had happened. He understood now how my behavior fit.

"Normal people would be outraged, but you were interested in the pattern. But you didn't feel outraged, didn't act on her cheating, and someone had to push to make you follow through. You're still able to read other people and to act on their expectations. That's good, and you could continue to function if you can maintain this level. If the FTD progresses, you'll become more distant, more apathetic, more everything of what little you are experiencing now, but I don't need to tell you horror stories. You know what this disease can do."

Chills quivered and shot through me. I knew all too well that FTD could make me a moral monster and would isolate me. A lot of us ended up in jail because we no longer could distinguish right from wrong.

"I'm going to give you a diet to follow. Some have had success with the Mediterranean diet because their symptoms of dementia diminished." He drew a deep breath. "But there's no cure, Dart. For someone who is in excellent health . . . you can live for quite a while with this disease, as you are in the very, very early stages. Don't quit your job. Stay at the university for as long as you are able to reason and deduce. Work with others so they can check your work. And if you are able, keep a journal of your symptoms. The medical establishment can use more information about what this disease does."

He reached out to tip my chin up so that my eyes met his. "You've always been driven, Dart," he said and his eyes met mine. "Empathetic. This disease will take that essence from you. You don't have children or a husband, but that's what the caregivers of people who suffer from FTD complain about most, that loss of empathy. The wife falls and hurts herself and the husband shrugs and continues watching TV."

"I felt Ellen's death here," I said, covering my heart protectively, "but I couldn't keep her in my thoughts when she had disappeared. And my work doesn't seem to matter anymore, and I've spent decades studying poverty."

"Poverty is a theoretical construct. It's not as intimate to you, and that's why, since it's tied in to a higher functioning part of your brain, it's easier to let that go than your deeper feelings for Ellen. Maybe the plateaus will be more frequent if you follow the diet, do the exercise, meditate, take the medication I'll prescribe."

"Plug all the holes in the roof, not just one."

Bring the rain.

He heard the whispered confirmation and the tremor in my voice. "The day will come when you won't remember to diet, to exercise, to meditate, but with your brain, Dart, and these behavioral and cognitive interventions, that will be years from now."

"I'm able to work since I got back from Illinois." Even I could hear the hope in my voice and, despite everything I knew about FTD, I still asked, "Can I get *me* back?"

Dr. McCloud drew in a deep breath and didn't answer.

His blue eyes blurred when I started to cry, because I could still feel grief, a complex, moral value that FTD had yet to take from me.

∿

Frontotemporal dementia.

The words meant death sentence.

Ash's hand gripped mine as we walked the beach, a slight breeze pushing us together. The day was sunny with no clouds. You'd never know it to be winter in North Carolina, like you'd never know looking at me that inside my brain, cells were dying. That trickle of dead brain cells no one could see would grow to a waterfall, isolating me behind the cascade from the rest of humanity. I shuddered with the thought of it, and Ash's hand tightened in mine.

"I'm going to open mailboxes, all the while muttering 'federal offense, federal offense.'"

"We'll move to an island, where there are no mailboxes."

"I'll see a handsome stranger and want to take a little nap with him. That's why they have sex in nursing homes, you know. All inhibitions are gone when the frontal and temporal lobes die."

"Any time you want to take a nap, I'm your guy."

"Why aren't you taking me seriously?" I stopped and turned to face him. The wind ruffled his hair, and I could feel it tugging at my own. The sunlight put his strength into relief against the cloudless sky, his broad shoulders shadowing me, protecting me. He was so solid, so steady, big enough that when he said the words that made the difference, I believed him.

He cradled my face with both of his hands, and kissed me on the lips, his own warm against the coolness of mine. And then he hugged me close. That was enough, and then it wasn't. The fear came back.

Behind the waterfall, I'd watch the world about me. As more and more brain cells liquefied, the waterfall would grow bigger, fall faster, cascade and plunge, the white noise of it drowning out any other voices. That's what this disease would do to me. My brain collapsing, falling and that's how. . . .

You'll drown, in silence.

"I don't want to die like this."

Behind the waterfall.

"This thing inside my brain, Ash, I'm not going to let it push me over a cliff like Ellen did, or turn my head to the wall like my dad did. I'll think of a way. I will, and then McCloud will be wrong, and the words he put inside my brain will go away. I just need a little time."

You don't have time.

I stopped and turned to face him again. "Ash, tell me that this will be okay."

His hand clasped mine and he tugged me closer to the water's edge where the sand didn't give way beneath my feet.

"Jennifer asked me the same thing." He looked away from me down the beach. "I told her that with the right diet, exercise, medications, research, we'd find a way. I think you've been fighting this disease and winning since your early fifties, because that's when FTD hits most people, but with that big brain of yours, it didn't even slow you down. I can promise you this, Dart. You'll have time to take your idea for The Raindrop Institute to Salzburg and launch that legacy you've been crafting."

"Robbie," I breathed his name as I comprehended what he'd told me. He'd go to college if I would stay healthy. Robbie thought I had more than six months of health left. He thought I had years because that's how long he would take to get his degree.

"Maybe if we can keep you at this stage, or even gain some ground with the right food and exercise, that will be enough time for the next pharmaceutical breakthrough."

I scuffed my toe in the sand. Water bubbled to the surface. I looked up at Ash. "That means no marshmallow baby chicks for Easter."

"Or rabbits, eggs, and cocktails."

"Chocolate is good for me."

"No hope for that either." He turned me around and pointed toward the pier. I looked into the sun, and the clouds that crested the horizon. Then I turned and started walking toward that sunset. Nuland had been right in his belief that the appreciation of beauty was an evolutionary adaption to coping with the chaos inside us and around us. Beauty could make chaos invisible.

I'd been wrong about Ellen if that were true. Maybe she'd sought out the spiritual leader in Mexico, not because he could heal, but because she instinctively felt the beauty of the area could heal. That's why Classy and Sandy were going back.

Perhaps that's what religion did as well—provided order through the beauty of cathedrals and churches. Man-made beauty as well as natural beauty resisted the contamination of disorder. Churches imposed order on chaos. No wonder people felt compelled to pray when they entered; they couldn't help their brain's response.

"Today's goal is to walk to that pier, Dr. Sommers." Ash pointed down the beach. The water's ebb went into flow and ebbed again, leaving behind firm, hard-packed sand. As the seconds passed, those grains of sand beneath my feet shifted as the water drained, but they also held together just long enough that I could walk into another second. That's how normal people built seconds into miles. And that was the path I'd take, always finding the firm ground of reason and insight inside my mind, until I couldn't think any longer.

As long as the sand held, I could keep going.

∾

The promise of rain didn't stop me from walking the beach the next day. Parking the car in Oak Island's designated public access parking area, I rummaged around in the back seat of the Volvo, found an old cap someone had given me, and tugged it over my hair. My fleece jacket would keep the rain off me for a while, but that didn't matter. The day was still warm, for January.

Mine was the lone car in the lot. Winter brought the locals out to play, but they had enough sense to stay in out of the rain, as my father used to say. Inside my head, he smiled and scooped away a handful of dead brain cells to uncover healthy ones. It was a useful figment of my imagination, that image of my dad. He used to shovel corn out of bins that way, the big silver shovel loaded with golden grain. Dr. McCloud called it brain atrophy. Dad didn't care what those cells were called. He wanted the mess gone.

But I hadn't come to think about that. I let Dad do the shoveling, and I started walking. That's the way insight worked . . . when it chose to do so. The beach stretched on and on, my eyes tracking grains of sand until the grains became a pencil whose sharp dark point punctuated the horizon.

I found the edge of the hard-packed sand and lengthened my stride. The ocean, sand, and sky blended into a monochromatic print of overcast and gray. Beautiful, surreal like my thoughts and, when the rain started to fall in fits and starts, I tucked my hands into my jacket and kept walking. Then wondered why and held my palms up to the sporadic splashes of cold so that I could feel the sensation of wet.

This wasn't the gentle, warm rain of September that fell like soft drops of petals against my skin. These occasional drops had the edge of ice, but they felt warm. The rain and the mist damped sound, and I walked further, deeper into the zone of silence and wet.

Blue-gray rippled against the edge of gray, and slashes of white crested and then disappeared. Maybe . . . and I stood, looking out over the endless, vast grayness and wondered what it would be like to keep walking . . . that way. But I'd told Ash I wouldn't, and the thought of suicide never had a chance anyway. My father caught its tail and whipped it down onto the hard bone of my skull. I'd seen him kill a snake that way once, grabbing the tail, whipping it high before it could coil and strike, then cracking the body like a whip onto concrete.

I kept walking on the hard-packed sand.

More raindrops fell. Soft splashes that my hat absorbed. When it got wet enough, I thought, when it got wet enough.

A brief look at the sky. Nothing to indicate more rain would fall and nothing to indicate that the rain would stop. Only gray all around me, but without thunder, lightning, or wind. Just *nothing* except for the movement I created, the footsteps I left in the sand, the breeze my mass displaced as I met and overcame the resistance against the gray that enclosed me.

Energy here, I thought, energy I could use to sweep FTD aside.

After two miles, I stopped, turned around, and started the long walk back to the car. The ocean had already erased some of my steps, and the hard-packed sand was higher on the beach. The tide must be coming in, as tides always did, but nothing seemed to move but me. The rain fell a little faster. No longer a gentle mist, the drops had mass and heft.

Now?

I stood for a minute, my head high, my broad brimmed hat level, my heartbeat loud in the silence. Then, I tipped my head forward and the water fell from the brim of my hat as a waterfall spills over a cliff.

From behind the waterfall, I stared at the world. Now I knew how the disease would kill me.

I walked on in the light rain.

Susan was home when I got there. She was the only one left since Lynn had moved out to be with Bill. I tried not to think about that because I didn't know how I felt about it. The old me would have been outraged, but the new me, whose moral limits were being erased didn't seem to care.

"Did your car break down?" Susan grabbed a towel and threw it at me, then grabbed another and wiped the floor where I stood dripping. The shivering had started on the way home, and I couldn't stop.

I struggled to answer her but couldn't because my teeth were chattering.

"Shower," Susan said. "Now." And she helped me into the shower stall, clothes and all. The warm water cascaded down, washing away the rain and the cold. I gave her my shoes, then closed the shower door and struggled out of my clothes, throwing them, dripping, one item after another over the shower door. Susan was there to gather them up and to leave my pajamas, robe, and slippers behind. Steam started to rise around me, and I leaned against the shower wall and let the warm water stream over me.

"Maybe I overdid the exercise thing this morning."

I heard a muttered "Ya think?" and then Susan left. "I'll make some hot tea for you," she said as she closed the door.

Bundled up and warm, a towel still around my hair, I joined her by the fireplace in the living room. The warmth felt so good. The tea Susan had waiting for me warmed up my insides.

"What's wrong, Dart?"

She knew me well, my friend did. "I got caught out in the rain while walking the beach over on Oak Island. Didn't seem so cold at the time."

"You do that when you have tough decisions to make." She stared at the fire then turned back to me and smiled. "What did you decide?"

"I'm not going to go to Mexico."

She straightened at that and put her wine glass down on the coffee table. "I didn't know you were considering it." Then she sat back, one arm outstretched along the back of the couch, the other in her lap, her legs crossed, relaxed, but her torso faced me squarely, and the time had come. I told her about the visit with McCloud, his suspicions, my own observations, and what I would tell Ash regarding our relationship.

"You should take some of that money Emory left you and travel, Dart. See the world, do what you've kept postponing all these years. Now's the time."

"Robbie's going to need that money for college. He told me he would go when I was home over Christmas."

Susan smiled at that, then grew earnest in her pleas for me to put aside my research and do what I enjoyed doing.

"I thought about that on the beach." I unwrapped the towel from my hair and ran my fingers through it. It would curl in the warmth from the fireplace, but I found myself unconcerned. What I looked like didn't seem so important now that I knew I had FTD.

"If who I am is what defines me, then I have to continue my research into poverty."

"Dart, honey, you don't stand a chance of solving the issue. There's not enough time, and why waste what you have struggling against something that's inevitable?"

"Death is inevitable, but we continue to live."

"That's different."

"We're all dying, Susan."

"Yes, I know, I know, but enjoy yourself in the time you have left."

My hair curled against my fingers, and I relaxed for the first time that day. "I don't enjoy teaching the MOOC."

"Odd, it's brought you so much recognition." Susan relaxed as well.

"I'll let Hendrix take over once she's back from sabbatical. She's always wanted to be where I was standing."

"Her office is cleaned out, Dart. She's not coming back." Surprise that I didn't know lingered in Susan's expression. "Her vita isn't on the website anymore." Susan thought for a minute. "She wasn't happy here. She hadn't been happy for a long time."

You might have been wrong about Hendrix.

You're not wrong. That voice I trusted. If Hendrix had believed herself to be wronged, then she would have fought and won. Instead, she had packed up her office and left the university without saying goodbye. Maybe she'd been relieved not to have to live a lie any longer. Or maybe they'd paid her off. Or maybe she'd had enough of university life and resigned. Or maybe someone had gotten sick, or maybe she was sick, or maybe she read my email and left. Whatever had happened to her, I hoped she lived what remained of her life with integrity. And I found it ironic that that might not be an option for me. Maybe Hendrix had FTD as well.

"You should let Lea have the MOOC," Susan said

"Great minds think alike." I felt warm for the first time since I'd gotten home. "I'll let her teach next semester. She'll have my notes from this semester and she can show my lecture tapes from this semester, and if I put in an occasional appearance, Ash won't be any wiser."

Both of us were pleased with that solution, and I savored the moment of shared insight that had solved that problem. Those would become rarer as the FTD progressed.

"If I'm lucky, Susan, my brain will still work on the theoretical. I'm going to lose my inhibition and self-control, but if people understand and treat me as if I have a disability, I think I can keep working. I'll just have to have an aide at work and a caretaker here at home."

"That would be me," Susan said. "I can shop for us . . . and the first order of business is a restraining order on wine. Once I drink up what's in the house, that's it."

"I'm going to draw up a trust and if there's anything left in my bank account when I die, that will go to you. Is that fair?"

"Depends on what you have in your account. Has to be at least a dollar left."

"In other words, you're not worried about it."

"I know that I can't take care of you when you need nursing home care, Dart, but I think I can keep up with you for a while yet. I'll make sure you're at Salzburg. That's critical, isn't it?"

"Yes, the Salzburg presentation will help others carry on the work. I'm determined to follow what Ash and I decided upon last night: a Mediterranean diet, exercise every day, and keep my brain engaged in the work."

Inside my head, my dad lifted another shovel full of dripping, decaying brain cells. This time the shovel scraped against bone.

"But if FTD makes that impossible, you'll have to help me."

"That's why you touch my hair."

I felt a momentary bit of shame. That was good to still feel shame.

"I can't help that." And that was bad.

"Even now you have fascinating patterns there, and my fingertips itch, they actually itch, to feel your hair."

"Are we going to become sexual partners?"

So lucky to have her understand. She'd laughed off the taboo, the anger that black people, herself included, felt when white people reached out to touch their hair as if they were exotic and different. "Don't laugh about this. It's possible. A lot of behavior variant FTD patients become sexually aggressive, but I don't know if I have bvFTD. It may be something else. But if it's any consolation, I've never found women attractive—although I like how they dress up in skirts that swish and high heels that click."

"Do you miss her?" Susan asked, and at first, I thought she meant Ellen but since she refused to look at me, her eyes on the flames while her fingers traced the rim of her tea cup, I knew she was talking about Lynn.

"I don't understand how Lynn could do that, and I don't understand why you aren't as angry as I am. Ellen was your favorite cousin. Doesn't it outrage you that her husband buried his wife one day and climbed into bed with Lynn the next?"

"You miss her."

"She's with him in Mexico celebrating Ellen's life. What a crock of sauerkraut that is," Susan said, getting up and leaving me alone in the living room.

After she left, I stayed by the fire, petting Brown Bear. Bill, Sandy, and Classy were down in Mexico for the winter, and Lynn had gone with them. Susan had a point. Why wasn't I outraged about what Bill had done?

They hadn't meant to harm Ellen or Susan or me, they said, but love found people in the strangest ways, and they, Bill and Lynn—I still couldn't believe it—were in love. The beauty of their romance tamed the chaos that had brought them together. That's what they believed. Nuland would have approved.

While I still had some morality left, some sense of right and wrong, I knew what I had to do. I just didn't want to do it. I sipped the tea, grimaced, and poured it out, filling a wine glass with the red I preferred. Wine wasn't on my diet, but I wouldn't drink it again after I made this decision.

I sat watching the flames, missing the crackle and pop of wood. The difference between Bill and Lynn and Ash and myself was that Bill and Lynn loved each other. Ash was still in love with his late wife. I couldn't drag Ash behind the waterfall with me. I wouldn't. He deserved a second chance at love, like Bill had found with Lynn.

SEVENTEEN

"**O**VER HALF THE FACULTY in this college suffer from some sort of dementia, Dart."

As usual, Ash was trying to multitask, and no matter how many times I'd told him that no one could multitask and trying to do so made him less efficient, he persisted. "I know it's here somewhere," he murmured, searching through a drawer in his desk. "Faculty are like little kids, you know." He shuffled some more papers around, peering under them and over the pile. "They'll promise you anything just to get what they want. Then once they have it, they leave this office and don't follow through. Well I'm tired of it."

I knew what he was looking for. Evidence. He had people sign promise slips, that they would do X and by a certain time, Y. Some of the faculty had started to jot down their own promise notes that he had to sign. That hadn't gone over very well.

"Thought signing promise notes was a good idea, but I hadn't known keeping track of the pesky things would be so difficult." He shut one drawer and opened another. "I know you have FTD. I was there on the beach with you, remember? I know McCloud's diagnosis is flimsy at best and that if you do have it, your big brain will take a while to falter. Too many cells up there that you like to use."

"Ash."

That brought stillness to the frenetic searching. He looked up, shut the drawer, and sat back in his chair, studying me, his fingers tented against one another as he considered. "I knew when you asked me to leave you alone to cope that this is what would happen. You're going to leave me, aren't you?"

He dropped his head in his hands and dug his fingers into his hair. Alarm flashed through me. I wondered what was wrong with him for a fleeting minute, then felt the disinterest slow my reaction. Although these last two weeks of the diet, the DHA supplements, hormone therapy, optimizing vitamin D levels, and strategic fasting to regulate insulin levels had lessened my symptoms, the disease was still there. The doctor hadn't been sure the regime would help, as this treatment was from a small study out of UCLA and done with patients in the early stages of Alzheimer's. FTD was different from Alzheimer's, but Doc McCloud had thought it worth a shot, as had Robbie, and I trusted Robbie.

The other thing I liked about the study was that it mimicked the work the Raindrops advocated for complex messy problems. We called it bringing the rain, while the Alzheimer's study referred to their approach as patching all the holes in the roof instead of focusing on just one. Alzheimer's results from deficiencies, imbalances, and inflammation, or at least that is the current prevailing wisdom, and the disease isn't polite enough to punch one hole in the roof. Oh no, Alzheimer's punches thirty-six holes in the roof, and you can't fix just one to stop getting wet.

"That fling with Bill and Lynn," he said. "You've got it in your head that I deserve a love like that."

"He's found happiness," I said, "and I want that for you."

"So did my wife," Ash said. "I'm cursed to fall in love with women who want me to leave them. I told you, didn't I, that she was fifteen years older than me. That was the first hurdle we had to get over. She was also brilliant, Dart, the smartest woman I've ever known, and I'm not so brilliant. I make faculty sign promise notes that I stuff into my desk and lose. Jennifer would be laughing herself silly if she were here."

He stood up, walked around the desk to me, and folded my hand in both of his. "When she got sick, she too wanted me to leave her and find someone else. As if it were in me to do that." He drew me close to him. Thank God the door was closed, but the window shades weren't. People could see in, and I started to struggle a bit, but not too much because, as always, it felt so good to have Ash's arms around me.

"You are my chance for redemption, Dart."

Finally. As if he hadn't given her everything he could.

He kissed my forehead. "Let me take care of you." I felt the light touch of his lips on my cheek. "This time I'll get it right, I promise you." He kissed me as if he meant it and dropped his hand to cradle the softness of my breast. My legs trembled and, deep within, pleasure started to tingle. I forgot what it was that was so important and kissed him back before I remembered.

He didn't deserve this.

"Let me go, Ash," I said, pulling myself out of his embrace. I put my finger against his lips when he started to protest. "You are a wonderful man, and I'm so glad that you came into my life, but I want someone who will love me for me, Ash, and you aren't that man."

He started to protest but stopped when I shook my head and stepped back, out of his personal space. The sad, bewildered look on his face almost undid my resolve, but I couldn't let that happen.

"The experimental diet, medicine, meditation, all of it will work. I'm already feeling better, and I listen now to her voice, the old me who is still there and insistent I do the right thing. She's the one who's standing before you now, Ash, and she's not sick."

"You are so stubborn. Don't do this to yourself, to me."

"With Jennifer, you would have said, 'Don't do this to us.'"

And he knew then what I hadn't been able to ignore. I turned to leave and he let me go.

Upstairs in my office, I noticed Brown Bear sitting on my desk where I'd left him. With Ash gone, he was all I had left. I picked him up and examined his kind eyes, his ratty fur, the bedraggled red ribbon, and that little stubbin' of a tail. Beneath my fingertips, his fur felt soft, and I held him close but realized I didn't feel the compulsion any more to keep him close.

Maybe everything I was doing was working.

I gave him one last long look; then I stepped onto the bottom shelf of my six-shelf bookcase, the one against the wall adjacent to the window, and stretched up to put Brown Bear on the very top of that tall bookcase. Brown Bear propped himself up against the corner. I stepped back down and Brown Bear shrank from sight.

That was good. I couldn't see him. I wouldn't be tempted. I dusted my hands and sat down at the computer. I had a program to fill for Salzburg, people to contact, and a speech to write.

And as I started to write, I remembered my father telling me to face what I feared. I'd always thought that meant finding the courage to do the right thing as I'd done with Ash, although my heart broke when I remembered the look on his face. I'd always believed that if I kept my brain engaged and active, it would take care of me. I'd been wrong about that as well. What my father meant when he said face what you fear is that it's always possible to go on, even though going on might seem impossible.

Wherever this disease led me, I'd discover a way to find the firm sand beneath my feet so that I could keep on walking. Every person struggles with something. My something just happened to be standing alone as I faced FTD, but I would go on.

～

Five months later, I stood in front of the crowd of well-dressed men and women of every nationality who had come to Salzburg to participate in my seminar on world poverty. One final speech to deliver, and my work at the Salzburg Global Institute would be done. The week had been amazing.

Gradually, conversation quieted in the cavernous room. Fresh flowers at every table accented the snow-white linen tablecloths and provided color. The wait staff had filled the crystal wine glasses with sparkling wine. Everything was perfect for the final festivities.

"We've had a wonderful five days together in Salzburg." Applause from the audience filled the gilded room and overwhelmed me. Many of these people had become more than friends and colleagues as the week progressed. I felt as if we were united now, engaged in a quest to make the future better for humanity.

Staring at all those expectant faces raised to mine, my legs started to shake a bit, but then as if he read my mind, Ash moved, and my gaze went to the table I'd shared for the last four nights with him and Lea, Susan, Lynn, Classy, Mary Beth, Carol Lee, and Faye.

I started to speak and heard the quiver gather in my voice. All the people sitting there staring at me. I would fail them all. The terror I felt grew and grew until I saw Ash take up his knife and wave it back and forth like a fan. Had he lost his mind? The question made me forget my fears. When he saw my attention focus on him, he smiled and tapped the crystal glass with the knife. I heard that sound, *somehow* I heard the noise that pounded at my confidence abate.

As the room quieted for me, he laid the knife back down, and nodded as if to say, "Well, go on. What are you waiting for?"

For five months I'd avoided him, but I couldn't avoid him in Salzburg. This entire week, he'd been there for me. When the electronics didn't work, he fixed the problem. When my confidence broke, he reminded me of the good work TRI had done. When a lecturer had been late, Ash entertained the people who had gathered to listen. Now he was telling me, with that little smile and level gaze, that I couldn't let myself down.

He was right. He was right about something else as well. I'd been a fool to let him go, but this was not the time and place to berate myself for that stupid decision. I had a final speech to give, and I didn't want to let these people nor myself down. I'd spoken in front of large groups of people many, many times before, and I told myself I'd look back on this moment and laugh for having doubted myself.

I drew a deep breath and said, "When I first started The Raindrop Institute, I had a new dean who didn't think my research was all that hot."

Ash looked surprised as everyone at our table turned to look at him and then everyone else in the room as well. Then he laughed and said, "I was wrong," and the audience laughed at the wry note in his voice.

"My tenure bid wasn't going well, and I needed something that would get me through the short term, so I started The Raindrop Institute and coerced my reluctant tenants—stand up please," I gestured to Classy, Susan, Mary Beth, and Lynn, who stood as the applause grew louder—"into letting me mess with their brains." All four of my very good friends bowed as people clapped. I'd wanted a moment when their diligence and insight would be recognized, and this was that moment.

"I wish I could tell you that we solved some very real problems, but last fall, I realized that TRI had fallen into the trap of short-term thinking. The first and worst place we lose the futures that will live beyond us is within our own heads.

"Short-term thinking is costly, and it keeps poverty alive and well. If you think it's not, consider that teachers can't spend quality time with individual students so, as a result, a high schooler drops out every twenty-six seconds. That means in the few minutes I've been speaking, almost ten students have rejected accomplishment and opportunity and accepted hopelessness, for many of those dropouts live in poverty."

The room grew quieter. "Thinking short term has prevented Congress from pushing for a real infrastructure bill. As a result, a bridge along the Mississippi collapsed a few years back, killing thirteen people. More bridges and tunnels and roads and electrical grids and sewer systems and water purification plants, like those in Flint, Michigan, will fail. The poor will suffer more because those of us who can afford to buy bottled water will, or we'll leave."

I paused and drew a deep breath. I'd decided last night that they needed to know what I'd pretended didn't exist during these last few days. "A few months ago, I received a health diagnosis that made me aware of just how very little time I had left to make a difference."

Heads turned as folks looked up at me. Brows creased with concern, the room grew quiet. I knew what they saw: a healthy, articulate, accomplished older woman brimming with vitality and intellect. "That forced me to think long term, past the diagnosis to what I could accomplish. I don't have children, but I wanted—want—The Raindrop Institute to grow up.

"I want TRI to become a way of thinking that doesn't rely on short-term fixes, like technology, or abating the symptoms instead of solving the problem. I want our mindset, our way of thinking, to build futures, not to be trapped within the present. Ari Wallach and others call this transgenerational thinking. It's a process of thinking about the decisions you make that avoids the memes and heuristics that trap us into a defined future.

"Used to be the high priests in Rome determined our future, and now it's the high priests of Silicon Valley. I urge you to push beyond that thinking. These days with me at Salzburg have illustrated how TRI has made that leap. Always think beyond solving the problems to envisioning what will our world be like when the problems are solved. Ask yourself, to what end are you making these decisions?

"And when you have defined that, people will go along with you, as you have come along on my journey, to craft a future for all generations."

I waited until the applause died down, but it didn't. Instead people rose to their feet, and I knew that the conference had been a success, and I'd given them the moral imperative they'd work to fulfill for the rest of their lives.

"Thank you," I said and I kept repeating that until the noise died away, and people resumed their seats. "We have a lovely dinner ahead of us and more work to do, but before we commence with that agenda, I want to ask my colleagues and friends, Faye and Carol Lee, who join us from the Busy Bookers book club in Anchor's Pointe in Southport, North Carolina, to speak for just a few minutes before dinner is served. They are going to tell you how The Raindrop Institute's way of thinking has changed their discussions, their mindsets, and the future of their community and county and possibly that of North Carolina and the United States."

I sat down at the table as Faye and Carol Lee took the podium.

Ash's hand reached for mine, and I didn't pull away as I listened to the Bookers discuss the growing number of book clubs that were transforming themselves into Raindrops. Yes, they still discussed novels, nonfiction, and other works, they told the crowd, but for a half hour of their meeting, they pushed beyond the short term to consider how they might bring about the eradication of poverty. And much to their surprise, they'd come up with some ideas that had impacted their community, the county around them, and given purpose to their own lives. I looked at the two of them standing before the immense crowd in this gilded room that glistened with gold in the soft lighting and I reveled in the emotion that swept through me. I felt hope for the first time that TRI would go on when I was gone.

EIGHTEEN

T HE NEXT AFTERNOON, my one free day in Salzburg before
I flew home, I walked toward the arch at the center of the
Makartsteg pedestrian bridge over the Salzach River that divided
Salzburg. Padlocks hung from every woven wire and chain link
in the fence anchoring the railing to the bridge. Far below, the
river gleamed gray-blue in the afternoon sunlight. A light breeze
stirred my hair as I stopped in the middle of the bridge and tried
to make sense of what I saw.

A novel had inspired this, a novel—and they say fiction can't
make a difference. Before me was tangible proof that it could. I
should have included that in my speech.

The locks symbolized unbreakable love.

I remembered reading about them the last time I'd been in
Salzburg when Christmas shoppers crowded the bridge and the
town's sidewalks. Today, the town was more crowded than before,
and the bridge had many, many more padlocks than the last
time I'd been here. So many I couldn't believe the bridge hadn't
tumbled down from the accumulated weight, but the fence hadn't
sagged and the arch hadn't weakened.

Around me, strangers pressed close as they rushed past.
Children dashed in and out among the adults moving from one

side of the city across the broad river to the other side. Surrounded by evidence that love is undying, lovers stood tightly together looking into each other's eyes, and, as if loath to intrude on that private moment, the crowd respected their space.

That might have been Ash and me, but I'd dismissed that future for myself as improbable. After my speech last night, I knew that to be a mistake, that I'd been so caught up in the short term of my diagnosis that I hadn't seen the possibilities. But it was too late now.

I pressed closer to the railing and the open woven fence beneath it, partly because the view from the middle of the bridge up the river was spectacular and partly to avoid being jostled and pushed. An older woman standing alone, in the way of folks who needed to be somewhere, wasn't a good place to be. An old fort sat high on the hill to my left and, to my right, beautiful white buildings gleamed in the setting sun with an ornate gilded clock tower dominating the business district.

My hands gripped the railing, the beauty of the spot holding my attention until an older couple stopped a few paces down from me. They both had silver hair and, from their dress, they weren't rich but neither were they poor. *Ordinary people, grandparents probably, no threat to you,* my Sentinel decided.

He withdrew something from his trouser pocket. She smiled, and I looked from her delight to his steady hand and the bright red padlock that he cradled there. He turned the key and the hasp opened. With a gentleness I couldn't imagine, he bent to affix the bright red padlock on the chain link fence. He had a bit of trouble finding an open spot, but persistence paid off. I watched him snap the shiny, silver hasp closed. Then he straightened and gave the key to his wife.

She held it for a moment as if to savor their pledge, then threw the key out into the placid but white-capped river below. Holding hands like the teenagers they used to be, they stood together, then moved on.

I moved over to the spot where they'd been standing. The red padlock faced outward, toward the center of the bridge. That's what had taken him so long, positioning the face just so. A rhinestone heart of red and white crystal gleamed in the sunlight and beside the symbol, their names, what appeared to be *Biefke*—or was that *Bigke*?—and *Osi*, or was the *s* an *a*? *Murz, 2011*, I could read, but I couldn't make out the other words.

I reached out and traced the heart with my fingertip, but stopped when I became aware of the man who stood on my right, slightly behind me, his broad shoulders protecting me from the hustling, bustling crowd. Had the older gentleman returned? I straightened to look at him.

"Ash?"

You left yesterday with everyone else. Hadn't he?

"What are you doing here?"

He moved to stand beside me. "When Jennifer and I came to Paris after she was diagnosed, we put a padlock on the Pont des Arts. They call them love locks there." He looked up the river and then his gaze went back to the locks. "In the summer of 2015, after she'd passed, Paris city employees started to remove the railings loaded with locks. They had over seven hundred thousand locks by that time and the fencing had started to crumble under the combined weight. Picture twenty elephants standing on the bridge, that's how heavy those locks were."

I looked up and down the bridge. Nothing like that had happened here. "How many locks are here, do you think?"

"Thousands." He reached into his pocket and drew out another padlock. "I don't think one more will cause the bridge to collapse, do you?"

I turned to go, not wanting to see what I already knew would never be mine, but he stopped me. "Would you help me find a space?"

I squared my shoulders and turned back to him, pasting a smile on my face as if my heart weren't breaking. "I wish I had a love like the one you shared with Jennifer."

He winced, but he didn't say anything.

"I never had what the two of you shared, not with any of the men in my life. My father loved me, but he loved the farm more. My husband—ex-husband—let me go when I asked him to. The very least he could have done was to fight for our relationship, but"—my hands gripped the railing—"I think he was as relieved as I was that we didn't have to pretend."

"He came home to you."

The river flowed peacefully underneath us, and a boat whistle sounded over the babble of voices all around us. "He had nowhere else to go, and he knew I wouldn't send him packing. I just couldn't, even though I didn't love him."

"You sent me away." His hand closed on the padlock he'd pulled from his pocket. It too was red, like the love lock the older couple had attached.

"You know why. I won't use you like Emory used me."

"You're in the very early stages of FTD. That disease strikes down much younger people. You're older, and you're getting better. With luck, you'll have a good nine, ten years before your symptoms worsen. I'll die before you do, Dart."

"Doesn't matter. There's no hope for me, Ash. You know that."

Let him refute what we both knew. I knew what was wrong with me even if he didn't admit it.

"Robbie agrees with me, that you're atypical. He says you've got nine or ten years before the symptoms interfere with your career, your life, with us."

"My brain cells are dying, Ash. Nothing is going to stop that."

"You're right, but you're compensating, Dart, and that big brain of yours isn't going to quit finding other ways to keep working."

"Even though there's no hope, she kept keeping on—is that what they'll say about me?" I turned away from him, to look upriver, unable to bear looking at his face because I had so wanted this relationship, this last chance at love with a man who made me feel alive in a way I never had before.

"I don't know if I want them saying that about me. I rather they talked about how she found one man who loved her, like you love Jennifer." But it wasn't meant to be, and I should accept that.

"Your love lock would look nice beside the other red one." If he had to have a memento of his love for Jennifer on this bridge, then I would help him find the best spot. "They were an older couple, you know, and looked to be very much in love like you and Jennifer were." My hands were locked now around the railing, as I faced forward, looking up the river, searching for the composure to keep my heart from breaking.

"By the red one?" he asked in that deep voice I would miss for the rest of my life. I'd made up my mind while in Salzburg that I couldn't stay at NCU in Wilmington because to see him every day and know what could have been made me miserable. It wasn't Ash's fault he didn't love me, but oh, how I wished he did.

"You'll have to help me," he said in a soft voice, and I heard him turn the key in the lock and the hasp swung free.

"Here," he said. "Hold this, will you?" He pressed the key into my hand.

My fist closed around it, first in reflex then in a desperate longing that flooded through me, a horrible hope welling within me that I forced back, my teeth clenched from the agony of turning away from what could never be.

The lock clicked into place. I looked down at the two red locks, both with rhinestone hearts. The rhinestones winked up at me. Only the names were different.

I looked away, my mind catching up to what my pounding heart already knew, and then I looked up into that dear beloved face. A gentle breeze blew several strands of hair across his forehead, and I reached up to brush them back into place. At my touch, he closed his eyes, and drew me close in an embrace I hoped would never end. Around us, the crowd surged but we weren't jostled or shoved or pushed.

"Will you throw away the key, sweetheart?" he asked and raised my lips to his and kissed me. "Let go, Dart, of what you think your life should be. Take a chance and embrace what your life is right now."

Oh, how I'd missed him, missed this. Maybe he was right. My brain might be dying, but in his arms, my heart could still live.

"Me, my heart, that's what is here and now, so let go, Dart, and love me back."

I kissed him, and then turned and threw the key. The bright silver tumbled and flashed in the waning sun and disappeared under the waves of the river.

This was a bridge for lovers, and that's what we had become, for Ash had inscribed on the love lock, *Ash, Dart, Salzburg, Forever.*

Author's Notes

ALTHOUGH DART'S STORY is a work of fiction, behavior variant frontotemporal dementia is a very real disease. Unlike Alzheimers, FTD doesn't erase memories. This disease takes away the moral self, that core of judgment and empathy that makes each human unique, that allows each of us to function in society, and that attracts others to us.

Researchers suspect genes may be at the root of FTD and there is a connection, researchers think, between ALS and FTD. The gene that triggers ALS in one family member can trigger FTD in another.

Unlike Dart's story, most who succumb to FTD have no idea what is happening to them. Until they have a diagnosis, caretakers suffer as much or more than the individual afflicted with FTD. Marriages end. Careers are lost. Money disappears. Some with FTD run afoul of the law. Lives are shaken upside down by this disease. That's why when I wrote this story, I had Ash care for his first wife who also had FTD. If he didn't have prior knowledge, he would have reacted very differently to Dart's symptoms.

There is no cure for FTD, but awareness of how this disease wastes the frontal lobes might ease the pain of coping with it. If you have a loved one who is not acting like himself or herself, consider researching bvFTD. It is one of a handful of diseases that can alter personality or judgment. For those of you who would like more information the Association for Frontotemporal Degeneration has published a booklet *The Doctor Thinks It's FTD. Now What?*

About the Author

JOANN FRANKLIN grew up in Illinois but now lives in North Carolina five miles from the Atlantic Ocean. She is a wife, mother, and grandmother who dabbles in painting, who loves to read, and who enjoys learning new things. She's fascinated with decision making and ethics and explored those many facets within The Raindrop Institute series.

SELECTED TITLES FROM SHE WRITES PRESS

She Writes Press is an independent publishing company founded to serve women writers everywhere. Visit us at www.shewritespress.com.

A Drop In The Ocean: A Novel by Jenni Ogden
$16.95, 978-1-63152-026-6
When middle-aged Anna Fergusson's research lab is abruptly closed, she flees Boston to an island on Australia's Great Barrier Reef—where, amongst the seabirds, nesting turtles, and eccentric islanders, she finds a family and learns some bittersweet lessons about love.

Again and Again by Ellen Bravo $16.95, 978-1-63152-939-9
When the man who raped her roommate in college becomes a Senate candidate, women's rights leader Deborah Borenstein must make a choice—one that could determine control of the Senate, the course of a friendship, and the fate of a marriage.

Anchor Out by Barbara Sapienza $16.95, 978 1631521652
Quirky Frances Pia was a feminist Catholic nun, artist, and beloved sister and mother until she fell from grace—but now, done nursing her aching mood swings offshore in a thirty-foot sailboat, she is ready to paint her way toward forgiveness.

Center Ring by Nicole Waggoner $17.95, 978-1-63152-034-1
When a startling confession rattles a group of tightly knit women to its core, the friends are left analyzing their own roads not taken and the vastly different choices they've made in life and love.

Play for Me by Céline Keating $16.95, 978-1-63152-972-6
Middle-aged Lily impulsively joins a touring folk-rock band, leaving her job and marriage behind in an attempt to find a second chance at life, passion, and art.

What is Found, What is Lost by Anne Leigh Parrish
$16.95, 978-1-938314-95-7
After her husband passes away, a series of family crises forces Freddie, a woman raised on religion, to confront long-held questions about her faith.